NOTICE

NOTICE

DUSTIN COLE

NIGHTWOOD EDITIONS

2020

Nightwood Editions
P.O. Box 1779
Gibsons, BC V0N 1V0
Canada
www.nightwoodeditions.com

COVER DESIGN: Topshelf Creative
TYPESETTING: Carleton Wilson
Cover design based on a photograph by Torry Courte

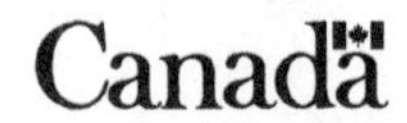

Canada Council for the Arts
Conseil des Arts du Canada

Nightwood Editions acknowledges the support of the Canada Council for the Arts, the Government of Canada, and the Province of British Columbia through the BC Arts Council.

This book has been produced on 100% post-consumer recycled, ancient-forest-free paper, processed chlorine-free and printed with vegetable-based dyes.

Printed and bound in Canada.

LIBRARY AND ARCHIVES CANADA CATALOGUING IN PUBLICATION

Title: Notice / by Dustin Cole.
Names: Cole, Dustin, 1980- author.
Identifiers: Canadiana (print) 20200213598 | Canadiana (ebook) 2020021361X | ISBN 9780889713840 (softcover) | ISBN 9780889713857 (ebook)
Classification: LCC PS8605.O434 N68 2020 | DDC C813/.6—dc23

CONTENTS

COV

III

EVENT

THEY unloaded the excavator off a scissor neck on Watson. People walking by missed the first raking motion of the articulated arm, cinder blocks crunching like booted steps, cedar beams snapping like bushfire. Through the buckled quadrangle of a sash in the last wall—the broken tombstones of its foundation, the nests of wire and shredded tarpaper, the severed curlicues of rebar.

From his unit in Bellevue Heights he watched the developer commandeer the parking lot next to Barney's to erect a showroom out of plywood and expansive glass panes. Inside, the simulacra of two dwellings. When the last condo was sold they pulled the showroom down with an excavator and redid the asphalt. The form carpenters parked here. Later on this was where the subtrades would park too. He watched them pump out the subterranean creek and divert it with PVC piping and shore it over, watched them tack mesh to the pit wall and watched the nozzlemen spray on the shotcrete.

A trio of excavators continued. Dump trucks queued up on Watson to haul the material away. The mast and jib of a tower crane arrived on highboys in sections and another truck-mounted crane was brought in to install, reducing the thoroughfare to a bleating column of single-lane traffic. They came in and out of Tim's at coffee time and lunch, muddy, mouths full of good-natured obscenities, returning to the pit, to pneumatic hammers and two-by-sixes, heavy sheets of form panel, ten hours a day plus overtime, Saturdays.

With the dogged certainty of automatons they described the involute parkade, building hollow irregular shapes and injecting them with liquid concrete. When the concrete cured they peeled the panels off and used them again. Spires of rebar were hung and their bases secured with twine, poking from the mass, each another promise, a foretaste of the tower to be. The side street was routinely closed to motorists as the workers poured slab after slab. Rolling drums of the cement trucks. Telescopic pump hoses reaching ever higher.

The slab-a-week routine was known as On Typical. The serrated edge canted outward as it rose, each week cutting out more of the dead-looking sky, every week the clangour of it getting farther away up there, every week the form justifying itself with more of itself.

▽ ▽ ▽

The worker stood on a stepladder. He had a scar the shape of a bass clef on the right side of his head where the hair did not grow. Wires dangled by his face and a beige collar with a black dome was attached to the wires. You never knew where the lens was pointing. Say cheese.

Levett walked down Tenth, phone to ear. A synthetic ring warbled. Twice, three, some of four.

"Hello."

"Is this Tom?"

The general contractor in charge of the Bellevue's renovations was quiet for a few seconds as he quick-changed into his building manager role. "Yeah."

"It's Dylan Levett, from the Bellevue—"

"I know."

"I need to organize a different time to pay my rent."

"I don't deal with the money," said the voice. It wasn't trying to be nice.

"Can I get the landlords' contact to arrange a different time?"

"I don't deal with the money."

"But you're the building manager."

"Yeah."

"Well."

"Well what?"

"I need a couple days."

"Rent's due on the first."

"I won't have it on the first."

"Then you'll get a notice."

"I need some more time."

"That's not my problem."

"So you're the building manager, but you can't give me the landlord's contact information and you don't deal with the money."

"Don't start raising your voice with me. You haven't got rent on the first, you get a notice. It's not my problem."

"I know who you are," Levett said.

"Who am I?"

"You're the contractor who doesn't finish any of his projects."

Along the dappled sidewalk of Tenth Avenue below arching boughs of oak and chestnut, virid moss scaling the knotted trunks, antic squirrels darting into the grass. Overhead two crows squawked in esoteric dialogue.

He could tell the voice smiled when it said, "Now you'll get a different notice."

Faint hiss of a dead line.

▽ ▽ ▽

Hammering filled the room, filled his head. He threw off the sheet, rolled off the bed and stumbled to the bathroom. He switched on the light. The light did not come on. More hammering. Talking somewhere in the building. Deep distorted voices like on a slow-motion tape. They weren't trying to be quiet.

Below his windows a large blue tarp angled down across the courtyard to the second-storey windows. It bellied loudly, whipping and popping in the wind. Rainwater from an overflowing gutter smacked on the windowsill.

Long yowling siren.

He thought the bulb was burnt-out. There were no spares. He unscrewed the closet bulb, replaced it in the bathroom and flicked the switch. Nothing.

He got up onto the toilet rim, looked down into it. Shit ring the size of Texas.

There was a lot of language going on in his head, all of it foul.

He unscrewed the bulb, standing on the pube-encrusted toilet rim in bare feet, got down off the toilet with the bulb and went to the walk-in closet where his bed was, stood on the concave mattress and screwed the bulb into the closet socket. Flicked the switch and no.

The refrigerator was silent. He felt the warm cellophane on some breasts. He peeked through the blinds. Lamplit venetians sliced the light of one window, muslin drapery diffused the glow of another. He leaned on the sideboard with his hand on a stack of envelopes, many unopened, some with the BC Hydro letterhead in the top left corner. One of the province's most robust corporations.

It was not the regular stubby shape. It was long. It didn't have the little window that showed his name and address. He tore it open and tore the letter. At the top a boldfaced heading: *Final Disconnection Notice for Total Amount Owing: $101.55.* And below, in case the heading lacked clarity, *We haven't received payment for the amount you owe. Please pay your balance immediately, or your service will be disconnected.*

He ran a bath in the dark. The tub's cool enamel shut his eyes. He imagined scourging Tom Ford with a cat-o'-nine-tails.

Later he ran into Magnus in the foyer. The building caretaker's lank white hair hung from a straw Bermuda hat. He wore a sports coat and golf shirt and tucked his sagging paunch into brown slacks. He stood with broom and dustpan watching traffic on Main Street through the glass doors. Eyes a pale, watery blue and the cars swimming through them.

"Hey Magnus."

The caretaker studied the young bespectacled man, bookish and broad-shouldered, in black jeans, black hoodie and a long black coat. To the caretaker he looked like a bardic assassin who had some growing up to do.

"There's the man, Dylan, Dylan the man. What's going, what's coming?"

"Something happened to my electricity."

"I bet it's those fuses, always going, blowing."

His eyes swivelled as he tilted a mendacious nod at Magnus.

"Are you going to be in your place? Say twenty minutes?"

"I can be."

"Okay, give me twenty. I'll come knock on your door."

The elevator doors shut on the old man.

Levett held the couch down for fifteen minutes or so. Then there was a rap on the door. Magnus stood in the corridor tapping an iPhone. "I'm going to call you from the fuse box, see if we can't get it back on."

The tarp outside his window flapped like a giant plastic wing.

Levett took up his phone. There was a new voice mail from Freedom. A chipper female voice said, "Hey there! Sorry, we hate to be the bad guy, but your balance is overdue. Pay up soon to keep your service active."

"Go fuck yourself," he said to himself. The phone vibrated in his palm.

"Hello."

"I'll tell you when to check your lights. We'll get you sorted out."

"Alright."

"You ready?"

"Yes."

Snap of a breaker through the earhole.

"Try now."

Levett tried the bathroom light.

"Nope."

"Really? Just a second."

Levett waited.

"They on?"

"Nothing."

"How's that?"

"No."

"That doesn't make sense. I've tried every fuse."

Magnus turned up at the door again with the smartphone still to his ear.

"I can't see what the problem would be."

"I owe Hydro a hundred dollars..."

Magnus shook his head consolingly. "If they cut it off there's nothing I can do about it. They control that. They know exactly what appliances you have and everything, what make, the year, all with those clever boxes."

▽ ▽ ▽

Blade Girl stood at the baked goods counter. Haggard man face, Levett thought, next in line. She had a guttural voice self-taught to go high. Neon-pink spandex, pencilled-on eyebrows, hair pulled up in a lavender scrunchy.

"Hot water," she barked. "Why won't you serve me? Why do you discriminate me? I'm Blade Girl. I'm here to stay." She had a lisp. Hard to tell if it was real.

She rolled back, tracing two opposing crescents on the dusty laminate.

"We'll get your water," said the Australian barista. She was strabismic and pudgy.

"We have nothing against you," said one of the Chinese Christian sisters who ran the cafe.

He looked at all the regulars pretending not to hear. None of them ever speak up, Levett thought. She's been berating the staff for a month. Then he said something—he wasn't trying to be a hero.

Blade Girl stared at him stunned, childlike. Then she disengaged. She coasted away and stood by the espresso machine, rollerblades shoulder-width apart. No one could fault her on technique. A pair of headphones clung to her thick neck. The kind with the foam coverings. She put them on, capped her travel mug with a strangler's hand.

The door was shimmed open. She tucked low off a single, perfect stride, arcing out of there, out of sight.

▽ ▽ ▽

In the foyer, a neon page had been tacked to the new corkboard management installed. Someone had already slashed it. You could see right through to the cardboard backing. The neon page was a memo. The entrance lock would be replaced. There'd be a key exchange.

In the foyer the following day two middle-aged men wearing matching white collared shirts stood behind two plastic fold-out tables. The taller, more garrulous man with the lumpy, outsized nose was Vaughn. The other man was laconic, short, and much portlier than Vaughn. The word "rotunda" came to Levett's mind. He was not introduced by Vaughn and did not introduce himself.

Vaughn compared the name on the rental agreement with Levett's ID. Vaughn's partner collected Levett's signature and gave him a new key.

"No definite day. Sometime next week. You'll be notified twenty-four hours in advance. Lost keys cost two hundred dollars."

Levett found it odd that this was billed as a key exchange but they weren't exchanging keys. "Steep price for a key," Levett said.

Vaughn's colleague replied by clicking a retractable pen and pocketing it, squaring off the papers, looking outside at traffic.

"We need to make another appointment. The landlords need your suite measured," Vaughn told Levett.

"How about tomorrow?"

"Perfect," Vaughn said. "How's about noon sound?"

"That works."

"I'm gonna text that to myself as a reminder."

Vaughn thumbed the letters and numbers into his phone, blocking the elevator. Levett took the stairs.

▽ ▽ ▽

The next day Vaughn texted, *I'm here*. When Levett got back from coffee Vaughn was not "here," which he expected to mean outside the building.

Levett heard Sadie's piano from the stairwell. She practised a descending chromatic run. A few solitary notes were struck, hung in the stale atmosphere, decayed, and she attempted the run again.

Upstairs Vaughn milled about in the corridor.

Vaughn offered Levett a cordial greeting, hand extended.

"I thought you'd be waiting out front," Levett said, passing Vaughn in the corridor.

"I've got the keys," the consultant said. "I let myself in."

"Come in, I guess."

Levett set out a chair for Vaughn and sat on the couch.

Vaughn stood in the middle of the bachelor suite, looking around, quite relaxed. He sat facing Levett, who expected a small-talk intro.

"Look man, I'm not gonna waste your time, I'm gonna be straightforward with you. You're living above a rotten beam." Vaughn leaned in and knocked on his thigh. "It ain't safe. The landlords got permits, they're gonna start replacing it. Everyone above it's gonna get a notice. You, guy upstairs, guy below," Vaughn said, twitchy eyes counterposed with earnest palm-out hand gestures.

Levett waited to talk.

"What would you be willing to take to move on?" Vaughn said to him as he looked around the suite again. Not move out, Levett thought, move on. "End your tenancy and leave clean, no hassle on either side. Because they're willing to negotiate with you, you three, the guy above you, the guy below." He pointed at the ceiling and at the floor with his retractable pen. Levett saw it was a custom pen, *Mac Bundy Consultation* printed down it. "The other two've already signed agreements, they're out." He pointed over his shoulder with the pen. "I mean, this could be a windfall for you. I'm not bullshitting you guys. Pardon my French. But also it just ain't safe." He wagged his glossy head. His large hand encompassed the pen. "If I come into somebody's home without a point to make, without a serious reason," Vaughn said, "you know, without a leg to stand on, guy's gonna tell me, 'Hey MacDunn, pound sand.'"

Levett had never heard "pound sand" before, but he thought about the proposition. He owed seventy thousand dollars in student loans, had defaulted on six thousand dollars of Visa debt on one card, five hundred on a second card. Add on myriad personal cash debts.

"Four thousand," he said, to test Vaughn's sympathies.

"I'm gonna do what I can to get that for you."

Vaughn's pendulous throat shook with each syllable, with each slap of his polyester pant leg. He slid out a yellow legal pad from what looked like a giveaway canvas valise, embroidered with a serifed *Mac Bundy: Solving Landlord-Tenant Problems*. He scratched out some figures on the yellow paper.

Vaughn looked around a bit more. In profile his nose was a mean-spirited caricature of a nose.

Levett managed to say very little. Instead of asking Vaughn to leave, he allowed him to natter on for informational and entertainment purposes.

"Hey man, I work for the landlords *and* the tenants. We can help you with relocation. You'd be eligible for this place again when and if it becomes available—but I can't tell you when that'd be, could be as long as three years, I don't know. Most people wanna move on with their lives." He spoke to Levett like an old confidant.

"It'd have to be no less than four thousand."

Vaughn visibly changed tack.

"I'm gonna try and get that for you. I *want* this for you," Vaughn said. His hand was slightly damp as he shook Levett's. Once he exited, Vaughn turned back not saying anything. He walked away down the corridor, never having produced a tape measure to record the dimensions of the unit.

▽ ▽ ▽

Blade Girl cut Levett off as he was walking into the cafe, zipped right in front of him on her skates. He tried to edge by her anyway and as he did, she knocked the laptop bag off his shoulder. He looked back. It lay there on the sidewalk. She gave him a challenging look when he picked it up.

As she passed the threshold, he pinned her in the door, one rollerblade inside the cafe, one rollerblade outside. He pinched her body there. She couldn't move. He realized he was clenching his teeth and putting quite a bit of weight into it and let her go. A couple sitting at the window looked on in horror.

He followed her in.

"Waah! Waaaaaah! My ribs! He broke my ribs!" She hopped up and down on her wheels, flicking her loose wrists.

In the corner some tourists in neon rain jackets observed the local colour.

"My ribs are broken," she whinged.

He sat down.

"Are you alright dear?" one of the tourists said.

"He assaulted me!"

"You're an asshole." Levett didn't see who said it.

He thought he probably shouldn't've done that.

She stood to the right, haughty and serene now. He glanced at that window couple going out, the word "monster" sharing their faces.

▽ ▽ ▽

A cumulonimbus towered far up in the bright blue air. It was the shape of a toadstool. Long tall sunlit windows braced the corner suite in Airport Square, with a view to a tangle of roads, a bridge curving over the river's north arm, aglitter with automotive traffic. The waterway was coloured steel. Passenger jets tilting skyward marked the quarter hour. Barges and couriers and long-haul power diesels were to the four identical eyes just so much digital currency in perpetual motion. Their desk made a horseshoe around the large office. Caden sat with his back to Terry on the opposing inner side of the desk, mirror image of his brother. He was a southpaw, his twin a righty. Caden manipulated a trackball with his left hand, Terry did so with his right. That morning they had, by accident, or through some kind of congenital telepathy, each put on cobalt and plum striped dress shirts. They did not care.

A five-tier relaxation fountain accented the low-noise dehumidifier. Terry flipped to the Bellevue feed. An empty grid appeared on the monitor. Views from in and around the building filled each cell, another one, another one, the building laid out like a mosaic of one-way mirrors, like an unfolded prism. In the first cell, Main Street, the labourers sit four wide on the front steps smoking cigarettes, drinking their Tim's. In another, Magnus sorts out the recycling, the paper from the plastic, appears in another cell emptying the garbage cans into the back-alley dumpster, locking the dumpster with a padlock. A gang of secondary school students rampaging along the side of the building down Tenth underneath the fire escape in one cell, their front view in another, having so much fun doing nothing, around the corner, filling the next cell, going to Tim's. A disembodied set of legs walks down the staircase, the elevator opens, somebody exits with a mountain bike. The labourers part in the first cell to let her by.

"Anything unusual?" Caden said.

"The workers took their second smoke break before their first coffee break, so, no."

"They're not expensive."

"We're paying them to be inconvenient."

Neither smiled.

A sparrow crumpled into the window. Thump of hollow bone and riffling plumage and the click of its smashed beak. The broken bird tumbled down along the face of the high-rise, a drop imperfectly helical. The brothers both leaned forward to watch it fall, observing without any particular feeling. In one of the cells Levett stared up at the camera, middle fingers extended, then stepped outside the frame. A red circle blinked in the monitor's corner.

▽ ▽ ▽

Hakim had his arm half in a checked shirt when the knock came. He knew who it was. He stabbed his other arm in the other sleeve, slack skin drawn over old bones. "Moment."

"It's Vaughn."

"Moment."

Vaughn stood square in the threshold beaming kindly. "How are ya?" Vaughn pumped out his hand, encompassed Hakim's. Not shaking, but squeezing.

"I just awoke," Hakim said, finally getting his hand back.

They faced each other. A reveille ringtone broke the silence.

Vaughn held his mobile up, whispered, "You don't mind do you?"

"Please," Hakim insisted, propped the door open with a sneaker. He sat at a small hexagonal table in the centre of the room, a lamp turned on beside it, nipped at a cup of mint tea.

"Certainly," Vaughn said. "Have them pick up the paperwork—that's right, and we've got a cheque written—exactly—and it's a done—" He rapidly clicked his pen. Hakim poured a second cup of tea. "They don't need that—it's not necessary—we've got it taken care of—just the keys—right—right on—well thank you—absolutely—it's become necessary—it's putting one foot in front of the other—right—great—okay—mmbye now—yep, bye."

Hakim looked out into the corridor. Vaughn smiled and rolled his eyes like the whole conversation was their in-joke.

"May I come in?"

"Yes, come, there's tea."

Vaughn stepped into the dim unit, the air redolent with incense, cooking spices and disinfectant. "Ah, thanks, that's very kind of you."

He sat down and made a covert visual assessment of the rental unit. Clean, tidy, some odd paraphernalia. He glanced outside the window. The tarp blocked any view outdoors. He was aware of it by hearsay. It was worse than he thought, for the tenant, which was good. Weak light filtered in through it that you could not read by. He slid out a legal pad from his promotional valise and scrawled in the middle of a clean page. Hakim's prayer rug with its built-in compass lay by the middle window. Man of faith, he thought, also a good thing. The compass pointed east. No need to pray to Mecca, Hakim, we've got you. Old green plush sofa with carved armrests along the south wall, a long silk scarf printed with three-dimensional mocárabe designs hanging above. Upon a walnut tripod at one end of the sofa threads of smoke curled through the vents of a tarnished mabkhara.

"So, my friend," Vaughn said, cautiously, tweaking the small cup between his thumb and forefinger. He sipped the tea. "Mm, mint."

Hakim smiled white and toothy. High cheekbones made two sickles of his eyes.

"Have you given any thought to the landlords' offer? I mean, thirty-five hundred's really—"

"I'll take it."

Vaughn stabilized the legal pad on his lap. At the head of the page he wrote, *$3500* ✓. He still felt the need to explain. "See, Hakim, we're getting you the maximum amount as a courtesy. There's no need for the landlords to compensate you on this, I mean, on a condemned suite." Vaughn looked outside at the lean-to structure blocking the windows. He pointed down at the floor. "And not to mention this rotten beam directly below where you and I are sitting."

"I understand. But still, I wasn't allowed back to my old suite after the Christmas flood. I was put here. I have no choice but to take the money."

"And that's neither here nor there."

Hakim wasn't smiling anymore.

"What we're talking about now is you making a choice, which you've made. You've made the right choice."

"You didn't give me a choice. It's leave without money, or leave with money." His shoulder twitched. His face turned into a smile again.

"That's exactly it. You can't fight this."

"I could, but it's too risky."

Vaughn uncrossed his legs and leaned in, knocking out a botched pentameter on the legal pad with the edge of his hand, in time with his words. "Let me be honest. This beam underneath you is like a soggy paper-towel roll. It ain't safe. You would never win. And I'd hate to see you walk away empty-handed. I'm bein' straight with you. I ain't lyin' to you. I wanna help you. Lotta people don't get what you're gettin'. They don't get squat. They get a notice of eviction."

Vaughn produced a single sheet of paper. "This here's an agreement to end your tenancy. Why don't you read it over, we'll get on the same page about a date for you to move out, I'm thinking the end of July, and I can get you a cheque for two and a half grand as early as Friday. You'll get the remainder when you turn in your keys. And don't forget, your last month here is free."

Hakim read the typed page. It specified in one sentence that he agreed to end his tenancy at Bellevue Heights, 210-2551 Main Street, and vacate the residence on the forthcoming date agreed upon with the landlords. The name of the occupant and the date were gap-fills. There was an *X*__________ below the sentence. He signed with his own pen.

Vaughn dragged it back, pivoted the page around and dated it, slid a foxed manila folder from his promotional valise, opened the folder from the top with a clawing motion, set the agreement on some other loose leaves and tucked away the folder along with the legal pad. He stood, taking another prolonged, and this time unveiled, look at the tarpaulin. A black distention where rainwater had pooled in the tarp bulged like a tumour, small frantic shadows orbiting there. Pigeons bathing in it.

"I'm not gonna linger here, Hakim. You did the right thing. For you." He leaned over and smothered Hakim's hand with both of his.

"What else could I do?"

"That's exactly it. What intelligent person wouldn't do what you did."

"Thank you."

"Thank *you*. I'm gonna let myself out, gotta be in the Tri-Cities by one this afternoon, not sure how I'll do it. Expect news of that cheque Friday at the latest," Vaughn said, standing in the threshold.

Hakim nodded as Vaughn softly closed the door. It was that easy. He poured himself another cup of tea and suspired, steam coiling off the brimming cup. He knew it was the right decision. For him.

▽ ▽ ▽

At nine in the morning four sharp knocks sounded on Levett's door. He plucked the earplugs out and lay there, fell back asleep. An hour later there were two more firm double knocks. He shot up again.

"Who is it."

"It's Vaughn MacDunn."

"I can't see you right now."

"Okay Dylan," the dismayed voice said. Steps receded in the corridor.

When he got up and checked his phone there was a text from Vaughn. The landlords had made an offer. They agreed to meet the following day at Kafka's, of all places.

▽ ▽ ▽

"What are you having?" Vaughn said, buddy-buddy. Levett looked for an expensive drink on the menu board.

They're tiny and costly, he thought, and said, "A macchiato."

Vaughn fisted his trouser pockets at the cash register. Levett sat at a deuce along the wall. Vaughn's back was to traffic. He sipped a black coffee, puckering his mouth at the hot brew, never really drinking it, a pleading look in his too-blue eyes, the colour of antifreeze. Skull like a polished knob.

"They've made an offer," Vaughn said, an officious snap to his voice. "Nearly what you asked for."

"Alright."

Vaughn slid out the legal pad, a few jagged lines of arithmetic scrawled in the middle of a page. "Now, remember, everyone has their price."

Levett downed the macchiato and stared at the consultant.

"They're putting twenty-five hundred on the table, plus your last month's rent free, so pretty darn good I'd say."

"I said four thousand."

"It's pretty close."

"Not close enough to end my eight-year tenancy."

"You're on a month-to-month lease."

The riposte caught him off guard. It took him a second to regain composure. "That's to my advantage. It's not a fixed-term lease."

"Look, I ain't bullshitting you guys. They gotta tear up all those suites. You're living over a rotten beam. This is better for you. I sure would appreciate a two and a half thousand–dollar windfall."

"I can't accept the offer."

"I can get a cheque made out to you as early as tomorrow. Not the full amount, mind you. You'd get the rest when you sign the agreement and hand over your keys."

"I'm going to arbitrate."

Vaughn leaned back and studied the cocky youth, prematurely grey it seemed. "You might not win. And then where will you be? No apartment, no compensation."

"I'll take my chances."

"I look forward to seeing your evidence package," Vaughn said. He took an actual sip of coffee, winced. "People don't always succeed."

"We'll see."

Levett went to Our Town after that and, by happenstance, bumped into Lane Roth, an acquaintance and recent law school graduate. Lane had made it known to Levett that he was interested in tenant advocacy. Lane and Levett had already talked about the landlords trying to bribe him out of his place. Lane thought he had a high chance of success if he arbitrated through the Residential Tenancy Branch.

Levett saw him along the banquette. Lane looked up from his laptop screen, two white rectangles in his glasses. He was pale with a pencil-pusher physique. His hair was a light ginger colour, as was his short beard.

"I was at City Hall again," he told Levett. "Last time I was there the clerk didn't give me everything on file. Today I accessed another one of the Lams' permits. The work permit was issued late last year. It might include your unit."

"It might."

"The wording's a little vague." Lane paused for a second. "Did they make you an offer?"

"I just refused it."

"You should consider accepting it. The permit I just looked at weakens your position to arbitrate."

Levett's face fell. He turned and left without saying bye, redialling Vaughn as he walked down Broadway, pressing the phone hard to his ear against the traffic noise. There was a long scream coming through him as the phone rang. It stopped ringing. He waited, finally asked, "Hello?"

"Hello," Vaughn said.

"I got some more information about the construction permits. I'll accept the offer."

Silence on the line.

"If it's still on the table."

"That's fine Dylan, the offer's still on the table. See. I'm not fibbing. They got the permits. They need you guys outta there pronto. It's not safe."

"Can you meet on Monday and bring the cheque?"

"Let me talk to the landlords. We'll see if we can't sort it out."

"Thanks," he said, icy droplets of sweat falling from his armpits, trickling down his sides into the waist of his pants.

"Thank *you* Dylan."

▽ ▽ ▽

A few days later he received a notice by registered mail. It was issued by the landlords through a third-party agent, Vaughn MacDunn, printed in full-colour ink-jet. On the back a box was checked and next to it, a phrase hard to get lost on: *The landlord wishes to demolish the unit.*

It's not something they really have to wish for, he thought. You'd think they could choose a gentler euphemism.

▽ ▽ ▽

Umbrellas out against a chill, slanting rain. Knots of people under store awnings waiting for the bus. Panhandlers squatting in their own detritus, creased palms held out to the passing crowds. An unbathed trio loitering on the wet pavement outside Guys and Dolls, cigarettes smouldering between their yellow fingers, waiting for the poolroom to open.

Mariana stood behind the cash register. "So you heard, right? The coffee shop is closing."

"For real?"

"Max only told us a couple days ago. Apparently the landlords don't want a coffee shop in their building anymore. Today's the last day."

"Today is the day."

"Yeah man," she said.

They looked at each other in mutual sympathy, she without a job, Levett without a haunt.

"But there's free coffee," Mariana chimed. "Sixteen-ounce."

He nodded.

"You can have a sandwich too."

"It's some consolation."

She torqued the porta-filter into the espresso machine, glanced over her shoulder. "I know, right."

On one of the benches he saw his neighbour Osman, muffin and coffee to go laid out before him, snapping photographs of the space on a borrowed iPhone.

A morose feeling permeated the rhomboid space. Levett had chipped away at an undergraduate degree in this coffee shop.

Lane walked in, black waterproof beaded with raindrops. He came to the table and took a place in the line of customers snaking around Levett. Lane smiled reluctantly, said, "Did you hear the rumour?"

"About here?"

"I wanted to verify."

"It's true."

"There goes the neighbourhood. I don't even think I can sit down and work."

With mute rancour Lane stared through the windows at the tower development. "Have you decided to take your landlords' offer?"

"Yes."

"You haven't signed an agreement, have you?"

"Not yet. I'm supposed to meet Vaughn this coming Monday."

"I'm about to send the letter I've drafted for you to the rest of the Bellevue tenants, so everyone can attach statements. I set up a cloud folder to compile individual accounts of tenant history in the building."

"I thought you said I should take the offer."

"Sorry. Afterwards I got to thinking about it. You have a pretty good case because there are empty suites in the building and the landlords haven't offered to relocate you. If you haven't signed anything, I would consider fighting it."

Levett shut his book. "I'll consider."

A doomy look settled on Lane's face as he glanced around and looked again through the south windows at the tower, up at the shadowy recesses marking each floor. "I think I'm gonna get out of here." Lane turned away and went back out in the rain.

Levett craned his neck. Air ducts ran at oblique angles along the ceiling. They were painted grey and their tops wore a thick fur of black dust. On occasion a piece of fluff would float down and plop into a cup of coffee.

He unzipped his computer case, brought out his laptop, checked his email. Lane's call for tenant statements sat unopened in his inbox. He clicked on it. The recipients' names and email addresses ran down the screen like a phalanx. He sat there watching the pissing rain. The foreign cars stopped and started, turning and going straight, a synthetic circulatory system, a poisonous pulmonary system, he thought, streaming music on his computer. He listened to Burning Witch's *Crippled Lucifer*, watching the brutal rain-slashed scene through this lens. The mug sat there on the table, tepid and half empty. He packed up his stuff and left the coffee.

People had their hoods on, heads down and collars up. He lowered his face. Rain drummed on the brim of his hat. Beneath the arched vestibule, three dust-covered workmen sat smoking on the marble steps. Double-doubles steamed in their callused hands. A young, stocky helper rocked on one butt cheek as if to fart when Levett stepped by. They eyed each other adversarially. Levett pulled keys from his pocket, a set of two, one larger, one smaller, and slid the large one into the front door. The new lock was tight and finicky. The old lock had been smooth and easy.

▽ ▽ ▽

When the sirens were very distant, barely audible, they sounded like a pinch. A door slammed somewhere. Two dogs howled in unison, meant to. He cleared a sizeable chunk of phlegm from his throat.

There was a message on his phone. "Hey there! Your payment is way overdue. We hate to be the bad guy, but we might have to disconnect your service—pay now online." He tossed the phone back onto the ottoman, cursing the entire communications-revolution joke.

It was two. He had to work at five. He swung his feet off the couch and planted them on the dusty floorboards, looked past his knees at the worn lacquer, the century-old hardwood.

While urinating in the dark he glanced in the mirror at his pouched eyes and frazzled curly hair. The toilet bowl was months overdue for a cleaning. The smell made him flinch.

He shouldered his backpack and locked the door behind him. Halfway down the corridor he turned round, walked back and checked he had locked up, turned the doorknob and pushed in on the door, turned round and descended the back staircase. He heard Sadie's piano filter through the corridor as someone passed from one hemisphere of the building to the other. She practised a phrase of stacked octaves with tritones.

A black Dakota cut him off crossing the street kitty-corner to the Federal Store. It had an unpainted canopy and a rooftop cargo rack with planks and plywood bungeed to it. The driver was Tom Ford.

Probably rendezvousing with the camera guy, he thought. The one with the scar. He had come back a few times and each time installed a few more cameras. Levett crossed Broadway, continued along the steady declination of Quebec Street.

The downtown skyline was like a mechanical implant on the land. Chrome-skinned buildings glinted in the cold light, and behind, scarves of mist wrapped around blue mountains. He faced it all with a frown.

An incident occurred just beyond Mario's Gelati, between First Avenue and Switchmen Street. Levett encountered a car, or rather confronted a car. It pulled out from the lane between a double row of condominiums. The car rolled calmly forward, blocked the sidewalk, while the driver texted.

Levett stooped over as the man's lapdog, a Pomeranian, scratched its ear and licked its genitalia. "Excuse me?"

"Seriously?" the driver scoffed in disbelief. "Walk around."

All the love inside drained away. All the hate rose up. "Look, motherfucker, you're on your phone, you're in the way, and you don't give a shit. Why don't you step out of your box for two seconds, come outside your pill of a life and consider the world around you? Your lapdog with its peanut brain and blind devotion shows more humanity than you do with your ass behind the wheel of this stock ride."

The man's jaw lowered incrementally. No opening in the rush hour traffic, no exit from the situation, no cover from the verbal bombardment. The Pomeranian planted its paws on the dash, panting as its head darted about. The sport coupe jerked ahead in fits and starts, power windows rising too slowly.

"Your windows are already shot. Is the gutless heap still on warranty?"

"Yer a fuckin' psycho," said the driver in a hollow, resigned half voice, inching forward, trying to merge with traffic, Levett sidestepping into the cyclist lane along with the car in an offensive stooped position.

"The only thing psychotic about this situation is the way you drive," Levett said, and in a dry, even iambic, "Get fucked. Drive your thirty-six-thousand-dollar piece of shit into the chrome grill of a Western Star." The dog huffed, pink tongue throbbing. The driver finally pulled out of the laneway, reaching over to pet the dog.

After passing Keefer, Levett walked through a weft of loitering junkies and pimps. Disoriented commuters stumbled off a rain-streaked bus crouching against the curb, blasting out compressed air and beeping frantically.

"Up, down, rock, rock," someone intoned.

He caught the urine stench of the alley running parallel to Hastings Street, unzipped the windbreaker and ninja-masked his t-shirt collar. An ambulance waited in the alley, an island in a river of aimless purgatorial figures. Through the bars of a doorway he heard Chinese elders singing karaoke. He looked up at the building as two pigeons emerged from a rotten corbel.

East Hastings. A soggy bazaar of the halt and afflicted. Gaunt putty-coloured people slipping and clapping around in flip-flops. Inundated plush purses, plastic stiletto shoes, scabby bruised thighs, hollow faces from the living crypt. A man in a wheelchair sat at the foot of a curb while a thin man in a black straw fedora and flared women's jeans worked at pushing his chair up a curb cut. Sidewalk dense with black marketeers and the vice-laden who supported this commerce. Someone huddled behind two open umbrellas arranged as a lean-to. The orange tip of a hypodermic rose above the edge and a dirty hand popped off the neon safety guard, plunged the needle back down below the lip of the shelter. "Can I owe you six bucks?" someone said, a strange inverted offer. Levett passed a dispensary. A man was asking anybody going in the SRO next door to "get Ryan to come down." He walked by the women's shelter. Beleaguered female drug users, single mothers, lesbian and transgendered couples all stood with each other, joking, offering moral support and information.

Gastown. A colonial statue glistened black under mild rainfall. The patios were closed all along Water Street. BMWs and Smart cars zipped over the wet cobblestones. Short half blocks opened up onto the marshalling yard. A trundling wall of orange, blue and green shipping containers scrolled along. He edged through sauntering tourists, some walking four abreast, thickening as the days rolled over into summer. A frail couple examined the picturesque and sublime images displayed on a spinning postcard rack. Asian gawkers aimed their smartphones at the steam clock. The clock struck one. Steam shot out the top as it chimed the Westminster Quarters.

▽ ▽ ▽

It was the first time the Oilers made the playoffs in ten years. The Wild Rose was an avowed Oilers bar. Levett was an avowed Oilers fan. He had to work all the games. Hockey highlights looped on flat screens in the bar's top corners. A miniature set of aluminum bleachers had been rolled out on casters to the centre of the Rose in front of the projector screen. A few disembarked cruise-line tourists stayed on in the Wild Rose. He noticed the servers carrying around debit machines as a hint. Bella was serving. He checked out her gear: backwards cap, tight white low-cut shirt, distressed denim, fresh Vans.

"How's it going?" she asked, tapping out an order on the touchscreen.

He tried not to look at her below the horizon.

"Not bad."

"Not bad? Come on now, why?"

"I don't know. I tell you what, though—it's a lot better now that I've seen you." They both knew it was lame, but she was always down for a quick turn of cheap wit and he tried to deliver as he pushed through the swing door into the kitchen's glare.

"Adding on: goon burger, fries; chicken burger, onion rings; quinoa salad," Jacob said. Vikram chopped carrot and celery sticks on the other side of the line.

"Okay, moon burger, chicken burger, quinoa salad," Vik said. "You gonna drop those fries and rings?"

"Yea-y-yeah, I got it," Jacob stuttered, greeting Levett with a nod, knuckling up his glasses as Levett crossed the line. Battered cod gurgled in the deep fryer. The *knock knock* of chopping knives punctuated the hearty guffaws and profane exclamations bleeding through the wall.

He cut his eyes at the dish pit. It was a greasy sty. Everything dirty and out of order. The sinks were plugged. Heaping bus bins lay on and underneath the counter. A painterly gesture of hot sauce spanned the wall tiles. He tried to spray it off with the nozzle but the water was cold and the sauce was dried on. He scooped dross from the drain catchers and flung it into the garbage can, let the catchers fill again as he rearranged the dishwasher racks and trays, three pronged, three flat, scooped more slime from the drains, washed his hands, dried them with paper towel and shelved the clean dishes, most of which were not even properly clean. He set them back on a mountain of filth: smattered inserts, caked wooden spoons, encrusted whisks, smeared share plates, hot sauce–stained oval plates, oil-pooled pans, spent sauce tubes, blackened skillets and burnt pots, paprika-dusted measuring spoons and floury measuring cups, furtive knives, stained cutting boards and baked-on-cheese lasagna boats, benign lettuce sieves, soiled mixing bowls, the treacherous mandolins and the tricky ramekins.

"How's it going Vik?" Levett said.

He walked up close to Levett, scoffed, "This place is a joke." Vikram was short and brown, of dubious origins. Levett once asked the cook where he was from. "Belgium; then I came to Toronto; after T.O. I went to Calgary; then I came here, Surrey; I was in Coquitlam; Burnaby now. You?"

"Northern Alberta."

"Alberta sucks. Didn't like it. Too many gangsters."

"Northside Edmonton."

"Calgary," Vik repeated, chin upturned, eyeing Levett through thick pinkish lenses. To Levett it always seemed like Vik was making an assessment. You were always being judged when you spoke to him.

Jacob stood at the threshold of the dish pit next to the organics bin holding a plastic insert, "This albacore smells a tad funky." He walked back to one of the coolers, lifted out another insert of boneless chicken breasts, pulled the saran off and sniffed it, shaking his head down the line. Levett heard them smacking the bottom of the organics bin.

"Can you save me any meat you can't serve?" Levett grabbed a sixteen-litre bucket from the storeroom.

"Sh-sure, I-I-I guess. What for?"

"My friend studies ravens," he lied. "They eat carrion."

"I see."

Jacob regarded the dishwasher with a small elliptical grin.

"Ravens consume several times their body weight every day. He struggles to procure enough meat." He dropped the slab of tuna in the bucket, fished out the chicken breasts, rinsed them off and set them beside the tuna, drew up a label with a Sharpie and a water-soluble decal saying DYLAN'S MEAT.

"That's quite an odd field of study," Jacob said as Levett capped the bucket. They cocked their heads slightly to one side, imagining it. They were imagining different things.

"Ravens are fascinating," Levett said as he went to the basement with the bucket, where he hid it in the far corner of the deep-freeze partly behind a rack. Upstairs he told Jacob, "The bucket's in the freezer corner to the left. If you remember, throw in any salmon, tuna, beef steaks, burger patties, chicken breasts or schnitzel you can't use. Avoid mentioning it to Henry if you can."

Warily, Jake obliged the request. "I can't promise Henry won't throw it out."

Levett shrugged and levered up the Hobart. A plume of steam scorched his face. He thought about how he basically assaulted Blade Girl. It was shameful, I shouldn't have done it, especially since she has cobwebs in the attic, he thought. I'm part monster, but everyone casts their shadow, he thought, and flashed a roguish smile at the thought itself. He let a stack of baking trays soak while he shelved clean dishes, still hot to the touch. Large plates on large plates, ovals on ovals, ramekins stacked within other ramekins, tiny columns at eye level.

Caught up, he fixed a coffee and stepped into the alley, its edges scabbed with litter. The sky had cleared, daylight waning. The marshalling yard spread out beyond a tall chain-link fence topped with a musical staff of barbed wire. The rusty rails crossed each other in neat curves or ran straight in tandem vectors, reminding him of bulging veins in a forearm. Neon graffiti emblazoned the CN freight wagons and well cars. Balloon letters and scrambled wild styles. A hooker trotted down the alley in precipitous heels. Beyond the trains, *Coral Princess* towered beside the cruise ship terminal. In the powdery blue, a flock of seagulls shrieked and scattered like a shredded plastic bag.

Anya, how I do this, how I know. I practise my English for job. We come here refugee, I have breast cancer, three child, what now? Mouse poop everywhere, Anya, each place, under stove, fridge, they run in hole in wall, just like cartoon, yes, Mickey Mouse, just like, Tom and Jerry, just like, yes, up the drape. They say they fix, we say No, No. Maja, Greta, Lena, each they testify. I testify. Judge say we get deal, half rent back five months, since problem, so we don't pay two months and pay half third month, korrekt, no, they say they fix mouse, still poop, now we owe now. How this, we refugee. I three child. I beated cancer. We testify again, manager company say mouse man come, two times irtó come. When, when this. They don't say he come at time, on day. We must be out. Go, they say. They say irtó comes twice, we no let them in, they say, we no co-operate, they say we want for free rent. I must be doing shopping. Manager company say mouse dead, all. Irtó no come but mouse dead. Still poop. Poop in corner, by toaster, by fruits, by tub, in bed. Judge say we want the deal, less for pay. We now evict. On Hanukkah. Send, Anya, send, kérem, kérem. Wire, wire. We two days need move. Wire, Anya, wire. Please Anya, áldjon meg az Isten. Köszönöm, köszönöm, köszönöm. Greta wants talk. She practise the English.

The air felt like a cool hand on his throat. He went unhurried by some derelict benches next to a park. A guitar was out. "Play anothern," somebody insisted. The guitarist closed his eyes, fingered a few open chords in silent rehearsal, then began to parse his way through "Wonderwall."

Levett's phone vibrated in his pants pocket. The caller was his friend John. He slid his thumb across the touchscreen. He heard John take a drag off his cigarette and it was like seeing him inhale the smoke.

"So whatchya gonna do?"

"You cuttin' straight to that?"

"About what?"

"About the notice."

"Any decision?"

"Maybe."

"You gotta really think about this."

"You think I haven't?"

"Not a lot of money they're offering you. Two and a half grand's gonna go in a snap, and then what?"

"I never considered myself a gamblin' man."

"You're a fighter. You never back down or take shit. You're the last person I see bending over to the Lam twins."

Levett felt it. His friend cared enough to reach out. "I've started grinding my teeth."

"Really think about it. Twenty-five hundo is nothing in this town. That apartment's a nest egg."

"Lane's willing to help."

"I know, I met him at the last tenant meeting. Everyone in the building is on your side, Dylan, we got your back. You gotta fight this."

"It's a chance to get into grassroots activism, I guess. Sorta doesn't gimme much of a choice."

"Hell yeah dawg."

"I'm not an activist, John, I'm an animal. Put me in a corner and I'm comin' through you. But it's still not a straightforward decision.

Sometimes I just wanna get the fuck outta here man. Fuckin' tech yuppie drones, the foreign capital, it's wack. Craft beer bullshit. Affluent white trash." He knew he could not escape all that. If he wanted to escape, he would have to fly to the moon.

"You gotta fight it, D."

"Say I do win the arbitration, the notice is cancelled and I get to stay, like, hypothetically? The dudes above and below have accepted the payout. They're gone. Mario's gone. Hakim'll be gone. If I win I'll have the right to live in a construction zone. All that goddamn noise, John." Levett imagined him twisting the end of his beard in thought. He heard a lighter's knurled wheel rubbing on flint.

John exhaled smoke into the receiver. "I'm not lettin' go, even in a situation like yours. I'd avoid the construction, go live up the coast in a cabin, do my research."

"You and I have different aspirations. I don't want to hide out in the woods. I've had my share of the woods."

John guffawed. Levett passed under the viaducts, the swoosh of cars overhead. Someone drove by with bluebottle exhaust, silence hung from the other end of the line. "Okay, but, you know, be careful about this decision. That's all I'm sayin' man."

"It's an impossible decision."

"It's not at all. It's easy. You're a fighter—fight."

"I may fight."

"They're gonna need awfully heavy machinery to drag me out of there. Wild stallions, yoked oxen, the Jaws of Life..."

▽ ▽ ▽

Blade Girl did powerful backwards crossovers in the empty lane. As they crossed the intersection she called Levett a woman beater. He remembered confronting her, her staring at him, the rehearsed coquetry of it, the studied emptiness. He really regretted doing that now. "Woman beater!" she shouted again. He pretended not to hear.

A big dude with a shirt that said WISH YOU WERE BEER stood to the side glaring at Blade Girl, cellulitic gut hanging out the bottom of the XXL. He said, "Somebody should get a slingshot and shoot some marbles back into your head."

Levett was smiling and chuckling about it. Lane wasn't. "We should take a bus," Lane said. "I think it closes at four and it might be busy. I still need to print out the forms."

"I'm flat broke. Let's walk down. It'll take fifteen minutes."

Lane silently assented. On a hoist in the bay window of Blue Star Motors, a blue Ford GT's clearcoat flickered in the weak light. Below it, a white Lamborghini Huracán sat in predatory shadow.

"Is your bank around here? If we got a receipt with your total funds on it, we could get your fee waived."

In his deep ditch of insolvency Levett cringed at the word "fee." "My bank's the opposite direction."

"There's other banks. Hopefully we can get a receipt. I think we still have time to submit anyway, if it's not packed."

Why did he say "I think"? Levett thought. Vaughn needs a good cudgelling, he thought, imagined the Lams in cement shoes at the bottom of the Fraser, tidewaters flushing out their eye sockets.

"I wouldn't be surprised if this all descended into violence," Levett said.

"I get angry hearing about it."

Autobody. Autobody. A propane dealer. Fine mist with intermittent drops of rain that accumulated on his glasses. In muted colours the downtown skyline shifted upon itself, as if with mirrors and pulleys, revealing, occluding, like the magic lanterns of yore.

They stepped over a dead pigeon coated with maggots, wings askew, entrails oozing from its split breast.

Looming golden arches, scent of boiling canola oil wafting under their noses. Amidst their shopping cart truckage, a tableau of ragged men stood along the eatery's disused patio.

In the viaduct's shadow. Along the low, worn ledges and the slant of the stone embankment. A man approached pushing a plastic shopping cart, all the hard living readable in deep face-lines, his appearance an inventory of personal neglect: the illegible logo on his sweatshirt, blue jeans a glossy brownish black, toecaps blown out, ballcap pulled low over his eyes, ashen hair, nicotine mustache, snuff-juice mouth corners. A couple of pop cans rattling around at the bottom of the brittle cart illustrated his lack.

"I'll try and get a receipt from these guys," Levett said, walking into a BMO. The bank vestibule was all glass. He slid his debit card into an automatic teller, tapped the touchscreen and requested a twenty-dollar bill. The machine pondered for a number of seconds, its innards humming and clicking. TRANSACTION CANCELLED—INSUFFICIENT FUNDS flashed on the screen. His red debit card stuck out from the slot like a tongue.

"I see an ATM sign," Lane said, pointing at a red-on-yellow sign reading Main Mini Mart. Dealers, peddlers and addicts milled about in front of a wrought-iron fence topped with fleurs-de-lys. A hooker slowly stepped onto the curb, her toes squeezed into a pair of high-heel sneakers. Slack belly, sore-ridden arms and thighs. It took her a number of seconds to get both feet from the street to the sidewalk. She was very stoned. Levett imagined her perceiving the surroundings as slow and receded, hardly touching her.

Two cheerful Indigenous men discussed who was going to buy off-sales at the hotel and who would go to the dispensary for weed and shatter.

Under a burnt-out marquee, a figure sat bent behind a rain poncho draped over half a cardboard box, doing cryptic activities behind the improvised shade.

A paucity of merchandise lined the racks of the Main Mini Mart. A woman in a black tank top stood beside the money machine struggling to pull on a fleece jumper, card in the slot and her balance visible in softly glowing white on a black background. More than me, Levett thought.

"Just a second," she said.

He turned away.

Her man stood balancing a suitcase on the crossbar of a mountain bike in the corner next to the windows. Wide windows plastered with junk print thwarted the drear daylight.

She finished dressing and finished her transaction. They left together, man with bike and suitcase following woman with cash.

Levett slid his card into the machine. A disclaimer about the three-dollar transaction fee. He requested a twenty-dollar bill, heard a stylus skittering inside the machine. The receipt curled from a hooded slot. *$0.00 Funds Available* barely visible at the bottom of the printout.

"You can't hardly read it."

"We should hurry," Lane said, looking back the way they'd come, toward the neoclassical edifice, a former bank now called Four Directions, an Indigenous job centre with a part-time Residential Tenancy Branch satellite office.

Around the corner on Hastings a security guard in high-vis apparel and a deer-bone choker talked to a man outside the entrance.

Inside Four Directions a security desk faced the entrance. The walls were painted a sandy colour; the wainscotting, rosettes and scrolls, a darker terracotta. At the back were niches with work tables, where the bank tellers used to stand. They walked around a corner to the left by a series of cubicles. At the end a woman sat behind an information counter.

"Where do we speak to the housing rep?" Lane asked.

"We don't do that," she spat back, nodding to a clipboard on the wall. Levett followed Lane back to the clipboard, wrote his name below other names.

They sat at a large round table outside the first cubicle. The security guard walked in whistling.

"How's it goin' guys?" he said, and they returned the greeting. He took off his sunglasses and said, "I wear these outside because sometimes people spit at me."

Lane turned to Levett with an amused look.

"Not inside, though," the guard added.

A voice rose out from behind the cubicle walls. Another voice made repeated attempts to confirm and clarify information. Levett flipped through one of the free dailies.

"I think I have time to run across to the Carnegie and print off the Application to Waive Filing Fee you need."

"Thanks for doing that," Levett said.

"Here's a pen. You can fill out this one." It was the tenant's Application for Dispute Resolution.

He took up the pen and filled out his name and address in the boxes. Lane was gone about fifteen minutes. While he was gone, Levett listened to the official going over the proper steps his client needed to take for a successful arbitration.

A man had come in. He spoke to the guard about leaving the city. "I don't do it, don't want to be around it, don't want to be around people that're doin' it," he said, setting his palm lightly on the security desk with each point, the guard's head nodding along. A north-facing sun penetrated the clouds, surrounding the two men in a corona.

Lane emerged from the flaring sunshine, took his former seat and began to fill in the other form. They waited there. The cubicle door opened and a woman exited.

The RTB officer picked up the clipboard from its transparent holder and read off the name "Loretta Tilbury." He looked around. No Loretta.

"Dylan Levett."

"Yes."

"Come on in."

He stood aside as they entered the cubicle, mostly desk, with three visitor chairs along the plain opposite wall. They sat down. The painted mouldings along the ceiling were visible above the partition. The officer was in his late forties, acne scars on his cheeks, a pencil moustache. He wore a sky-blue, short-sleeved dress shirt and jeans. Business casual.

"So what are we doing today guys?"

"I'm disputing an eviction notice," Levett said.

"When did you get the notice?" he said, fingers laced on the desktop.

"I got it on, like, April twenty-sixth. It was issued on the twenty-first. I have the form here, but I need to get the fee waived."

The officer's head tilted slightly as Levett placed the ATM slip on the desk, its faint print all too real now. His hand moved across the desktop palm down, hovered above the slip, and took it up close to his face, said, "This is an ATM receipt, but you need two months of bank account statements. Not to worry, though, you've got time. Your submission doesn't have to be in yet if you received your notice on the twenty-sixth."

Lane leaned forward. "I just want to double-check that I can amend the application after it's already submitted."

The agent looked at Lane, at Levett, wondering about the nature of their relationship. Lane continued, "I'm wondering if I'm correct about being able to amend Dylan's application with a statement and evidence."

"The amendment is the evidence package, and that's what you need in your hearing. The purpose of the form is to book a hearing. But you've got time to do that. And you need to go out to our main office to either pay your fee or receive a waiver." The agent looked at Levett, then Lane, again at Levett. "Are you guys computer savvy?"

Lane nodded.

Levett scoffed.

"Well, I have to ask. Trust me, you'd be surprised, you really can't assume." He meshed his fingers on the desktop again. "Do you have a BCeID?"

Levett shook his head.

"Come on over to this side of the desk. I'll show you how to get one, then you can register for a hearing online."

As they stood up and shuffled to his side of the desk, the agent opened the door of the cubicle. They squinted at the sunlight reflecting off the floor tiles. He rotated his screen so it faced them, pulled his mouse and keyboard over, brought up the web page and scrolled down to the link: *Register for your own personal BCeID.*

"See that," he said, and clicked on it. A new window popped up on the browser. "You can register with a driver's licence, a passport or a birth certificate." He clicked on *Start Registration*. "You can select your documents and continue on to your contact information." They stooped in front of the screen nodding. "I understand this stuff is a snap to you young guys. It's just that, you know, the government is going paperless."

"Thanks," Levett said.

"You're welcome. Have a nice day, guys."

"You too," they said, suddenly outside the cubicle.

▽ ▽ ▽

Her face was nigh perfect, something out of a Dutch masterwork, he'd told John. Spearmint-green eyes. Two rows of straight white teeth, an orthodontist's deft handiwork, perhaps. Large enticing smile painted with tart red lipstick—the colour of alert, of emergency, the colour of exits and blood and the inner depths of remembered fire. After their first interaction, engineered by Levett, he imagined falling in love with her, played it all out vaguely in his mind: the West End apartment, the rescued kitten, an exotic holiday planned well in advance.

The cooks called her Kristine.

Instead of ordering his staff meal directly from the cooks, he went to the front of house saying he needed to look at a menu. Kristine stood at the corner of the L-shaped bar. She was doing cutlery roll-ups. She set a fork and knife at the centre of a napkin with measured intensity, folded one corner over the bottom of the utensils, rolled them in the napkin, and set the roll-up neatly with the others in a clear plastic insert for the dinner service. He liked the undivided attention she gave to each of her several duties, from punching in orders on the touchscreen, to tearing the receipt off the debit machine. She arranged the pint glasses on a round tray then poured water into them with a pitcher instead of using the soda wand. Efficient, he thought.

"Do you know where the menus are?"

She sidled around the L and leaned over to look at the lower shelves. She's stocky, he thought, but curvy.

The invisible down on her neck and shoulders glinted in the afternoon sun coming through the patio atrium.

Her hair was pulled straight back in a high, tight ponytail. It was tastefully plain. She had a beauty mark, a small mole above her left upper lip.

He thought these things while attending outwardly to the plotted exchange.

"I'm bored of clubhouses," he said.

"What about a BLT?" she said, leaning there with him, her head tipped sideways to read the vertical text.

"Too much like a clubhouse."

"Reuben?"

He shook off the Reuben.

"Chicken tenders?"

"Not filling enough."

"Goon burger?"

"Lasagna," he decided.

"Mmm."

By the time the cooks got to cooking his lasagna and he ate it, she was off work, posted up at the end of the bar next to the L. "How was your lasagna Dylan?"

He liked this attentive gesture.

▽ ▽ ▽

The steam clock whistled its quarter. He sipped coffee in a wedge of shade. Shunting railcars behind him, their couplings clashing and echoing like titans at war. The diesel engines bawled. His ass got cold on the parking block. Halfway down the cup he went back inside, wondering if his team would advance to the conference finals. They had Connor, the best player in the world.

Vik cursed on the line, one bill up, two buns on the cutting board. The kitchen was dead quiet.

"What's up?"

Vik shook his head, averted his eyes and, gripping a knife, darted back and forth from one side of the line to the other, to the grill and the cooler, to the toaster, back to the cutting board, grill to the cooler, accomplishing nothing.

A chain of bills came up all at once. Then he recovered. He tore up lettuce leaves to fit the burger buns, fanned sliced tomatoes over the lettuce, placed red onion rounds on top, spread Dijonnaise on the other side of the bun, laid Gruyère to melt on a smoking vegetarian patty with intent, lifted fry baskets from the spitting, popping oil, turned on tiptoe pulling three dishes from the top shelf with a long pair of tongs, arranged them on the stainless-steel counter opposite the flat-top, garnished each with a lemon wedge, a sprig of parsley next to a diced strawberry.

He rang the bell. At the sideboard he took a swig of cola, long since flat.

Vik walked over to the Hobart, levered the door open. Gouts of steam rolled out from it.

"Can I help you?" Levett said. He didn't like people in his territory, small as it was.

"As if."

"You seemed upset."

"Want something to eat?"

Levett turned away puzzled.

The daytime bar manager Lowell swung through the kitchen door with a cordless phone to his ear. "No, we don't reserve tables on game nights. It gets super packed in here, people line up to get in, we can't even let friends save seats." He hung up with an indignant thumb. "Fuck, people are stupid. We've never made reservations on game nights, like we'd start taking rezos for game seven. He shook his head in disgust, roughly pushing through the swing door without a knock of warning to staff who might have been on the other side.

Crowd thickening, increasingly raucous. Both teams faced elimination. Levett thought of the phrase "sudden death," thought there was mercy and dignity in it while at the same time being utterly humiliating.

No sign of Kristine. It would have been creepy of him to check the servers' schedule. He was tempted, went and checked it. She had the night off.

Portioning was written on the whiteboard beside his name. He slid the dish rack underneath the steel counter, squeegeed the countertop into the gaping dish machine, gathered a green toylike scale made of plastic, a box of clear freezer bags, and checked the portion-weight chart tacked to the kitchen wall. Seven ounces for onion rings.

He slit the case tape with the point of a scissor blade, pulled the plastic bag around the box flaps to expose the manufactured food. The frozen rings left a greasy film on his hands.

Vik would always reach around him for one-litre containers, or a whisk, or one of the large stainless-steel mixing bowls, muttering curse words at unknown targets. He would pace up and down the line shaking his head, return to the dish pit, something there he needed but he didn't quite know what. He'd look around, walk away empty-handed.

Levett turned around, the short glowering cook's face was five inches away from his own. Vik didn't say anything though; he just stared like someone does when they challenge you to a fist fight, his cloudy glasses reflecting the overhead fluorescent tubes. Without a word he walked away.

Some minutes drained out of the shift, but not many, not enough. The kitchen started getting orders. A dirty container flew into the dish pit, hit the wall and spun on the clean stainless-steel counter.

Levett asked Vik what was up.

Something about whites. He went for a smoke. Levett heard the clash of trains through the open back door.

"If he keeps throwing shit by me I'm gonna hose him down with the nozzle."

Jake laughed warily. An image formed in his mind, visible on his face, depicting the volatile consequences of this proposal.

"He really shouldn't be doing that."

"If he keeps doing that he's gonna get wet. French fine dining background or not, I don't give a fuck."

Vik sauntered back onto the line.

"Don't throw things by me into the dish pit."

"Haha, sure, okay," he said, smiling and nodding.

One by one, night servers arrived. A swelling din as they entered through the swing door. Anna came, a sweet haute goth studying fashion, from Russia, via Atlanta and Dallas. She had a Psychic TV stick-and-poke tattoo on her thumb.

"I can't. Believe. How. Retarded people are," Lowell said to Anna. "They might eat, they might have a drink, they might stay… fucking morons." His tone was scalding.

Hoots and hollers. Game time. A low, ominous chant bled through the walls. During the playoffs the kitchen had seen a drastic increase in chicken-wing sales. Henry had written it on the board. The case lay in readiness on the floor of the basement cooler, bound with two plastic straps.

Levett lugged it upstairs, straps cutting into his hands. He mixed flour, salt, pepper and steak spice in a bus bin, grabbed a chopping knife off the magnet and cut slits in the two bags of tightly packed chicken meat, battered and trayed them, latex gloves soon caked with clumps of bloodstained flour.

The wings smelled of sick death. He retched, pushed it down, continued to batter and line them up horizontally, top to bottom, left to right, on the large baking trays.

He heard voices crescendo out front. Eruption.

The booming welter of voices faded. He went out to check the score. Out there it was orange and blue, orange and blue, orange and blue. Score one–nothing Oil. Lowell brought a full bus bin into the kitchen.

Back in the dish pit traying chicken, he heard rough, merry cheers out there. Even the women sounded masculine. He imagined not a goal, but an act of sanctioned violence. A punishing bodycheck, Plexiglas flexing and clattering, audience wincing on the other side of the warped pane, their mouths shaped into small Os, a player slow to rise up onto his skates again.

As he prepped wings, Levett wondered whether or not he would win the arbitration hearing, whether or not he had made the right decision. It was too late now. But two and a half Gs weren't shit.

He finished one of the vacuum-sealed bags. He peeled off the caked latex gloves, dropped each into the garbage can and snapped on another pair. Clutching another tightly packed wad of poultry with fresh gloves, he felt the cold deadness, felt it in his palms and wrists, felt it pass through his elbows and up to his shoulders, his neck, down the spine to its base. He remembered walking by the chicken processing facility when he worked at the lighting shop, thinking of the veiled carnage inside, the zigzagging conveyor belts and the refined disassembly process, remembered the stacked cubic pens and a forklift driver wearing coveralls and a face mask with two cylindrical filters on the mouthpiece like that was how many you needed, in there. Stray feathers. Collar of a laundered t-shirt over his nose against the putrescence, the noisome effluvia, rushing past the bay doors, each time fording a sluice of rotten fluid, hurrying away, only to enter into the dain of a fish processing facility just up the street.

"Hot," Vik shouted, bursting in with a pot of soup he set in the sink. He came back with a pail of ice he spread around the pot as a coolant. "Try this," he said, and put a small bowl on the shelf by the solvents.

"What kind is it?"

"Bean and bacon."

"Thanks."

"Yeah buddy." He sounded calm again. Chits chittered from the miniature printer. Anna called out orders. A lot of hot wings, barbecue wings, honey garlic wings, poutines and cheeseburgers. The front-of-house staff were slammed with food, beer and cocktail orders. Lowell walked in with another bus bin and slid it under the sink.

The crowd let out a cry of collective disappointment.

"Tie game now," Lowell said.

The bar was at capacity. A line had formed at the door in vain.

Levett stuffed the bloody plastic bag in the garbage can.

As he crossed the line, Vik said, "Hey, I dare you to yell 'Connor McDavid sucks' through the door."

They laughed. He was the best hockey player in the world. Everyone knew that. There was a consensus. Winged feet and the softest of hands. Not only could he skate fast but he could change direction laterally, instantly, almost teleport, doing things a human body shouldn't be able to do. That's what pro athletes are for, he thought. They do things physically regular folks can only imagine. Connor did astonishing things with the puck, all manner of deke, made defencemen look like they were standing still, turned goalies inside out. Here's McDavid in full flight. Jersey parachuting. End to end. Scores. There was a massive eruption out front and it rose up in him too and he cheered without having seen it.

Anna brought some empty sauce bottles to the dish pit.

"Hey Anna, back in Atlanta did you ever hang with Gucci Mane?"

"He was my babysitter."

"What about 2 Chainz?"

"We lived next door to him."

"You ever meet Quavo?"

"Quavo took my sister to the prom." She said it deadpan.

The shift wore on stagnantly, fryer hiss and patty sizzle, the dish machine groaning as if it housed everyone's complaint, moaning along with the dull tinkle of nozzle spray on crockery, Levett squeezing, aiming, holding the jet on an area of baked-on cheese crust.

The rabble let off dismayed exultations every time the Oilers missed a scoring opportunity.

People stopped ordering food and committed themselves to alcohol. Anna and Vik flipped the kitchen, broke everything down to be washed, rotated the sauces. Vik scraped the dirty oil off the flat-top into a trough with a special black brick. The drain fed into a stainless-steel insert that made Levett shudder when it was taken out to be emptied and cleaned. He saw the grease slosh around and imagined the hair above his temples paler, his skin saggier and his clogged arteries buckling.

"Can you fill up sauces?" Anna said.

"Sure, I guess," he shrugged, hated dicking around with sauce bottles at the end of his shift. He aimed the barbecue sauce in the squeeze bottle, wiped the threads with a damp paper towel, capped the squeeze bottle and the bulk sauce jar, then poised himself to direct tzatziki into an open squeeze bottle with a rubber spatula, thick condiment dripping down the sides. Curry mayo clung to the outsides of a squeeze bottle. You just had to hang the mayo-slathered spoon over the bottle mouth and let it cloyingly drip inside, the whole finicky task an insult to Bachelors of Arts everywhere.

Gulping once, twice, the dish machine fell silent. He pulled the last load of dishes out from its steaming maw. Then he changed. He wet his hair. He put on a hat.

He gathered his beer from the walk-in cooler. The large steel scoop lay on top of the ice machine. He shovelled cubes into the plastic bag. This is how he did it since they cut his power.

Pushing through the swing door he said good night to Anna and Vikram.

Anna said, "Night," in a sweet voice. Vik stared and said nothing.

The pub was still busy. Blue-and-orange people sat wasted and crestfallen over their warm pints. Two yuppies sat in front of the soda fountain opposite where he was squirting himself an ice water.

"How's it goin'?" one said.

"Not bad. Who won?"

"Oilers lost bud, didn't you see it?"

"I was working in the kitchen. Maybe I could get a radio and listen to the games."

"Pff, a radio," the yuppie scoffed. "That's a joke. Get a tablet. At least."

"Too late now," the other one said.

Fuck off, he thought.

Highlight reels looped on the big screen. One of the Ducks getting creamed. Instead of slowing it down, it looked like the network sped it up. He walked out onto the damp flagstones.

He delayed a cab crossing Water. At Cambie and Cordova a linguistic cross-section of the touristic species rose up from the Cambie's patio: laid-back Brazilian Portuguese, backlander Australian English, carousing High German—all mingling and dissipating in a pall of blue dopesmoke.

He went eastbound along a parkade and then by the film school. Up ahead the illuminated outline of El Choza's cactus signboard. The traffic lights on Abbott and Cordova changed. Green to yellow, yellow to red in electromagnetic semaphore. A grey-skinned man pushed a beat-up stroller with a vacuum cleaner in the seat. Panhandlers leaned along the closed shops holding cardboard-and-felt-pen signage in their quavering hands. Unpunctuated messages in block caps. *ANYTHING HELPS GOD BLESS. HOMELESS HUNGRY LOST MY GIRL TO FENTANYL.*

A listless chattering throng gathered outside the Grand Union Hotel below the old hand-painted sign. *Vancouver's Favorite Country Music Pub* in letters done to look like nailed-up lumber. Night people lurked in shifting permutations around the gaping bar threshold. Rail-thin hookers catcalled for dates. Scabby dealers straddled BMXs. Young couples trudged by in off-brand sneakers and t-shirts, dragging their feet, the seized wheels of coffin-sized luggage scraping behind.

Winged curses of frustration and desperation ricocheted off the buildings.

A hulking man sauntered through oncoming traffic to a leitmotif of car horns and squalling brake pads. He yelled over his shoulder in stride, "Right over there in the doorway, just go in, you'll see him."

Among a clutch of young adults smoking outside a club an elderly man held a floppy ballcap out for change. Hollow cheeks and puckered lips, no teeth.

In a corner store window across the street an OPEN sign emptied and filled with cherry light. Next to the bodega people stood along a ledge with a chain-link fence peeled open at the corner, asking each other "where Frank was" because "he had oxies yesterday."

A siren flared up and began to howl terribly somewhere nearby.

Fragments of dialogue accompanied his passage like bad scenery you only ever hear about: "She's a fuckin dry cunt bitch"; "He took my scooter, five bills and my phone"; "Tell 'im I'm lookin' for 'im and he's gonna get shitkicked"; "Goof! Goof!"; "Don't be fuckin' favourin' her."

He continued eastbound. The vestiges of a narrow-gauge rail line embedded in the pavement ran blind from International Village and disappeared into a gated condominium terrace on the north side of Pender. At the base of the Chinatown gate a pair of foo dogs stood guard. They were decorated with aerosol names. *Cree Thug. KAZ. Lefty.* Someone had painted their eyes pink as if inside them were death rays charging.

A young burnt-out couple walked past. The man trailed the woman. He pushed a plastic shopping cart laden with their effects. Atop the load a guitar case had been secured with a length of severed electrical cord.

On Carrall a lady pushed a two-tiered shopping cart down the bike lane. It must have seemed to her like Levett was staring. She eyed him down, let out a bitter snort.

"Have a good night," he said.

"Thanks." Sardonic tone.

"It's a warm evening. No rain."

"That's about it," she scoffed. Turned west. The cart's rattling heralded her long shadow, slanted upon the high concrete wall and moving inexorably forward.

Across the street, people were camped out on the benches along the soccer field. A man slept with his effects set out around him. No dog to sentinel. He looked to be in his twenties. A gaping mouth showed few teeth. His unwashed face wore lines of hard living. Of homelessness and crack smoking. Days without food. Like the titles of tracts about suffering.

Chinatown Plaza's colossal neon sign burned scarlet and gold forty feet up the side of the parkade. Popping ollies echoed over the soccer pitch from the skatepark.

Headlight cones drifted along the viaduct.

He sat down to rest on the curved ledge at the southernmost end of the skatepark.

Overhead the hushed passage of cars. Everywhere there seemed a tranquil somnolent motion. The swelling clickity-clack of a train rose and died away as it dipped below the viaduct along a hedgerow and curved westward. A constant sweep of traffic on the boulevard.

Skaters cruised amongst the viaduct's transverse columns trying tricks. Switch stance disasters to fakies, kickflips, heelflips, hardflips, bigspins and backside tailslides. All of them speaking an idiom he still knew. He used to be able to do the tricks too, but that was years ago. He wished he hadn't quit. They were having so much fun. They were crewed up on a warm night, smoking joints and crushing beers.

He looked into the empty, illuminated expanse of the parkade as the soccer pitch floods went out one by one. The path lamps burned on. The only features he could make out in the distance were a guy's bare folded arms and two triangular nostrils. A mangy bitch slept tits up on the dirt beside him.

Levett pulled a silver can beaded with condensation from his bag, cracked it and lit a joint. He poured a long draft of cold beer down his throat. A light breeze played on the damp of his neck.

Hardly audible urethane wheels on glassy cement polished by years of these same gliding wheels.

No birdsong. Pigeons didn't count.

No sooner had he sat down than a lone figure in baggy shorts and a loose tank top coasted out of the shadows.

The skater rolled to the ledge and sat down adjacent to Levett. He had sharp Indigenous features. "You got a smoke?"

"Don't smoke," Levett said, took a hit off his joint, held it out to the stranger.

"That's cool man." He sat for a moment then spoke again. "It's good to get out and skate anyway, relaxes me."

"It's a good outlet."

The skater nodded, pushing his soaked hair back into thick spikes. "I'm livin' with my parents right now. Well, my dad. I can't wait to get my own place. Next month I think. I gotta move and then look for work." His forehead was quartered by two lines of worry, an x- and a y-axis.

"You thinkin' construction?"

"I thought about construction. Never done it, though. There's cranes sticking up all over the place. Could be good." He pushed his hair back again. "I'm from Alberta—Edmonton."

"I'm Albertan."

"I'm not originally from Edmonton."

"Where else you live?"

"Swan Hills, Barrhead, then Edmonton. Edmonton's rough though, fuckin' gangbangers are harsh there. Doesn't seem as bad here. I mean, over there," he gestured toward that notoriously sketchy area two blocks away.

"People are alright," he said.

He cut his eyes over at the skate posse.

"You'd find trouble if you were looking," Levett said.

"I don't know much about it. Moved out here with my dad a couple months ago. He was doin' good for a while. I hadn't really seen him in four years. Cuz he was all cracked out."

Levett didn't react. Not that he didn't care.

"It's pretty disappointing."

Levett introduced himself. The guy's name was Justin.

"You wanna beer?"

"I'd drink a beer."

Levett took a cold can from the plastic bag and handed it over. A silver-plated bracelet dangled off Justin's wrist, clinking against the can as he took it. The curved plate on top featured a red enamel hexagon inset with a caduceus. His forearms were dotted with cigarette burns.

"I'm allergic to bee stings, what are you allergic to?" Levett said.

"Nuts."

"Cashews?"

"All nuts."

"Almonds?"

"Every nut."

"Even like, half a peanut?"

"I'd be on the wrong side of the dirt if I sucked on half a peanut. I can't even be in the kitchen when someone opens a jar of peanut butter."

He pulled out an EpiPen from a cargo pocket in his shorts.

"I'm supposed to have one of those."

Justin put the needle back. He cracked his beer.

Levett looked up at the massive Ts of the viaduct columns, the faint seams where the form panelling touched. They diminished toward the stadium and the downtown core. There were ledges with coping built around the bases of the columns; a low, sharp wedge-like bank with a waxed edge people did salad grinds and bluntslides on. *HOSER* and *LUTZ* and *G4N*—Good 4 Nuthin' Crew—aerosoled on the columns. An image of Satan rendered on the large bank. The paint wasn't red enough. It looked more like a Minotaur.

"Did you work in the patch?" Levett asked.

"I had a couple oil-patch jobs. Insulating wellheads was the first thing I did. Then I did seismic. I filled in for a buddy on a service rig for a couple weeks."

"I swamped on a picker truck off and on for five years, hauled drill mud for a winter. That sucked."

"That fracking stuff is hard on the environment. All those chemicals contaminate the water. I don't get it. We treat the earth like shit when really it's—"

"A big machine—"

"A big organism."

Justin jacked one knee up to his chest and braced his shin.

"Switch frontside pop shove-it," a skater said and rolled out into the open with a beer bottle in one hand and a cigarette in the other to attempt the trick. The board shot out from under him and he landed on his ass, remaining there, palms flat on the cool cement, the bottle and the cigarette set down slightly out of reach.

"I can't stand my dad's girlfriend. All she does is hang around leeching off him. My dad won the lottery." Levett was kind of tuned out, but this got his attention. "Like half a million." Justin looked Levett straight in the eye. "It's almost gone. He got it last year, no, like less than two years ago. Bought a big-screen TV. Did a couple hundred grand worth of blow. Bought a brand-new Dodge Challenger. Wrecked it. Ten minutes after he got it out of the body shop he wrecked it again. Then like, you know, everyday expenses." He said it all smiling, but with a discernible warble in his throat.

Levett didn't know what to say.

"And his girlfriend just sits around spending his money. 'Let's get some down,'" Justin mocked. "She's a user. He's just her next score. Doesn't give a shit about my dad. Once his money's gone, she'll be gone. It's good to get out of the house."

Neither of them spoke. The passing train left its long weighty sound, its intermittent screeching.

There was a swelling clatter, not the train, but a desiccated man in Asics and black shorts who pushed a heavily laden Costco cart. Garbage bags bulging with aluminum cans hung from multiple points around the conveyance. Calves bulging. There were some piled quilts, a suitcase, a yoga mat, a tent, a folded tarp, a rolled tarp, a tankless propane burner. There was a plastic fan rake poking from the miscellanea of his load. He had a jouncing Budweiser flag for an ensign.

"Are you native?"

Justin nodded out of his trance, drank. "I got my treaty card. I can't remember my number though. Kind of embarrassing."

Levett relit his joint.

"Most guys know their number by heart, in case you lose your card. It's like your social insurance number, you should have it memorized."

"What's your band?"

"I can't even say it."

Levett cracked another beer. There was one left. He didn't offer it.

"It's hard to remember, Kap... Kapaw... Kapawe'no, or something like that."

"Do you miss your nation?"

Justin chuckled nervously, unsure whether or not he was being fucked with. "I got a couple friends are treaty, but I'm not really in touch with the culture." He chuckled again, drank, set the can aside. Then, in all seriousness: "I just got a card. I'm just part native. It don't mean much besides having a card."

His skateboard rolled back and forth under his shoes, bearings grinding. He seemed to be watching the dark skyline for something that might turn up there.

"I'm gonna peace dude," Levett said.

"Take it easy." Justin sounded forlorn. He sighed. "It's good to get out of the house." He kept saying it, like he needed to remind himself, or he didn't quite believe it.

Levett looked down at his bag. Ice water was draining from it. Over the coping down the ledge into the corner embroidered with litter. Levett rose with the dripping bag. They shook hands. Justin had a strong handshake but his hands had gone soft from idleness.

"What's your name again?"

"Dylan."

"Oh yeah, sorry."

"Okay."

"Later."

"Bye."

Levett sidled through a gap in the park fence and went on in the dank air, went on parallel with the elevated track. A cyclist pedalled by. There was a skunk sniffing around on the knoll next the parking lot with its tail erect. The lighted vertices of Telus Science World's geodesic dome shifted gradients on a timer, from yellow to orange to red to violet to pink to yellow to orange over and over again.

He walked the promenade at the head of False Creek. A sailboat called *Mizzy* lay anchored in the black water, sail furled, cabin portholes shuttered. Science World's red base feathered in the rippling water beside the vessel. A man with a fibreglass canoe over his head came by.

Another man chided him. "You walkin' back to PoCo with that, Canoehead?"

"I live in the city."

"Back to Walnut Grove," said the josher's girlfriend.

Levett laughed about that coming up the long hill.

A warm wind started up. The leaves of a weeping willow shimmered in the streetlight like a dancer's hair.

Across the street he saw another skunk. Its back stripe blended with a patch of lilac, hyacinth and daisy, aquiver as it disappeared through the bush and the bars of a slender architrave that doubled as a shed for garden tools.

Cab drivers slept in their taxis on Main. He approached the Bellevue.

The foyer's sharp light stung his eyes. Now they had installed a video camera above the elevator in the corner facing the entrance, and another above the main entrance facing the elevator. A ceiling tile had been removed above the elevator and a black bar with mounting holes speared down from the dark rectangle.

I've lived here for twelve years. Seven bills for a one bedroom. It doesn't get much better than that. Not here. They tried to jack it up to twelve. All this when I was working on the Venom costumes. Like, I had zero time for anything, right? You know how it gets in film. One day you're eating chicken, the next day feathers. I knew it wasn't legal. The advocate I got through the church advised me to suggest I let them do the renovations, and when they were done I could move in again. They weren't havin' it. Instead we had an RTB *hearing. The arbitrator upheld the notice. I took it to the Supreme Court. Meanwhile I'm packing up my house. I've been pounding the pavement trying to figure this out. Of course, the advocate, he's not a real lawyer. He hasn't taken the bar. On top of that I'm blasting out masks and crests and capes left right and centre. Custom sewing jobs. Short turnaround. Like same day–type shit. That's why it looks like Armageddon in here. I would totally smoke a joint. Now it's in the appeal stage. Now what's in question is the arbitrator's decision. It's not even about the notice anymore. That's exactly what my advocate said: they won't renovate, they're not renovating. Oh, my, god, I totally needed a hoot. Can I offer you a glass of wine? I've got three different reds, a couple white. Just point to the one. The Riesling. Me too. Hot out, eh. And the smoke. Do you have a lot more deliveries? I'm going on and on. They tried to show the apartment last week. They've communicated with me by mail this whole time and then out of nowhere they knock on the door trying to show the place. I totally made a scene. The couple who came to view it felt really bad. The manager's eyes were kind of vibrating. It looked like he was calculating. Not like, figures, not like long division or something. Moves. Chess moves. Thank you so much for the ganj. I know it's mine, like I paid for it, but… Seriously, look at me, look at this, I'm boxed in here. I've been crying off and on all day. My Pfaff is what's keeping it together. Everything. I don't know where I'm gonna go if they deny the appeal. No dude in the picture. My dad lives in Mississauga. We haven't spoken in ages. He hates that I'm gay, but he should just step out of his glass closet already. He's a nonagenarian. Good luck. Anyhoo. I'm like, one of the go-to people for costumes right now. There's the film biz, the theatre biz, private events. I know I could. But seven hundred. It's a chill overhead. And you know, feast and famine. Some months you're hemorrhaging money. You can light that again if you want, I'm good. Oh you have to go. No. I totally understand. You've got a job to do. Respect.*

Levett ordered a coffee, sat down and opened his laptop. He refreshed his browser. There was an email in the Bellevue thread from Kaitlin.

> It's hard to say this in an email, but I'm scared. Forward this to anyone else in the building you think has not received this email:
>
> Virgil, my neighbour, has kept me up every weekend since I moved in. Mainly he just blasts music, often screeching at his visitors and slamming things around. I hear Magnus, John, I'm pretty sure Dylan's involved. This is from two to five in the morning usually. Virgil has regularly creeped in the courtyard with other males next to my window late in the night, until they put up the tarp, thank you.

Levett almost spat out his coffee at the computer screen.

> A single woman lies alone on the other side of the curtains. What he's doing out there? I don't know. He's asked me over for drinks out there a few times, extending the invitation through my open window. I very nicely say no thanks.
>
> The other day he was working up to another spaz and I pounded on the wall obviously,, He got quite nasty, it edged into hate speech. He shouted "Go fuck yourself, BABY!,," then he proceeded to revile me publicly,, ((I mean, we're basically in a common space with these thin old walls)) and in a condescending tone lecture me from his apartment to mine. "For YOUR information, this is how the Bellevue functions."
>
> I wrote him a letter to doc that I felt my apartment was no longer a safe space. Virgil came by the next day. He was extremely apologetic. He invited me for a drink,

again. I reluctantly said yes. He was really sorry, said he'd make a strong effort to accommodate me, and insisted if it was ever too loud I should come over and say so. By all means he assured me. Since I've lived here out of about a hundred disrupting late nights I knocked seven or eight times. Sadly, this problem at home is impacting my mental health. I'm helpless all alone at night and this feeling is extremely intense, scary and unfair,,

Today at three in the morning he woke me again with his music. Usually arena rock, but this time it was Kate Bush, and I love Kate Bush, so that's weird. I waited half an hour. When he obviously wasn't going to shut it down I went and knocked. Virgil agreed to "dial it back,," "I'll dial it back, I'll dial it back," he said. But then he started pacing next to our common wall and babytalking me: "Pwease," he said, "your tunes are way TOO loud, turn it down, you're so diswuptive." He carried on saying how insane it is that I don't let him "DO HIS THING IN HIS OWN HOUSE." At about four this morning he yelled, "Get a load of her having sex, I hear her all the time, do I whine and bitch about it?" Then he screamed at me "I HEAR! Hear THAT?! FUCK OFF!"... And he kept doing impressions of me... mock sounds of a woman doing it ,, At six in the morning he came out and shouted gibberish outside my door then said quite clearly: "Buy ear protection and ZIP IT." Besides knocking the one time I did not participate in any dialogue with him,,

He wondered why she so favoured the double comma.

Obviously I didn't want to get management involved because I don't want to undermine anyone's living situation,, He's clearly an alcoholic, though I'm being empathetic beyond all reason. I can't excuse it anymore. I made a complaint in writing to the landlords and filed a report with the police department. I'm at the end of my tether, really disturbed by it all. Just so you all know, an extreme situation involving noise has now become sexually threatening. I no longer feel safe at home.

▽ ▽ ▽

A robed old lady stood motionless up in the pedway spanning the lane, clutching her walker, presiding over the alley, the donation porch at the back of the Sally Ann. She had a big lentigo on her forearm you could see through the tinted window.

He went by the undertaker's. It seemed they built the old folks' home directly across the street to make their near future clear, not skirt the issue. In case it crossed their minds to exit samsara, the Buddhist monastery was right around the corner.

Looking north he saw masked workers high up with power sanders, dusty and diffuse in the open cubes of the tower. Blades of sunshine lit the raw concrete as they negotiated their harnesses. Levett grimaced at the incidental beauty of the image.

Flag girls refused traffic down the side street, waving and twisting their reflective paddles to catch the light. Pylons cordoned off three semis end to end. In the spaces between: stacked form panels, waste tanks, hoses, lumber scraps and cut-offs, gravel piles, gravel skids.

Day labourers—people of colour—unloaded Bosch and General Electric dishwashers and stoves from the corroded China Shipping containers.

He felt a pang in his abdomen, had felt it to the DQ and back. Hot tong feeling in his stomach as a compact share-car cut him off crossing the street.

▽ ▽ ▽

The transom above Virgil's door was ajar. When he had male callers the transom was always closed. You could hear music inside. Contemporary jazz. Levett knocked.

"Hello," said the voice inside.

"It's D."

"Come in."

He tried the door.

"Hold on a minute."

A bout of coughing.

The door swung open. Long hair tied back. Tall, thin, Cree, in his early fifties, skin a bit loose from drink. He wore his rimless spectacles. "I'll get you a drink."

"I brought a joint."

"Thank goodness."

Virgil reappeared with a tumbler of vodka soda, a wedge of lime bobbing on the surface. He set it on the glass table below his loft bed. He sat down in an old hydraulic barber chair, desert boots planted on the discoloured Persian rug. He made a stung face. Braced his temples with a thumb and forefinger.

"Did you happen to, um, read an email that Kaitlin apparently shared with the entire building?" Virgil asked.

"I did," Levett said.

"I can't believe it," Virgil said, forehead cupped in the palm of his hand.

"Neither could I," Levett said. "You two've been going at it—"

"Don't tell me what it said, what she said, that fucking little cunt."

"What's been going on?"

"Thursday night I had Magnus and John over, his gal Willa came with. We were having some drinks and of course *knockety-knock*. I said 'Okay, I'll quiet down.'"

"What'd she say?"

"She went back into her place. In an hour there's another knock at my door."

"Who was that?"

Virgil put a cigarette in his mouth, lit it with a Bic and inhaled deeply. "She called the cops on me."

"The cops showed up at your door."

"Eeeyeah. The guy was really nice, kind of a young buck, pretty hot actually. So he says, 'We got a call from your neighbour Ms. Brown. She's made a complaint about the noise.' And I say, 'Look man, I've been havin' it out with her for months. I work nights, this is my weekend.' 'Perfectly understandable,' the cop says, then he tells me, 'She's accused you of sexual harassment.' I say, 'Excuse me officer? I'm gay. You know that, right?' I say, 'She knows that, right?' He was like, 'Look, we believe you. You didn't do anything wrong. We've got to follow up on this stuff.' And I was like, 'This is my home of going on twenty years. I work nights. And I'm queer. She can add it up.'

"'It's alright. Live your life,' he says. 'Try to come to an understanding with your neighbour.'"

"Why'd she call you out on the thread if she already reported you to the police?"

"That's what I was wondering," Virgil said, voice worming through the words. He exhaled a cloud of cigarette smoke that flattened against the ceiling. "Can we smoke that joint please?"

Levett fired it up.

"Thank you. It's good to see you. Thank you, Dylan. Thank you for coming to see me. I'm so embarrassed. I'm so hurt by what she did."

"She said some harsh sh—"

"I don't wanna know."

"Sorry."

"It's okay."

"I mean, just reading it made me—"

"Don't tell me," Virgil said. "Just leave me out of that."

"You're the subject—"

"I don't wanna know."

"You're kinda like a frat boy."

They laughed.

"Stirring the pot," Virgil said, and rolled his eyes.

"Trying to relive them Jasper days eh?"

Levett's stomach felt better once they started kidding around.

"Oh, yeah, definitely, yeah, that's right." Virgil shook his head and smiled.

"The cop told me to keep it down after eleven. What time is it?"

"Just after five."

"We really carried on in Jasper. I tell you that. This spoiled brat next door hasn't seen shit. At one point I was working for Jasper Park Tramway, and I was roommates with the owner's son."

"Like a little narrow-gauge track and engine up into the mountains?"

"No, it's on a wire, you know, not a funicular, it's a… a… it's a cable car." Virgil snapped his fingers on the word "cable."

"A gondola."

"I've heard it called that, if you want to get all European on me."

"You know I'm straight Eurotrash."

"You're tasteful Dylan, there's nothin' trashy about you."

"Me and my roommate, we, we'd get fucked up and take the tramway out at night after hours. We'd take LSD and ride it up into the Rockies."

"What'd you see?"

"It was pretty dark."

"Ever get caught?"

"Not doing that. But me and Brett, Brett Markson, that was my roommate's name, we had a shaker at our house, you know, a real house-wrecker. The cops came. It was all over town. I mean, Jasper's so small, right? Brett's dad fired me."

"Why?"

"He said my behaviour reflected negatively on the company."

"You're just a shit disturber."

"I guess so." He stuck his middle finger up at the wall he shared with Kaitlin Brown.

"Is she home?"

"I heard her leave around noon. Good riddance."

"Have you had other disputes in the Bellevue?"

"Fifteen years ago, but it was one time and we worked it out."

"You've had enough to deal with in the last year, with Shane, excuse me mentioning it, and then your mom."

"I know. I know Dylan. Thank you for saying that."

The tarp started to pop and roll like a synthesized ocean.

"Not to mention my garden," Virgil said bitterly. "Does the spoiled brat know? Just two months ago I looked my own mother in the eyes and she didn't know who I was. I held her hands, I hugged her and said 'It's me, Virgil, your son.' Nothing. She didn't know her own son. And she didn't even know her own husband. Does that little priss have any idea what I've been through, and what I do for a goddamn living?"

Levett knew what she meant, though, at least about the noise. There were a few times when Virgil and his late friend Shane Stork carried on into the wee hours. "You got any drawing paper?"

"I have beautiful paper."

"Have you got a pencil?"

He rummaged around in his closet, pulled out a ream of watercolour paper. Then he pulled out a Venus pencil from the rolltop bureau. He sat down at the glass table.

Levett pushed the paper toward Virgil and set the pencil on top.

"Draw your garden."

"I could easily draw and label my garden."

"Let's see."

Virgil pretended to be inconvenienced. Soon he was fleshing out the diagram. Somebody knocked on the door.

Magnus stepped in wearing a Greg Norman Bermuda hat, white hair shooting out from the back and sides. Ashen blazer overtop a turquoise tennis shirt of 1970s vintage.

"Hello Magnus," Virgil said. Levett wondered if there were acrimonious feelings between the two of them presently. "You look thin," Virgil declared.

Magnus stood in the door frame, four fingers of each hand tucked into his blazer pockets. "Walking fifteen miles a day," he said, "and twelve days into a nineteen-day cleanse, thirty push-ups a day, spread throughout the day, an old guy like me has to be careful, messing around with too many cata-stenichs—"

"Calisthenics—"

"Too many cata-sthenics at my age will give you a heart attack."

"Would you like a drink?"

"Yes please, a drink, a drink, just a small one, two fingers." Magnus set himself down on the leather sofa. "Aah, there's the man. Did you get your power back on?"

Levett shook his head.

Virgil's head poked out from the kitchen. "How the hell are you living without power?"

"It's not that bad in the summer."

"You can't live without power."

"You can."

"How much do you owe them?"

"About two hundred. That includes the reconnection fee."

"Pay it," Virgil demanded.

"You're down at the Wild Rose now," Magnus said, "working steady, free fish and chips, good fish and chips, the best in town, the best in the world, you should be able to get your power back on."

"Why should I get—"

"Why should you get your power back on? Because it's a good idea! You need your fucking power," Virgil barked.

"Quit interrupting me."

"Seriously."

"You're terrible for that."

Virgil covered his eyes, body hanging slack in the barber chair. "Go on," he said. "Go on now," he gesticulated dismissively. "I wouldn't want to *interrupt you.*"

"Why get the power back on if I'm going to get evicted in a month or two anyway?"

Virgil and Magnus looked at each other, conceded, nodding in unison.

"Why don't I run an extension cord up from my place to yours? You can use my power," Virgil said.

"I'll think about it," Levett said. "It's a bit of a heat score." If he went for it, it would be another thing he owed Virgil. There was already the eighty bucks.

"The Lams wouldn't find out. They didn't even know I had a garden out there for *fifteen years.* We could run it under the tarp and up through your window."

"It's actually a good... it's a good temporary solution," Magnus added. "I've got no input anymore. They've taken my keys to the boiler room and storage areas. All I do is floors and garbages now. Do it. I wouldn't say anything."

The tarp slanted up from the foot of Virgil's windows. It fluffed again and settled. Magnus let the straight Stolichnaya play on his palette, rested the glass on his knee. On the shelf behind Virgil there was a cork diorama with a pagoda and cranes. He had a collection of cork dioramas. They all had intricate temples inside and subtly carved plane trees, miniature rustic folk with mattocks and donkeys.

There was an urn next to a clay sake bottle holding white orchids. A Japanese ink painting leaned against the wall atop a small ceramic tripod. The image was of a solitary figure somewhere dark.

"You know," Magnus said, sucking on his teeth, studying the invisible truths evident in the glass of vodka, "last night I was reading. A magazine. You know, one of them science periodicals, and would you believe it—"

"What, Magnus?" Virgil said, with a languid inhalation of the cigarette and a histrionic rolling of the eyes.

"Did you know Walt Disney had himself mummified?"

"Bullshit," Virgil said.

"No, he did, he did, mummified, frozen, mmkay, and he's having his favourite string quartet played on a loop until they can revive him. Said so right in the magazine."

"He had himself cryogenically frozen," Levett confirmed.

"Yep, yep, cryo-generically preserved in a special mummification liquid, a substance, and they're piping in Haydn mmkay, old Walter Disney's got a direct feed of Haydn going on and on until they figure out how to revive him." Magnus studied his vodka. "Won't be long, either, twenty years, twenty-five tops and he'll be back."

"Sure Magnus, what*ever*."

"Are you sure that wasn't just something you dreamt you read?" Levett said.

"No," Magnus said, "it was clearly stated in a reliable scientific periodical."

"Are you sure it wasn't a comic book?" Virgil joshed.

"No, it's real," Magnus stated unequivocally, straightening up. "These days, with what they got. There's a machine the size of a thimble, no bigger, what tells a person's thoughts."

"Bullshit, Magnus."

"I'm serious, a thimble-sized thingamajig what tells a person's thoughts, their secrets, see, it's spy technology, unavailable, right? I mean, the havoc a thing like that would cause with your young couples, your sweethearts. Johnny likes Sandra, but he's going with Rachel. What a mess that would end up being. Relationships wouldn't last long enough to have kids and raise—"

"Shut up Magnus," Virgil snapped.

"Hey, I'm relaying reliable stuff here, this is real science fiction, mmkay, real stuff, not just novels and films and comic books. We're talking real capacities, real capabilities."

"You've got quite the imagination," Levett said.

"I do, yes, that's true," Magnus admitted, "but this new technology is not the stuff of fantasy, it's reality *now*."

"You're dreaming Magnus," Virgil said.

"I'm not, this is real mind reading and mummification technology, twenty-first-century stuff, Cold War–era stuff come to fruition."

"I had a weird dream last night," Levett said.

"What was it, Dylan? Tell us, tell me," Magnus said, and he squared himself toward Levett. "Share it. I'm an interpreter of dreams."

"I had this dream I was on tour, playing music. We were stopped somewhere, hanging out in this house, in a room. There were a lot of gig posters on the walls, nice arty bills, and I started getting anxious, saying, 'We're not going to make the next show. Let's pack up the van.' Nobody I was with seemed to care. I didn't recognize anyone either. There was a mattress on the floor. Light filtered in through a bedsheet pinned over the window. And we were all in there, hanging out. There was a weird dude, sitting there on the floor at the foot of the bed, sort of like half dog. He was sitting there like everyone else. He had a snout and floppy ears, but human eyes, and he just chilled out quietly. I don't know what to think of that dream. I'm always having dreams where I'm in a strange house, usually some modular or mobile home, white-trash shit, cheap wood panelling on the walls or something, but with an endless sequence of rooms. This one was irregular. That dog boy..."

Magnus steadied himself, the glass set on one knee. He nipped at it purposefully. "This is a simple dream, Dylan. Really very simple to read. It's very important to understand, the dog boy, this little guy, that's you." His eyes lit up on the word "you."

"I never thought of that."

"It's true, it's really very simple, uh-huh, mmkay Dylan. That little guy is you. You're in a transitional period of life. But that's okay. You're struggling with money, borrowing money, like what Virgil lent you, the eighty bucks or whatever it is he keeps mentioning."

"Which I *need* back."

"You'll get your money, man." Levett faced Magnus.

"When?" Virgil said. "A year from now?"

"Soon."

"It's the principle," Virgil stated.

"The little dog boy is you," Magnus said, "halfway through a transformation. What it means is, that studio you got down there, with your friend—"

"Dion."

"Dion, that's right, Dion. Well, what the dream means is you got a lot that's going to happen for you, cuz you're smart, you're a little genius, a little Freud, just too deep, you need to rise up to the surface with everyone else. And the way you'll do that, is down there at the studio, with your music. That's what this dream means."

"Never thought of that."

"That's why I'm here. I can tell you what your dreams say. I can translate them. This one, though, this is a very simple, straightforward dream, easy to interpret."

"I'd love to get back in the studio. Dion hasn't been getting back to me."

Magnus waved that off as inconsequential.

Levett looked at Virgil's initial sketch. There were a couple of windows, some three-dimensional rectangles, some tapered cylinders.

"Speaking of dreams," Virgil said, "I had one with you up there looking out your window. This is the view you had of my garden."

Levett took up the paper. Virgil had neatly drawn a small table with an ashtray holding a cigarette, a thread of smoke rising up off the tip.

"See, I've just stepped in to mix another drink. My cigarette is still burning. Would either of you like another drink?" Virgil said.

He mixed another triple. Soon it would be time to go.

The pink setting sun flashed off the Lee Building on the other side of Broadway, into the courtyard, off a piece of mirror set outside Virgil's window. A prism hung from some fishing line tacked to the window sash opposite the mirror. A faint wind spun it round. Spectra played over the nicotine-stained walls.

▽ ▽ ▽

The mice had gotten brazen. They would run by him when he sat drinking beer and smoking weed beside the window, moving easily from the kitchen to the closet, making regular circuits around the unit. He thought the matter through. Traps are cumbersome and ineffective. A snap trap with peanut butter or cheese is just a convenient snack. A mouse might as well eat all the peanut butter and save just enough to write GET FUCKED on the wall. Glue traps have them writhing and squealing on the red gelatinous surface as you dispose of the animal. Steel wool in wall holes does not mean you don't have mice, it means they live and die in the walls and decompose there. Rodenticide is effective, but again, the dying in the walls. Cats are lethal, but then you have to have a cat.

Levett settled on buying an air pistol. Fun to shoot. He'd perforated dozens of beer cans, murdered scores of whisky jacks and squirrels. His grandfather wanted to get him on a treestand with a .222 so he could shoot a deer during hunting season for the freezer. One time when he was thirteen, his grandfather made a target out of a square piece of wood and nailed it through the bull's eye halfway into a birch tree. Levett held the rifle up and, with one shot from twenty feet away, standing without a rest using open sights, drove the nail into the tree. That was about as proud as William Levett would ever be of his grandson.

He never shot a deer or an elk, never a raven or crow. Crows remembered your face and bore multi-generational grudges. Ravens flew away when you held up a gun. Ravens flew away when you held up your hand in the shape of a gun, with the thumb up and the index finger extended, or when you pressed a pretend rifle to your shoulder. A very cautious animal. Ravens always fly away.

His dishwashing paycheque was there in his account every other Friday at twelve a.m. That Friday morning, he got up and went for coffee. Outside, a cloud hung in the sky like a cancerous white lung. After a quick read with his coffee he went to Canadian Tire on Cambie. The firearms section was tucked away in the northeast corner of the big box store. He stepped by the vertical glass cases, by the shotguns and bolt action deer rifles, a decent selection of twenty-twos, pellet guns, and half a dozen air pistols zip tied to a pegboard: a Baby Desert Eagle, $84.99 on sale; an American Classic Pump air pistol, $94.99; a Crosman 1088 RepeatAir Action pistol, $126.99; a Browning Mark URX pellet pistol, also $94.99; a Stoeger XP4, $139.99.

"Do you want to check anything out?"

The clerk looked up at Levett with hard eyes. You could tell the clerk had been one of those kids who had to fend for themselves. He wore old floppy runners, over-worn jeans, an imitation-leather belt and a red Canadian Tire golf shirt. Oily uncut hair pressed flat down on a flat skull. His name tag said *Clarence*.

"What do you recommend for air pistols?"

"If you want something good but not super expensive, I'd say the American Classic."

"That's what I was thinking. Some of the other ones look kinda gimmicky. Baby Desert Eagle."

"Don't get the Baby Desert Eagle."

"The Beretta looks upsetting too."

"It's actually pretty sweet, just a little costly. What's your budget?"

"If I could get a good air pistol for a hundred bucks, fairly accurate at, uh, point-blank range, I'd be happy."

"Well, the Classic, but also the Stoeger XP4, anything with a longer barrel is going to be more accurate, though, easier to aim. That'd be the Crosman 1088."

"How's the Classic—in your opinion?"

"It's solid, it's on budget."

"What's the difference between the two?"

"The Stoeger is really nice, it feels great, shoots real accurate, and you can mount a laser on it. It's forty bucks more though."

Levett looked at the Stoeger zip tied to the pegboard. It looked like a real gun.

He thought about the last mouse prone on the glue trap.

"I think I'll go with it."

Clarence unclipped a mass of keys from his belt loop.

"Do you have the laser sight'll go on this?"

"We got a laser sight'll go on there. Do you need pellets and air cartridges?"

"I need all that."

As Clarence knelt to unlock the storage chest below the display cases, they heard a voice from down the aisle.

"Clarence, we need you."

"I'm busy with a sale, Russell." He set the items one by one on the floor beside him.

"We need you, Clarence," said the fluty voice.

"I'm with a customer, Russell. Get Angela to help." He withdrew the gun from the storage chest, slid the case closed and twisted the key. He patted the package, handed it over. There was some weight to it.

"I'll meet you at the till," Clarence said, stacking the scope package, the CO_2 cylinders and the pellet tin atop the Stoeger. Levett walked by the camping and garden aisles, the wagons, bicycles and lawn mowers, the sconces and other light fixtures, the doorknobs and handles, the packing tote aisle, the motion-sensor spotlight aisle, the paint aisle, to the tills lined up near the tall windows. He went to a self-serve checkout. A man cleared his throat in one of the lines. "The express clerks are out of order."

Levett looked back at him. The man wore all new running gear. Silkscreened abstractions that somehow emphasized musculature, implied speed and evoked technology. He gripped an oblong box. An UPPAbaby graphic slanted down over an athletic white couple behind a minimalist pram. The man turned and looked behind him after Levett wouldn't stop staring and scrutinizing—the guy's gear, his purchase. Levett visualized him emerging from a garbage dump in tatters, covered in slime and fishbones, gym socks and wilted lettuce, tormented by seagulls.

The queues stretched back into the extension cord aisle. It had turned into a conference back there. Someone somewhere said, "We can't do anything for ourselves anymore." It wasn't a sarcastic comment. The person sounded genuinely dismayed. "I'm all for automation, AI, VR… Bring. It. On," his interlocutor said. A trainee tried to scan a barcode, passing the item over the scanner, shaking his head, trying again. He kept paging for help.

Clarence motioned toward a closed till. He swiped his key card and punched in an ID code on the touchscreen, executed a few more key commands and scanned the items.

"I had to override the firearm safety function," Clarence informed. "If you were buying a shotgun, or anything beyond an air rifle, I'd need to scan your firearm licence to complete the transaction."

"I figured I could get this without."

"Oh yeah, me and my buddies were getting them at ten years old with a parent's signature."

Levett looked over his shoulder at the queue. Now the man in running gear was staring at him.

"Is he buying *a gun*?" a blonde woman whined. There was a strange modulated whip to the sentence, a stuck-up affectation he didn't really get the point of. It just sounded like the person was brain-dead. Levett looked back at the other queue. Another woman stared too, deep bags under her eyes, hungover, well off, clasping a trowel and a tub of putty. She was getting her hands dirty this weekend.

"That comes to $206.87," Clarence said. "But I like you man, you're cool, so I can just…" He tapped on the screen again. "I can give it to you for… $151.87."

Levett held out his debit card.

The two of them looked over at the stalled queues. There was a devious glint in the clerk's eyes. He struck another key command.

"You're ready."

Levett tapped his card to the keypad display. It beeped once and the screen said APPROVED. That's the word he liked. Clarence held out the bag, smiling. "Later man. Come see me any time."

He headed for the door.

"Don't forget your Canadian Tire money," Clarence said, holding out a wad of funny money, same playful malice in his eyes. Levett took it and stepped out into the blanched light. Out of the doorway into a mirror. Instead of the street he saw his surprised reflection. Two movers had been carrying it by, had stopped for one of them to get a better grip. It didn't shatter but Levett left his greasy nose print.

▽ ▽ ▽

Dopesmoke throbbed against the ceiling. A wet mop dragged in the corridor. Levett didn't hear it. He was with a cold can of beer. His laptop sat open on the couch. His earbuds were plugged into it and plugged into him. Earth's *Extra-Capsular Extraction* streamed on the internet. The name of the internet signal was Chrysalis. He filched it from a router in a neighbouring unit. He did not know whose it was but the network was never locked. It was another way to cut costs.

He favoured the minimal drums and the linear chug of Earth's guitars. He was into music that sounded like a small-town weed dealer brooding alone on a rainy Monday night in a rented room in a house in which he was not wanted, riffs like sentences in your head that would never end.

The slap and suck of the mop receded by increments. Magnus whistled atonally. Levett heard neither the mop nor the whistling.

A mouse darted along a baseboard riddled with tiny divots. Nose twerking. Cautiously toward the large open closet containing Levett's bed, a few shirts on hangers, a clothes hamper and teetering columns of papers: lecture notes from his time in university, abandoned manuscripts, journals—all destined for the incinerator. The mouse sped toward this lettered safe zone wearing a red bead of light. Levett held the gun with two hands, nudged the safety off. It was already loaded and cocked. Squeeze, never pull. You learned that from the movies. Sound like a pneumatic hammer.

The mouse tossed against the baseboard with the report. He scooped it up with a dustpan, tipped it in the toilet, watched it vortex away tail-first.

Osman had never commented on the shots and they shared a wall.

A shadow appeared in the light spilling in from the corridor through the gaps between door and door frame.

Levett plucked out the earbuds and opened the door.

It was John with a tallcan. His eyes were bristling and his hair and beard were grown out.

"What's this, D?" John said, a vigilant lilt to his voice. "You packin' heat?"

"You can borrow it if they get to be a problem again."

"Is that some of the legal?"

"I smoked one."

"You could lend me this."

"It's fun as hell."

John rotated the gun in his hand. He looked around the dark unit.

"Still no power?"

"Negatory."

"You don't even want it back. You're getting used to it," John said. "Have you been using my place at all?"

"Every once in a while I hung out up there."

"At least you had the option."

John examined the pistol more closely. "Does this have a laser sight?"

"Fucking rights it does."

John held it up against the wall.

"I just capped a motherfucker."

"Where is it?"

"The shitter," Levett said. "Mind the artwork."

John shifted the gun, sniggered malignly. "I got a beer for you. Let's go outside man, it's a beauty night."

They stepped out into the corridor and walked down the back staircase to the alley.

"Did you see me lock my door."

"I'm pretty sure I saw you lock it."

"I should double-check."

"You locked it. You gettin' into that whale tranq tonight or what?"

"Smoke strong dawg."

John pulled out a cold one for Levett.

They stood against the planter ledge along the government building. Hydrangeas loomed in the rank odour of their bloom, the reek of urine mingled with their fertility.

He popped the tab. Slurped foam. They toasted. Levett poured a third of it down his neck and felt the velvety wash of alcohol in his system.

John placed his palms on the pebbled concrete of the planter ledge, John Deere cap low, nodding in the direction of the Orthodox church, its large carved doors ajar, its gold interior visible from across the street.

Sonorous waves of chant drifted out, gaseous and super-intelligent. Long woven tones drawn over the tiered flower beds. Plaiting their dialogue.

Occasionally the glissando of a small car.

"You see the cameras?" John said.

"I did."

"My truck was parked out front last night. Someone broke into it looking for cash or computers or whatever."

"They didn't take the CDs?"

"Nah, they rooted around in the console and glovebox, left everything."

"No shit."

"I called Tom Ford, asked him if the landlords could check the camera footage."

"What'd he say?"

"'They're not for that.' He said, 'They're not for the tenants.'"

"He needs the rack."

"Dude's got it coming to him."

"He needs a Hells Angels beatdown, a few broken bones, contusions, some hospital time."

John laughed, watching the church doors.

"I was out doing my field school. I slept in a traditional longhouse."

"Rest easy?"

"Like a newborn pup."

They laughed. They watched the church doors. They watched for some figure of grace that might depart from there but it was only the sound departing. But the sound itself was a kind of figure—thyroid cartilage rocking against cricoid cartilage. The chanters had cycled through the hymn twice now and renewed it again with variations. As creeping mist, it fingered through the carved doors, beneath the icon, then fell like a raiment over the tiered planters.

"The river's fierce up there dude. I went fishing with these guys. The currents! It's really swift up there in the canyon, compared to the river down here—all tidewater backwash, polluted as fuck. Anyway, there's these barrel currents, they go down, meet another current, join deeper, meet another current, join, get sucked deeper. Guys drown." As John explained this hydrological phenomenon, he illustrated it with two index fingers, one representing a current, the other index finger a new, deeper current, animated and synchronized with his exposition, eyes blazing with an ardour for knowledge. "You should see it D, roiling like molten lead." He drank. "There's also a standing wave. It's a block-like wave that rises out of the water and sinks again."

"A big cube of water rises suddenly from the river?"

"Suddenly. The people I was with see them. Sometimes they surface really close to the boat and the boat capsizes."

"No shit."

"No, seriously."

"Leonardo drew water, different permutations."

John did not know about da Vinci.

"How's the thesis?"

"There's some interesting stuff at the archives. Been getting into some letters, the correspondence of this bishop, George Hills. From a promontory he looked down on Vancouver in its earliest days, when it was nothing, said, 'A city on the hill shall be a light to the world... but if the light in you be darkness, how great that darkness.' Look at this city—that statement's prophetic."

"He could've been a prophet, or maybe he knew the human heart, its fallen nature, in his age and the next."

John nodded, smiling, agreeing.

"So you're balls deep in the archive," Levett said.

"Not as much as I'd like."

"Finish your coursework and she'll be screaming for more."

"What about you man? Your Wilby project, that autopoetics stuff, it's great. Technological heroism, fuck man, excellent stuff. You got it made if you wanna do history. Not many people can call themselves a transportation historian."

"History is more fictional than fiction."

John smiled. He agreed but he wouldn't say so. For him it was too real now. He was in the annals. When you were in them they were real, and when you left them they turned to vapour, no more here than a particle of dust. History. The past as it presented itself now. All the ephemeral moving parts working upon our subjectivity—the primary sources and the secondary sources, the imagination and mental rigour and the lack thereof.

"What will you do?"

"Write a long narrative poem."

"What kind?"

"It'd be set in Yorkist England. A lad's baby sister is mortally ill. She's beyond the help of the villagers. They know of a monk who practises medicine at a nearby monastery. They go for him but he is unable to cure her. Prayer doesn't work. The lad goes with a couple of friends on a journey to find a reputed sorcerer, as a last-ditch effort to save his sister. He would gladly trade places with her, she is so dear to him and to the family. He has a few shillings with which to buy a spell."

"So, historical fiction."

"It's a road story. In verse."

"Sounds solid." John looked away. "How's the case going?"

"Me and Lane are going out to the RTB in Burnaby Monday morning to book a hearing and get the fee waived."

"Good man, good on you." John clapped Levett on the shoulder, looked him in the eye. "I'm glad you're fightin' it, D. They offered you fuck all, it was an insult, and they sicced some ex-pig on you, tryin' to take it off you."

"Vaughn was a cop?"

"Fuckin ex-RCMP officer, a cop. You know I hate cops."

"Where'd you hear that?"

"He told me."

"Damn."

"Pound sand."

They laughed.

"Did you hear about GG?" John said.

"What about her?"

"Vaughn's tryin' to get her to take a payout."

"Never heard that."

"He's on her now too. She shouldn't leave the Bellevue man. She's on disability. I remember back in the day, she'd set her desk up outside her door. I'd be coming home wasted, see her out there, I'd be like: 'Hey GG, whatcha doin'?' 'I can't think in there,' she'd say, 'I'm working on my business plan.' 'Right on GG. Lemme know how that goes.' 'I just can't think in there,' she'd say, and be all focused on her proposal."

"Remember when she had that young sketchy boyfriend?"

"Yeah!"

"They'd be banging non-stop to *Club Traxx* or some shit."

"That was the golden era of GG. She was killin' it back then, swaggerin' around," John said. "Anyway, I'm glad you and Lane are doin' this thing, and fuck the Lam twins man. Fuck Ford."

"Fuck Ford is right."

"How's your job? How's the Hobart?"

"Sucks shit."

They laughed louder.

"Makin' shit shitty an hour, scrubbin' burnt pots. 'Behind you, behind you,'" Levett whinged, mimicking the kitchen protocol. "I can't fucking stand it. I can't even get fired. They won't fire me dude. Even if I throw a cutting board in the sink or shove the dish racks around and curse and whatnot, act like a total psycho, can't get fired."

They laughed again, filling up the night, tipping the cold beer down their throats.

Levett reeled, half-cut. "Fuck." He spat the word out like a toxin.

"You know," John said, "I quit a dishwashing job in the Rockies, that's why I know about the Hobart, that's why I know you."

"That tripped me out when you mentioned the Hobart just now."

"Not just the Hobart. I quit a dishwashing job and moved to Edmonton. Then I went to the North Country Fair in Joussard and met you watching Luke Doucet, and then you tried to jump on stage and hug Tanya Tagaq."

"Don't remind me."

"If it weren't for that truck-stop job I never would've got pissed off and moved to Edmonton, went to the fair and met you. I'll never forget that thing with Tanya."

Levett watched John remember it, replaying the haywire scene: Tagaq on stage throat singing, but kind of beatboxing, then Levett flipping out on psilocybin over this beautiful Inuk vocal artist and trying to barge the stage, and a female security guard roughly pushing him back into the damp grass.

"Don't remember my past."

"Or the time you shattered the pickle jar on that guy's front lawn New Year's Eve. Dude was pissed. He made you clean it up. By that point you couldn't even wipe your own ass. And you're bent over picking up broken glass in the dark."

"I wanna get into your brain and rewire it. I've done other dumb shit too. You'll never find out about it from me."

John chortled softly. Levett thought of that thing with Jim.

There was a long-term tenant in the building, Jim Auerbach, who had been there even longer than Levett. They were friends, dope-smoking buddies, but the relationship had cooled since the Christmas season, when Levett had accidentally lit Jim's beard on fire while they were high on mushrooms. They had been doing shatter hits with a blowtorch when Levett got too close to Jim with the torch, as a joke, and flames began to flicker around Jim's face. Then the stench of singed hair. Levett couldn't convince him that it was an accident. High on mushrooms, Jim was positive Levett had done it on purpose.

"Maybe you did what everyone wanted to do, but wouldn't let themselves do," John suggested.

"I'm just half-crazy mate. It could have been someone else, and I wouldn't have to be on the losing end of your paradigm."

"Winning end."

"I was young and blasted out of my mind on psilocybin mushrooms. I could plead insanity. I wanted to hug her while she was performing."

"Don't regret that."

"Now I got Blade Girl on my ass. She rolls by when I'm chilling having coffee and says to the people around me, 'You're talking to a woman beater,' and I have to, you know, roll my eyes to whoever I'm talking to and shrug it off."

"The other day someone cut a lady off turning right on a red by Timmy's. Blade Girl was there in her skates. She put her arm out in front of the lady, sort of guarded her like a hockey player protects the puck, kinda hip-checked the share-car. I told her it was great. You know what she told me?" John said dryly. "'Get lost asshole.'"

Levett lost his shit. He laughed and laughed with his back arched. Laughter shooting up like pyro into the sky. He ripped the world down and built it back up again with his laughter. That's all he'd ever had, all he'd ever have. His coffin would be filled with it. There was a proper flower for it.

"It's what makes you great," John said. "Your instinct."

"Basic instinct."

John fluttered his eyelids and shrugged. He put down a draft of beer. One of his dismissive gestures. That there was nothing more to add.

They listened to the chanters.

"Glory Be to Thee."

Levett thought the phrase would end in a plagal cadence—fade out on the tonic. Instead it moved back to the fourth as one harmonic mass and the great doors closed.

He looked west at a diminishing series of lampposts, the circles of yellow light pooled on the sidewalk. A tall figure neared wearing grey slacks and a blue track jacket. His hands were clasped behind his back. It was Hakim. He turned and smiled at them. "Hello," he said.

"Hey Hakim," they said.

He held his arms out palms up.

"A perfect night."

"Totally," they said.

"Hakim," John said.

"Yes."

"Are you gonna fight that notice?"

Hakim shrugged. His hands fell down to his sides.

"Because if not, you should think about it. Everyone's going to bat for Dylan. You'd be no different."

Hakim's smile disappeared. "I already signed."

"It might not be too late," John said.

"I signed." Hakim turned and walked away toward the Bellevue with his head hung low and the brim of his cap aimed at the sidewalk, then regathered equanimity, tossed his head up high, straightened his posture and tugged down the waist of his track jacket as he passed beneath a pivoting video camera.

▽ ▽ ▽

She was small next to the form carpenter. Reflective tape was sewn onto her coat. The worker still wore his reflectives, coming from the building site, the slab-a-week routine, On Typical. The two of them burned bright amid the damp placid faces. Building windows went by like a film strip in fast-forward. They sat edgewise on the side seats at the back of the double-long B-Line express. She was to his left, closer to the front. She wore a floppy pageboy hat and anodized burgundy glasses. Her flared workout pants were frayed at the heels and soaked to the back of the knee. A set of keys hung from a lanyard round her neck.

The bus yawed. The dirty form carpenter pressed against her. Mix of B.O. and fuel. So, so hot, she thought. The bus slammed to a full stop. Her nipples got hard, her clit tightened. It was simple Newtonian physics.

"Pardon me," he said.

"I liked it."

She looked back at him over her shoulder like she thought a movie vixen would do it and he looked sorry.

She threaded through a knot of riders crowding the closing back doors, stuck an umbrella in the shrinking gap and hopped out, padded through the Lee Building's malodorous colonnade, caught the last few seconds of a red and jogged across Broadway.

The light was ashen.

The rain pounded down.

At the Bellevue she retracted the umbrella. Some of its ribs were broken, didn't fold in, had put tension on the canopy and ripped it near the edge in places. She turned around on the slick parquet steps and shook it off.

She stood in the foyer looking at the elevator and then the flight of stairs, the elevator, the flight of stairs, noticed the camera and the black shaft coming out of the ceiling, decided to hoof it, sloshing up the steps in her soggy trainers.

Rounding the landing between the third and fourth floors, she looked up and Vaughn was there leaning on the banister, as casual as can be.

She tried to slip by.

"GG."

She stood beside her door, 410, with the lanyard dangling in her hand. "What?" she said, avoiding eye contact, looking down at the brass mail slot.

"We agreed to meet today, didn't we?"

She met Vaughn's eyes.

His head looks like it's made out of fibreglass, she thought.

"I said maybe."

"We agreed to measure your suite at the key exchange. Don't you remember?"

"I said fifty-fifty."

"It'll take five minutes, GG."

"I haven't cleaned."

"I need to take measurements."

As he inched up to her during the dialogue, she became aware of a large boil on Vaughn's nose.

GG fidgeted with the key.

"Why do you want to do that, measure my suite? What's the point?"

"I'm doing it on behalf of the landlords."

"What's the point?"

"They don't know what size it is. We need to know."

"*We.*"

"They."

"Who cares?"

GG felt the deadbolt click. "This better take five minutes."

"Maximum." He followed her in. "Wow."

GG's unit configuration was an ailed sequence of piled junk. The result of slow accretion. A tall steel shelf flush with the door extended to the kitchen like a corridor. Wall made of stuff.

"You kinda got a hallway entrance here, nice."

"See," GG said, voice husky, tone righteous, "it's a mess, you gotta gimme time to clean, man."

"That's fine," Vaughn said. "No worries, you keep it how you want to keep it."

GG let her packsack slip off her shoulders onto the floor. "Well?"

"Come again?" Vaughn said, glancing through the shelves at the lanes of detritus snaking through the apartment, eyes darting at the luggage, magazines, wall units, stuffed animals, objects wrapped in plastic bags, plastic bags full of plastic bags, clothing, three skateboards, two unicycles, one exercise bike, a brittle pair of mounted stag horns, packaged food, at least six beanbag chairs, two couches arranged like a sectional in the far corner, divers paintings, manifold prints, various maps, entire archives of board games, LPs, CDs and cassettes, a shopping cart topped up with science fiction and fantasy novels, one guitar, two organs, three banjos, four ukuleles, all in disrepair, cardboard boxes and plastic totes stacked up to the ten-foot ceiling, crockery and cookery, makeup sets, felt pen sets, tea sets, a miniature spoon collection, a mob of random figurines.

"Well," GG paused, shoulders shrugging, palms upward, "aren't you gonna measure it?"

"That's what I needed to talk to you about."

Vaughn simpered. He stole another peek at the hoard.

His nose looks like something gnawed on it, she thought.

"I'm here to let you know that you're going to get a notice, GG." He clicked the retractable pen.

"What are you talking about?"

"The landlords need this suite empty. They're gonna be ripping out the wires. All the electrical and ventilation is getting redone. Eventually the landlords want the entire building vacant. What I need to talk about, is how much you would expect for compensation. I mean, you're not going to walk away from this empty-handed."

"What notice? What's that all about?"

"A notice of eviction."

"Evicted? Really? What'd I do? I pay my rent on time. I can't afford anything else. I've been on disability for ten years. I've lived in the Bellevue for fifteen. I can't leave."

"You have to, GG." He said it like he was her bestie. Like he was coaching her through a minor setback.

"Call before you stop by, man. Seriously. Unbelievable."

"No need for hostility GG."

"I said maybe. And you're not even measuring anything."

"Oh. Okay, we're back there again. GG, look…"

"Quit repeating my name."

"You'll receive a notice." He clicked the pen. "We need to talk. About compensation. You need to give me a number and I'm gonna relay that number to the landlords and we're gonna go from there."

"I can't move. I can't afford anything else. I'm gonna fight this."

"You can't fight this."

She rolled her head toward the long steel shelf. Something like terror began to stir on her face.

At that Vaughn held up his vibrating cell. "I did not intend to blindside you. They don't have to compensate you, miss. But they will. Text me."

He let himself out, cell pressed to ear.

The worst was New Year's Eve 1999. Y2K. We didn't know what was going to happen—every computer on Earth crashing. To think what that'd've done to logistics alone. Supply lines kaput. We had a gig at the Grid Iron in Railtown. We billed it as the Stephen King Trio's Y2K Throwdown—Three Sets of Doom. It was because we were a quartet that we liked the name. Plus it sounded tech metal and we were more stoner metal. Just, you know, straight fuckery. The landlord wanted me out on the thirty-first. That was the basement suite on Balaclava. You've been there. The new spot was on Fourth. I had to borrow the band van. All good when I asked the guys in November but it was a different story on gig night. Nathan our drummer had the day off. I thought I could get his drums out of the way first thing in the morning to save ourselves time later. He had his partner over, said go ahead, just be careful. He played a 1965 Gretsch Catalina kit, always the kit this, the kit that. I was surprised he could play the way he did on it. Huge. It was the way he hit. Otherwise the thing sounded like a little paper piece of shit. No. Nate is savage. I'm real careful when loading his kit, cymbals in the right cases, everything, nice with the hardware and everything and I go on over to the Grid Iron but it's not open until suppertime. So I take the drums to my soon-to-be old spot, take out the drums, take out the seats, and hump a good amount of my stuff into the van, then I think I can get it all, and I do, I get all my worldly effects in the van, including my books. My rock docs alone have their own shelf. I get it all in the Econoline twelve-seater. I stashed the seats in my old place with Nathan's drums. I went in the bathroom for something, looking for something. I went to the van and looked in a box near the back doors and what I wanted was in there. I had a halfer in the van first. I got time, I thought. I was out of that dank basement suite. I guess I just drove away. The schlep up to my now-former third-floor unit winded me, and at the time I was playing a lot of rec hockey, yeah, oh yeah, beer league for sure. My cell rings. It's Conrad. Says the guys are meeting for some burgers at that pub, Clevis and Field, and I'm all over that. So I lock up my then-new, now-former pad, pretty stoked. I'm thinkin' that went smooth. I hop in the van and go meet the guys. Spirits are high. The gig pays well. It's going to cover our mastering fees, an album four years in the making, we called it

The Lost Novel, *in and of itself a lesson in hubris, yeah, like how many times do you need to hear backing vocals on the same verse with and without reverb. But yeah, we were primed for our Throwdown. I automatically drove to the jam space after we ate, even though we were a lot closer to my old spot, exactly, the one on Balaclava, so, a little bit of a detour, my bad. We get to the jam space. Nathan confirms that his drum set is at the Grid Iron. I say, "No, but like, no worries, it's at my old spot." "Why is it at your old spot?" he asked. Bryan wants to know where the van seats are. "Ditto, my old spot." "Why?" they want to know. The Grid Iron wasn't open yet so things got shifted around. We're driving back and they're really hemming and hawing, Conrad especially, sittin' on the floor. Nathan called shotgun. Plus Nathan frets about his drums in the rain. He was really ringing his hands. It's pissing, right. You can't turn the wipers on high enough. We get to my old spot. As we're walking around the side of the house I see the white door, ajar, half my key chain hanging from the deadbolt. We go in. The place is empty. That right there bro was the real* Y2K.

Levett had the night off work with a bank balance of forty-eight cents. He walked directly to Save-On's frozen foods section. There was a new brand of meat pies called Piper's Pies. They came in lots of flavours. There was butter chicken curry, homestyle chicken, steak and kidney, traditional. He picked them up one at a time comparing the flavours. The butter chicken curry was tempting. When the man by the ground beef turned his back Levett slid two personal-size meat pies in a tote bag. He went to the canned food aisle and set a can of chili in with the meat pies, glanced up at the shelf. A pale porous face looked back at him. Festoons cupping yellow eyeballs. Levett blinked, and the face was gone. He turned toward the bakery, continued on through the produce section, by the cantaloupe and honeydew, lemons and limes. The stocker came round from the opposite end of the aisle, jogging in Levett's direction. Levett power-walked toward the large opening at the express lane, the clerk growing in his peripheral vision, gunning to intercept at the candy racks.

"There he is, Ray," the clerk said from the bulk nuts. His colleague pointed to a street guy wearing two ballcaps stacked on a toque.

He looked away from Levett at the ragged figure lurching by the romaine, spun, sprinted back the way he came as a third employee materialized from behind an apple bin and stepped in front to block, got punched in the jaw. The stocker tackled the street guy. Upon impact, half a dozen oranges and a roast chicken spilled from the guy's parka. Levett passed through the express lane, the cashiers and customers all turned to the commotion below the sprouts and watercress, demands to "Let go!" fading as the automatic doors closed behind him.

▽ ▽ ▽

Lane paid Levett's transit fare. The platform was being renovated. Plywood sheeting blocked the street view from Commercial–Broadway

SkyTrain Station. Advertisement placards covered the wood. A train whined to a stop. They sat opposite each other along the carriage windows.

Lush tree crowns and brown shingled rooftops scrolled over Lane's shoulder. He suggested Levett save time by filling out the forms en route.

The language used on the forms was hostile and ugly. Levett started filling in his personal information on the Application for Dispute Resolution.

Lane consulted a map on his phone.

Levett burped. He had curry-flavoured dyspepsia.

Indigo mountains set against a clear weightless sky. In the foreground, a streaming blur of houses, intermittent trees, chain-link fencing. The parallax of sagging power lines, retrograde in the middle distance. An empty baseball diamond appeared, disappeared.

The voice recording said, "Nanaimo Station." Chimes played with the spreading doors. Worn white panels, rounded ceiling corners, brown floor tile, stainless-steel ventilation grills, behind them all the ugly—the electrical, the drainage. People waiting and people waiting.

"I'm kinda lost on this one, mate."

A train shot by. Lane had to raise his voice over the squeal of the carriage as he looked at the form, where it said *Landlord's use of rental unit* under the heading *Cancel a Notice to End Tenancy*. Levett checked it off as the train pulled into Twenty-Ninth Avenue Station. Then Joyce–Collingwood Station. The recorded voice said in a regal staccato "This—is an Expo—Line train to—King George."

On through tall condominiums and mirrored office towers, newer and more numerous the closer they got. Layers of white paint chipped off the tubes of geometric pipework at Metrotown Station. It was a geodesic pattern, like Science World. Expo 86. Buckminster Fuller.

A freshly chalked soccer pitch. Across the street from the field, the rental fence and backhoes of an excavation site.

They got out at Royal Oak. They tapped out. The turnstiles flung open and whipped closed again before you were through.

The gable window in the old peeling M&B Grocery was like a rip in the fabric of spacetime.

The boughs of a Douglas fir drooped over the warped surface of an empty parking lot.

Inert car wash. Red, white and blue colour scheme. Hoses coiled up, wash wands horizontal on the racks like firearms.

Shout and body thud of the dojo. A car drove by with its windows open and its stereo loud. Kick thump, bass drop, sixteenth-note hi-hats, trap music. They crossed Imperial Street. High chain-link fencing interlaced with a fuzzy green material. Aqua Zone. Hot tubs. Inflatable pools. Crompton Brothers Automotive. *We accept all insured collision claims.*

The driver of a five-tonne transport truck waited to make an illegal left turn on Kingsway. Behind him a lady leaned on her horn until traffic thinned and the truck could turn. It was a long single angry note. They crossed Kingsway and turned left, passed the 7-Eleven, Denny's, Tuesday's Drycleaning, the African Hair Gallery, Moneytree Cheque Cashing and Payday Loans.

"I think it's in this building," Lane said, thumbing his phone, looking up at the building from the map on the screen, from the screen to the building again. It was called Marlborough Court.

In the foyer an artificial bamboo tree was stranded midway down a long bare wall. A woman sat behind the security desk wearily polishing her glasses. There was an unmarked hallway to her left.

"Are we in the correct building for the Residential Tenancy Branch?" Lane confirmed.

She replaced her glasses and gestured to their right. "Through that hall, third floor."

A red ring glowed around button 3. You didn't feel the elevator. The doors just opened up to a different place.

No signage or directional prompts on the walls. There was an active murmur to the left.

The pale-green walls were brightly lit. Another fake tropical plant in one corner. A couple stood there looking mystified. Others focused on their casework at a carrel in triplicate. Another carrel in duplicate had computers, where an RTB support staff member was showing an old lady how to set up a BCeID. "How will I ever *use* this? I don't *have* a computer," the old lady said, as if to an uncomprehending child. "I need this landlord off my ass, dear. I need a *person* to help me."

Four tightly spaced rows of armchairs were bolted together in the middle of the room.

Lane and Levett sat down.

To their left, black stanchions with red belts traced out a queue. The mystified couple came and stood there, unsure why. At the end of the queue, a sign said PLEASE WAIT TO BE CALLED. A beleaguered man sat behind a high white counter with square column mouldings that didn't even try to reference antiquity. He wore a burgundy ski fleece and told people, "This is kind of like a courthouse, you need evidence," or "Where does your landlord live? He needs to provide you with an address, some kind of contact information, somewhere for you to respond by registered mail," or "Here's your number, wait over there until your number is called, then you can talk to an officer to book your arbitration hearing."

Levett filled out a Monetary Order Worksheet. He checked off the *Applicant* box, entered his full name and the conflict address.

"What is my amount?"

"Check off the *Separate Damages* box and write 'Loss of quiet enjoyment' in the description field. It's a negligible amount of space to describe damage, but just write what you can. Under the heading *In support of your claim, you are submitting copies of the following documents,* check off the boxes for *Eviction Notice, Photographs, Letters/ Statements from Third Parties.*" After Levett checked the boxes, Lane took the pen and wrote *FORTHCOMING* beside the *Photographs* box. On the back of the form a table ran the length of the page, provided to describe all monetary recovery claims. Lane dictated, "One-year loss of quiet enjoyment for ongoing construction, nine hundred dollars; loss of water service, four hundred dollars; stress and loss of income caused by baseless issue of notice for landlords' use of property, five hundred dollars."

Two little boys with long hair climbed on their parents and alternately played with the bright toys beside a carrel at which a man sat. He wore drugstore reading glasses and flipped through his arbitration papers undaunted.

The red numerals of a digital counter glowed on the wall. A fly buzzed in front of the numerals, continuously swooping out and coming back to the red glyphs on the black screen like they were some kind of insect idol.

"Should we get in line?" Levett said, shuffling the papers, making sure they were in order and he knew exactly what he had, and what he needed to say, slightly on edge, shuffling through them again, scanning their contents.

They joined the queue. A tall man in sweatpants waited ahead of them. An older couple spoke with the information officer. Levett double-checked with Lane that he had his story straight.

"I can do most of the talking if you want."

"If he starts grilling me and I don't know what to say, then sure."

Lane nodded.

As they waited, other RTB employees made inquiries with the officer. He appeared to be somewhat of an expert on policy, judging by the way his colleagues deferred to him behind the counter with clear nods, almost bowing, then returned through an open door to what seemed like a much larger, hidden office space. The official reclined in his swivel chair. Levett set his paperwork on the countertop.

"Hi."

The man lifted his chin, regarding them.

"I received an eviction notice from my landlords. I'd like to file for a dispute resolution and book an arbitration hearing."

"Do you have your notice?" the officer said.

Levett said, "Yes," shuffling to the document and handing it over.

The man read it. "Why are you disputing the notice?"

"Because my place isn't listed on the permit they cited in the notice."

"There was no mention of his suite on the permit," Lane said.

The officer looked at the second page and nodded. "That'll make good evidence. Alright, take this number. When we call the number you can speak with someone and they'll schedule a hearing."

Levett accepted the tapered slip numbered *B-211*. "I need to get the fee waived."

"They do that." He waved off the issue with a brushing-away gesture, a flicking of the fingers, the back of the hand.

They returned to the raft of chairs.

"I wasn't aware this would be a two-stage reception process," Lane said, smiling, and brought out his laptop, opened his word processor, altered a line of text, closed it and slid it back in his tote bag. He looked at the alphanumeric display, the fly flying into it now, hitting it and flying away again.

Red digital *B-207, A-178, D-109*.

Levett went over to the water cooler and filled a paper cone and drank it. The cold water stung his teeth. He crushed the paper cone and tossed it in the wastebasket. "I hear there's some weird stuff about taxation forcing landlords to jack up the rent," he said.

"Say you've got a two-storey building with three retail units and a handful of residential units, as you commonly see. There's many in this town. Realistically, only so much money can be made from that space, yet the owner can be taxed according to the speculative value of the property as a seven-storey building with a London Drugs at ground level in the retail space."

The display blinked *B-209*. The no-less-mystified couple made their way behind a glass partition.

That green fly meandered through the space.

"It's a sly practice," Lane said. "Lawyers crunch some numbers based on development statistics to properly tax the value of an empty lot that could potentially, eventually have a building built on it. But this practice is being applied to properties which have existing buildings in neighbourhoods where speculation is happening. I'm not anti-taxation, but we need a more accurate and accommodating policy. That way we're not turning smaller, older buildings into a financial liability for owners—small old buildings that give neighbourhoods a sense of place and support low-rent residential and commercial tenants."

The seconds dragged.

The display showed *B-210*.

Levett exhaled. He got Lane to check his phone. They had been there for twenty-five minutes. It felt like an hour. "It's just what I expected," Levett said.

"What's that?"

"The inertia."

Slipping the temple bar of his glasses into the neck of his hoodie, the older man walked past the computerized carrels with his manila folder and was let through an unmarked door as if expected.

The display beeped again.

Levett checked his number against the number on the wall. It was a match.

Behind them a windowed wall ran along a series of partitions. Behind the partitions a long window looked out at the old condominiums, the blue mountains, the bluer sky. In one cubicle an African man and a Persian woman sat opposite an officer. A man stood up in a cubicle farther down marked *B* with a placard jutting out of the wall. He had a preened beard and a gelled coif.

"Hello, how can I help you today?" His voice was coldly professional, yet disarming.

"I'm here to book an arbitration hearing. I think I'm being wrongly evicted. I have the notice."

The officer went back around to his side of the desk.

"Can I see it?" Levett handed it across the desktop.

He looked it over without sitting down, flipped the page, scanned it, flipped the second page back and set the document on his desk, looked up, glanced at Lane and back. "The filing fee is a hundred dollars."

"I have a form to not get the filing fee," Levett said.

"You need two months of bank statements."

Levett set the form and the statements on the desk. Lane had orchestrated it all.

"How much do you make a month?"

"It depends on how many hours I get. Now that I'm done school I'll get more shifts."

"We need to know how much you earn to approve a filing-fee waiver," the official said as he perused the bank statements.

"I'm not sure, it varies."

"Where are you working?"

"At a pub called the Wild Rose." He pointed to one of the deposits from his employer on the statement.

The official looked from the bank statement to Levett. "So you make about twelve hundred a month."

"Since I got out of school. Before that I was on student loans."

"What about these other deposits, these transfers, two hundred dollars here, two fifty there."

"Those are monetary gifts from my mother. My loans ran out before I finished the semester. She helped me a few times when I was finishing my coursework." He could feel his face changing colour, his heart pounding in his ears.

The RTB official deliberated silently. He stood and walked along the sunlit window. He returned with a form and a large spring-loaded stamp, placed it in a square on the form and pushed down. The stamp lowered slowly through its framework and made contact with the document, producing the mechanized sound of administrative finality. He initialled and dated the stamp and pivoted it around for Levett to sign.

"We've waived the fee."

He signed.

The officer circled his arms around the pages as he keyed in the information on his computer.

From cubicle D the man's voice raised in ire: "Our landlord showed up at three in the morning banging on the door, saying 'Open up nigger!' We had no plumbing in the kitchen for two weeks—three weeks." His partner confirmed with a nod.

Levett looked at Lane, who pretended not to hear then looked up at the official and said, "Just one thing, we need to attach an amendment to the application. I'm Dylan's advocate. We're still working on the evidence package."

"That's not an amendment," the official corrected. "That is the evidence package. You have two weeks to provide evidence from the date the application is filed."

Lane nodded.

"It's fourteen workdays, so something like late May, May 28 I think," the official said.

"That's plenty of time," Lane assured. "I'm thinking I'll have it done by the beginning of next week. Provided we get all the tenant statements by then."

"Your hearing will be on July 15, there isn't anything sooner. Do you have a preferred time? We have either nine or eleven in the morning."

"Eleven works."

Again the officer walked along the narrow space beside the windows. He was not gone long and returned with copies of the forms and a tenant's Application for Dispute Resolution, respondent Vaughn MacDunn.

"You have to send one to the consultant and one to the landlords within two days."

"I'll get those out by registered mail today," Lane said.

"What's your name?" Levett said.

"Jay."

"Thanks Jay."

"No problem." Even if it wasn't a problem it still sounded hollow.

They walked along the cubicles. The female official explained a piece of legislation to the mixed-race couple, standing now.

At the elevator Levett held the doors for the couple, and smiled at the man, implying some notion of fraternity, while the resentful look on the man's face said "I know you feel sorry for me because I'm black." They rode down in silent discord. Levett spared them the awkward courtesy of first exit. As the doors broke apart he edged out. Lane let the couple out and followed mildly behind. The security guard was eating a pear. Levett was already outside.

It was muggy. The sky warped in the mirrored face of an office high rise. A continuous stream of cars hummed past in both directions.

The same couple waited on the corner, speaking privately, avoiding eye contact.

"What do you figure?" Levett said.

Lane was silent. It was hard to get him talking.

He might not become my friend, Levett thought, but this is the friendliest thing anyone has ever done for me. This is the utter pinnacle.

They headed down Kingsway toward Royal Oak.

Cars. All drivers like one generic driver, close by and so distant behind the windows.

On Kingsway there was a barn-shaped Kentucky Fried Chicken packed with people lunching.

They walked by a mini-mall. The Cruiseline Centre. Bohemia EuroDeli. Designer Zone Nail Spa. Floatwell Floatation Spa.

They walked by a laurel topiary bursting over the cinderblock cap of a retaining wall.

Buildings in progressing states of desuetude. Old asphalt. Fading signage. Crossed-out graffiti. They crossed Imperial and walked on past the M&B Grocery. Cartoon totems of ice cream ran up one margin of the building. In front of the shop under the shade of a corrugated awning: roses and tulips, calla lily and oriental lily, mandevilla and zonal geranium, arranged on a double set of steps upholstered with artificial turf.

Lane bought Levett another transfer with his debit card. They tapped in. On the middle landing, below the concrete undercarriage of the platform, Lane snapped a picture of the eroded corner store.

"That place makes me want a Coca-Cola," he said, almost to himself.

On the stairs to the platform Levett winced at the anti-pigeon spikes running the length of a light fixture. Some basketball kids with Afro fades, matching sweatsuits and Jordans waited for the train.

The train arrived and they got on.

An orca mural panned away.

"I heard about another maddening occurrence involving Vaughn MacDunn," Lane said. "Apparently when Hakim was speaking with a housing rep about receiving priority rental relocation assistance and the lady he spoke to didn't quite understand his situation, Hakim called Vaughn, of all people. Then Vaughn spoke to the woman and proceeded to sabotage Hakim's ability to get priority assistance."

A jaunty triad ascended as the doors slid open.

The voice said, "Joyce–Collingwood Station."

"Seriously? Vaughn did that?" Levett asked.

"Yeah. Not only is Vaughn the agent of Hakim's displacement, but he's also obstructing his attempt to relocate. I don't know the exact details, but it sounds like Vaughn is doing more damage than he was hired for."

Levett imagined punching Vaughn in the nose, traumatizing the cartilage of that grotesque proboscis.

Lane stared out the window. Levett listened to the high-pitched whir of wheel friction, the rapid shudder of rail joints, the rattle and suction when the doors sealed closed.

An elderly lady with a walker shouted again and again asking if this was the train to King George. Multiple people tried to explain to her that she needed to change trains, she was going the wrong direction. She kept leaning on her walker, shouting "King George, King George, King George Station, King George!" The doors clamped and re-clamped on her walker as she struggled to get out.

▽ ▽ ▽

He initialled his name beside the number *102* in a spiral-bound pad. He folded the five twenties and slipped them in his wallet, pocketed the change.

On Commercial Drive a garbage truck blocked the alley next to the McDonald's, its backup beeper on and its back end jutting into traffic. The front forks and hydraulic arms lifted and tipped the bin into the compactor. The machine seemed to have an impatient personality, the forks like mandibles shaking and jerking overtop the tall loud smelly vehicle, trying to dislodge garbage packed at the bottom of the dumpster.

"What's this now?" Levett said impatiently. He was going to get his haircut. He loved to get his haircut; every time it felt like a fresh start.

A tall stooped man with slack skin turned to Levett.

"He's too big to wrastle with."

The man turned away and stared at the broad green side of the garbage truck reversing into flowing traffic.

A throng of passengers boarded and disembarked at the bus stop. Levett cut through them. The stooped man walked into a methadone clinic. Levett crossed Commercial Drive. On Tenth he heard the bass and kick from the open door of So Icy.

A whiteboard between the first two barber chairs with a list of names. Byron, the stern Rastafarian owner, nodded at him.

"How's it goin'?" Levett said, writing down his name at the bottom of the list.

"Not bad Dylan, come to get it worked out now?"

"Yeah dude, gettin' somethin' real funky today."

"You and homeboy makin' another video?"

"Naw, just for fun, you know, summer stylings."

Byron laughed and so did the fellow in Sandra's chair.

"No, I'm serious bro," Sandra said. "You wanna get on a real self-actualization tip, wake up in the morning, or whenever, any time of the day, and look at yourself in the mirror, straight in the eye, and say to yourself, 'I am an exceptional person.' Try it," she said while shaping his sideburn into a knifepoint. "Yo, it ain't actually that easy, it's not. You cringe, you actually can't say it without looking away, or you laugh or whatever. I'm tellin' you, once you start sayin' it, and believin' it, you start to become it."

"I'll try it," her client said. "I'll try anything. Anything I can do to ball, I'll do."

Levett sat next to a tank with a listless catfish floating inside. He watched its fins wimple. It seemed depressed.

He looked around the shop. Three barbers worked. Two chairs were empty, aprons draped overtop the backrests and arms, a small plastic window in the lap of each apron so a client could check their phone. Levett thought that was a clever touch.

They had taken out the ceiling panels to heighten the space. The new ceiling was painted black. Bright fluorescent light fixtures without diffusion angled down toward the chairs and mirrors. The gradient of a fade had to be just so and you needed good light to do that. Six different clippers.

Byron never cut his hair. Byron cut whom he wanted to cut and gave the other barbers what was left over, a lineup sometimes four hours long. And people would wait.

Football on the flat screen directly across from Byron's chair. He watched a replay and alternately lined up a guy's beard, took a break, let the guy sit there, watched a field goal attempt. Levett watched the ball miss the uprights in Byron's mirror.

Byron's dreads were plaited elaborately into one mass and hung down his back.

"So what you want?" a barber said to a lanky stoned teenager. Levett didn't know the barber's name. He wore a white Polo cap and a baggy white Polo shirt, stonewashed Diesel jeans, white Vans. They don't all dress like 50 Cent, he thought. Nothing against Fifty.

"High fade, number three on top, I'll get a part line too, left side." The teenager had rehearsed saying this all day.

The barber nodded. He tied tissue paper on the kid's neck and fastened the apron. He pumped up the chair twice, flicked on the clippers and was at it, roughing in the sides with a number two guard, then switching to a different pair of clippers for the neck and around the ears. When this was finished, he set up a different pair of clippers with a guard and took down the top, switched clippers and blended the top with the sides so at the end the kid's dome was one seamless gradient from the crown of the head to the nape of the neck, from the temples to the ears, hairline gently rounded.

Byron and Sandra finished each of their clients. An old black man with an Afro like a halo came in with his wife.

"You Peter?" Byron said.

"Yeh, that's me."

"Whatchoo wanna do today?" Byron said as he fastened the apron.

"Little off the top I guess," he said, looking at his wife. She sat on a seat near the door, leaning forward with her hands neatly on her lap, smiling at her husband.

"Sides?" Byron said.

"Yeah, the sides," the man said.

"He's so handsome with a haircut," his wife said.

Byron got to work on him. "What'd you get up to today?"

"We was out shopping. I got a couple records."

"Oh yeah, what'd you get? You a rap guy?"

"No I hate rap."

"Oh yeah, that's cool, that's cool, whatchoo go for then?"

"I listen to disco."

Levett smiled. Moroder was a personal hero.

Byron stood in the glare of the sun from the window brushing out one of his machines. "Whoa," he said, "man, you can't seem to hold onto that thing."

"What's that Byron?" Sandra said.

"Guy out there keeps droppin' his beer on the sidewalk. Maybe he should take the signs," he said, now brushing out the white Afro and running down the comb with the clippers. Little fluffs fell to the floor like down.

"Alcoholism is a mental illness," Sandra said. She blew a bubble and popped it loud.

Levett looked at the large catfish floating there. It seemed to have achieved maximum stasis, alive only for its diurnal feed.

The barber looked at him. "You Dylan?"

"Yeah."

"You up."

He took off his Oilers cap and sat down in the chair. The barber swept up the clippings. Levett set his glasses on the countertop.

"What we doin'?" the barber said, looking at Levett's wiry greying hair.

"I want a sort of mullet, faded from the front to the back on top, and on the sides." Levett made motions with his hands down the sides of his head. "Not too long in the back either, but contrasting with the top and sides.

The barber looked at him.

"Is that weird?"

"So you want a short mullet and fade on top."

"And the sides," he said, doing the backward motion with his hands.

"So you want me to keep this at the back," and he grabbed the chunk of hair at the nape.

"Yes, except, you know, clean it up, and clean up my neck. But I don't want a faux hawk, though, whatever you do, don't go past the back of my ears with the clippers."

"Oh," the barber said, "you want a Napoleon."

"Is that what it's called?"

"Yeah. That's not weird, man."

"Alright then, let's do it."

The clippers vibrated through his teeth and jaw. The barber turned him away from the mirror. Sandra had another young man in the chair.

"Fade it up," Sandra's client said. "Real short on the back and sides, not too short on top."

"Just fuckin' hurry up Sheldon," his companion said and laughed. "Make him hot awright." And she French kissed him in the chair.

Levett knew there was a swear jar. No one said anything.

"Go wait outside with Blair and Martine," the guy told her.

"Let's move!" she slurred and stumbled down onto the sidewalk, tummy bulging out of her spaghetti-strap top.

"How's that?" the barber said, and turned Levett toward the mirror, front to profile, front, a little of each. Held a hand mirror up to reflect the reflection so Levett could see the mullet.

"A bit more off the back. I like it above the neck, let's accentuate that."

The barber snipped at the back some more and showed him.

"Yeah, great. Okay, now, I want you to fade backwards, from my hairline."

"Really?"

"Yes, fade it back, on the hairline, so it's a fade on the top too."

"Okay, okay, I hear you. Yeah, *that's* weird."

"You wilin' out Dylan?" Byron said.

"Hell yeah."

All of his curly grey hair lay in a circle around the chair, lay clumped in the folds of the apron. It had greyed early but at least he still had it.

The barber tested this, showed him.

"Great, go further, further back man."

The barber shrugged, kept fading back from his hairline, turned him around.

Levett looked in the mirror, turned his head to the side, turned it to the front again, bowed his head.

"Love it," he said.

The barber made some final adjustments.

"Can you put some lines in there?"

"Like what?"

"I don't know, surprise me."

He flicked his clippers on again and started carving designs on both sides of Levett's head. One side was like a network of songlines from the Dreamtime, the other side two vectors in tandem coming back from the temple. The barber put some foam on his neck and rubbed it in and it burned.

"That's twenty-eight," the barber said at the cash register.

Levett tipped him five dollars. On the way out he was wondering if he really should have let the barber improvise the lines.

▽ ▽ ▽

On skint days he drank coffee gratis at the Wild Rose. He had not seen Kristine since their first interaction. It was a busy Friday lunch service when he saw her again, bent over a thick book near the L.

"Mind if I sit down?"

Palms flat on the open page.

"What do you got there?"

"It's an anthology of surgical reports."

"Light afternoon read."

"I have to keep studying."

"Are you studying medicine?"

"I'm still an undergrad, anthropology, plus all the science electives. I plan on going to medical school." She looked down at the back of her hands, bits of text between her fingers. "To be a surgeon."

Levett nodded at Lowell who held up a slime-green coffee mug. Lowell set the mug down and filled it.

Kristine tried to get back into her book. On her wrist a tattoo. Levett could not make sense of the design, an equilateral triangle with a horizontal line running through it just below the apex. So many tattoos are like whims that last you the rest of your life, Levett thought.

He asked her if she was at one university but she was at another one nearby. He didn't care about universities anymore.

She made a show of inserting a slip of marbled paper into the gutter of the open spread but did not close the volume. She said something about fees. Anything about a university made him stop listening.

"I didn't know there was much difference."

"I went with the cheaper option."

She adjusted herself on the stool and peered at the arcane text. A fragment about controlled bleeding.

"I just finished a degree," Levett said, yawned. The coffee was hot, full-bodied and rich. He did not intend to let her keep reading.

"What did you study?" she asked, more out of politeness than sincere interest.

"History."

"Did you have a specialization?"

"Transportation technology." He left no space between her "specialization" and his "transportation."

"I didn't know there was such a thing."

"There's no stream of courses for it, I just focused on that for my projects." He wanted to get off the school topic.

He looked over his shoulder through the atrium glass. It was an overcast day, sky a pale ash colour.

"So you're just here for the summer?"

"Yeah. I'm staying at a friend's in the West End. But she's hardly around. She's *affluent*," Kristine said. For her the word had an aura. "She travels all over the place whenever, wherever she wants. She's a firecracker."

He did not understand the connection between affluence and being a firecracker.

They talked about hometowns. More boring, he thought. At least he could hit a couple free cups of coffee.

"I'm a prairie person too," Levett said.

"Where-boots."

"Northern Alberta."

"I was in northern Saskatchewan once, for the summer, working at a fishing resort. I did not like it."

"Too buggy."

"I had serving experience but they made me bus tables. The owner's niece and daughter got to serve, with no experience. There were a lot of bears, too, so I couldn't take walks. I just didn't appreciate the lifestyle. A lot of binge drinking and satellite television." She tried to find her paragraph again.

"What are you getting up to?"

"Like, in Vancouver?"

He nodded.

"I take walks, or hang around the apartment and read."

"Do you go out for drinks?" he asked, expecting she did, hoping to ask her out for a drink, so he could see what she was really about.

"I'm not much of a drinker. My friend tries to drag me out for drinks. I finally gave in and went the other night."

"You have to be dragged out for a drink?"

"It takes me basically one drink to get drunk. And I hate spending the money. I have four jars, for different savings."

He finished his coffee.

The Wayne Gretzky clock behind the bar read quarter to four. "My shift starts in fifteen minutes. I should refresh," she said, woodenly.

Not what he hoped. Square, he thought, passing his empty coffee mug from hand to hand on the lacquered bar. In a few minutes she returned.

Lowell gave her a six-top of disgorged cruise-line tourists. She walked over with a stack of menus.

"They all want waters."

She poured a tray of iceless pints and spread them out among the senior citizens, all in neon workout gear. Liver spots plagued their withered skin.

She did cutlery roll-ups. Her face kind of glowed.

Something about the tilt of the earth's axis toward the sun following the vernal equinox, the increased concentration of radiance in the northern hemisphere, that tickled awake a dormant libido.

Levett's and Bella's breaks coincided. Then Kristine walked out too.

"Hey Bella," she interrupted, sitting next to him, so she had to speak past him, adamant about hijacking the conversation. "Do you have a cigarette?"

"I bummed this one off Heather," Bella said.

"Do you smoke Dylan?" Kristine asked.

"I smoke strong."

She tilted her head, not getting it.

"Lowell's cute," she told Bella, across him. "Does he date?"

He went back inside.

He stopped sitting beside her before and after his shifts. As time went on, he warmed up to her again, started to be attracted to her again. She was inclusive with all the staff, greeted each of them and asked how they were. She was invariably in a good mood, and tried to be kind to Levett.

But then there was the issue of her legs. She had flabby knees and giant calves. He got a clear look at them down the line whenever she was running food. From the dish pit he would look at them and, as he warmed to her again, would debate whether or not, when it came down to it, the legs would arouse him. He wondered if her pussy was amazing—Could it be some cosmic recompense for the gams God gave her? he thought, turned around, cringing at his own douchebaggery. Plus she wears those metallic pink flats all the time, like every second day, he thought. Those legs and funny shoes.

"You're not wearing your magic slippers," he joshed once as she set piping hot plates on her forearms. Her response was a lowering of the eyes and a reversal through the swing door. He thought she might have been at one time a victim of bullying, by the way she turned inward when you teased her. Another time Lowell asked her if she was in heat. She stomped off without a word.

It dawned on him that a rotating door of kitchen staff was the norm. Bobby was back, rehired, according to Henry. She was a butch punker. Green mohawk. Two lip rings. Drawn-on eyebrows. Her style kind of punched you in the face.

"Vik got fired," Bobby told him in the alley during a lull.

"I can live with that."

"He came downstairs and reamed me out when I was slicing the roast beef. He was like, 'Get the fuck up here and deal with these dry ribs! I don't touch pork. I'm Muslim.'

"'I don't care if you're the Prophet fuckin' Muhammad, don't fuckin' talk to me like that,' I said to him. I called Henry. Henry fired him. You know what he said?"

"What's that?"

"'*You whites sure stick together.*'" She sucked on her smoke. "I don't care if you're black, yellow or green," she said, exhaling. "I don't care if you have two pussies and a dick. If you're an asshole you can't hide behind your difference. You're still an asshole."

An image dropped into his mind of Blade Girl flashing made-up hand signals at motor vehicles as she coasted by.

"And Anna quit, after five straight no-shows. She promised Henry each time that she would be at work. Sure," Bobby said, looked down the alley, "I'll do coke every once and a while, but not days at a time. Anna's spending a lot of money she doesn't have. Eventually she's gonna have to dig herself outta that hole, and it's not easy. I know, I've done it." She anxiously flicked the ash from her cigarette. The ground beneath their feet trembled with the passing train. "And she's been hanging out with Matt lots, cuz he moved in with her."

Bobby added a caveat: "She got kicked out of design school."

"I knew about design school, didn't know about her and Matt."

Around the time Matt was fired from the Wild Rose he was also moving out of his apartment down the street on Water. He claimed at the time he would sublet a houseboat. Apparently the arrangement fell through.

"Did they know each other before he started working here?"

"No. I introduced them," Bobby said, hunched forward, taking big hasty drags. "I don't care either way, it'd just be nice if she didn't fuck over her co-workers. Like, take the time off if you need it. No one's gonna hate on you for that."

Matt the smooth loud talker from Windsor, Ontario. He would show up three hours late for work on two hours' sleep. In his first hour of work he'd take four smoke breaks, bum the cigarettes, and when he was on the line he was dragging his heels, talking about how that morning he had been wasted at an after-hours party when he realized he worked at nine, boasting but also complaining, then he would peel a few carrots, slowly, and break again to cook himself a steak sandwich.

"What happened to Matt?" Levett had asked Henry.

"That guy is worthless. I guess he's an artist. Can't lift a finger."

Matt took the first opportunity to brag about being a painter. He would unplug his phone from the kitchen's communal speaker and pull up a JPEG grid of his paintings for anyone he realized he had not told. Levett had looked them over, mostly illustrative pop art and Dali rip-offs. He nodded and handed back Matt's phone.

Close to the end of his Wild Rose stint, Matt had showed up characteristically late and tasked himself with telling the whole kitchen staff about the night before, when he participated in a live painting auction. He made "three bills" off an image of umbrellaed silhouettes on a rainy day.

"I just figured it was, you know, Rain City," he said, nonchalantly, standing in places where there was no work at hand then vaunting to the next passerby.

This time Levett did not spare his feelings. As the arbitration date got closer and closer he became more and more indignant. He wondered what would happen in the event he had to move. He sprayed off and racked stacks of circular plates, a few ovals, a stack of sharing plates, some ramekins, a poutine boat and three hummus bowls, jaw locked, holding his face away from the splashback, cursing the Lam twins, Tom Ford and Vaughn MacDunn in rotation, playing out in his mind the prospect of cooking on a hot plate, showering at the YMCA pool amongst the other downtrodden men, their horking and spitting, their pubic hair, seminal fluids and mucous clogging the drains, their bad intentions and their missed opportunities, warm water well above the ankles, ringworm, dermatophytosis.

Matt dragged his heels over the dish pit's rubber grip mat to spray mayonnaise off a whisk. "Hey Dylan, I did this live painting last night and sold it for three bills dude."

"Why would you ever do that?" he snapped.

"To make money," Matt whined.

"It's a good way to damage your credibility," Levett said over his shoulder. He scoured a pan with a wad of steel wool. Matt shrank away down the line and slouched by the coffee maker. Matt sucked on his soda straw with a languid arrogance Levett had not encountered in the dozens of entry-level jobs he had worked over the past twenty years. He racked the pan and started work on a large burnt chili pot, spraying the carbonized kidney beans, loosening areas with the steel wool, spraying, dumping the black water and repeating. Matt pouted by the coffee maker, feebly holding half a grilled cheese sandwich with both hands.

The swing door opened and a new cook appeared in a Vancouver Island tourist cap. Ponytail. His t-shirt was white. Under the black chef jacket it looked like a priest's tab collar, the chef jacket a faded cassock. William had a weary, benign look to him. They got along at first.

Bella brought back a bus bin. She smiled at Levett, crouched and slid it underneath the counter. Above the waist of her jeans he caught a glimpse of black thong.

"Thanks Dylan."

She melted him like a wedge of brie.

Kristine greeted each of the cooks with a singsong hello as she manoeuvred through the chicane of bodies along the stoves and counters.

"Last night this guy was like, trying to chat me up," she said to Levett. His apron was soaked through to the shirt.

"I checked his ID. He was like, nineteen. I don't wanna date anyone with 'teen' in their age."

She stooped slightly as she tied her apron. He got a good look at her ample cleavage contained in the black low-cut blouse.

"Did you get a mohawk?"

"It's more like a mullet."

"Take your cap off."

He took off his cap. "It's a multi-stage process. Next I'm gonna bleach it, then fade it again so it goes from my grey frosting to the bleached blond."

"Since it's so short it'll grow in again. Less risk."

▽ ▽ ▽

Kristine started calling him Trouble. "Hey Trouble," she would say over the bar, waiting for her shift to begin, as he refilled his one-litre. Cranberry juice. Ice. The soda jet made it froth pink.

She started saying "What's up Buttercup?"

If they crossed paths during a shift, sometimes when she peeked through the swing door to see if an order was up, she would say it, one or the other, or when he was shelving ovals, or when he was plucking latex gloves like Kleenex from their box. She said it with a lilt that charmed him despite his better instinct. He caught her saying it to a server. Some wannabe actor. Levett always forgot his name.

The seconds, minutes and hours of each shift would drain away like a bag of ice.

Often it was William and Bobby who worked the line evenings. Bobby was a stomper and a shouter. Every time a chit came up, she would call, "Adding on!" William took naturally to his line-cook position, flipping patties and dropping fry baskets, fanning out tomatoes, ladling soup into bowls, all with natural ease. He claimed he had no kitchen experience. During an after-work drink Levett found out William's parents owned and operated an Irish country pub.

"Irish pub is dead," William said, a Guinness in front of him.

"Isn't it a social institution?" How would Levett know? All he knew about Ireland was what James Joyce, Samuel Beckett and Flann O'Brien had told him.

"There's new liquor taxes. People just stay home. It's cheaper to drink there."

"Same as here," Levett said. "Did you hang out at the pub as a kid?"

"I was always there." He pronounced "there" as "dear." "We lived right o'ertop it."

That explained his aptitude in the kitchen.

"You can't get way from the pub."

William smiled and drained his Guinness. He ordered a Rickard's Red.

"Did you work in the pub?"

"Yeah, pullin' pints 'n all, right from a wee lad."

Levett laughed. "Dude, I'm gonna get a shirt made up for you at Bang-On. It'll have a big mug of beer on the front, with PUB LIFE printed on it. And on the back, *Cradle to the Grave*."

They laughed.

"Nice calligraphic script on the back, Latino style."

"Brilliant."

"I'm gonna make that, mark my words."

Baseball highlights looped ad infinitum. A batter hyperextended his knee running over first base. The network showed it frame by frame. Levett fought back a gag reflex.

"Oooh, I love that stuff," Kristine said. She was wiping off menus.

The network showed a close-up frame of the injury paused on the instant of hyperextension when the lower leg goes the wrong way at the knee like a two-way spring hinge. It hurt just seeing it. Kristine watched it with delectation. You could have taken it as a red flag—sadistic tendencies, an affinity for body horror.

"So, William," Levett said.

"What's that?"

"Be straight with me."

William set his pint down. A serious look came over his face.

"Are you sure you're here on a working holiday visa..."

"Ye..."

"...and not gathering intel for your IRA overlords?"

They laughed.

Kristine got cut early. She sat at the L with the same screwdriver from an hour before. She'd been nursing it on the sly, its volume hovering between three-quarters and half full. He saw her take micro sips, probably fake sips, placing her lips around the straw and taking them away without applying any suction. They were on beer three.

"Where do you stand on the car question?" Levett said.

"The car question?" William said, perplexed.

"Do you believe cars are a problem?"

"They pollute."

"My friend," Levett's eyebrows arched over his frames, his eyes kind of bugged out and magnified in his glasses. "They do more than pollute. Cars should be phased out of the city, period. Cars do nothing for the city. They do not belong in the city."

"Good luck with that."

"William, listen to me. You're from the Old World." As he gained verbal momentum Levett began to sound like an orotund car salesman. "There's a struggle for space over there, in Europe. Why is there a struggle for space?"

"It's all used up, nowhere left to go but up."

"There's a struggle for space because cars and roads are taking up almost a third of our urban space."

"Seems like a steep estimate," Kristine interjected.

"A quarter of the space then—a significant amount," Levett said. "Get rid of the car. The car must go. It's a spatial problem, it's an ecological problem, it's a social problem."

"It's not a temporal problem," Kristine said.

"But how is it a social problem?" William wondered.

"Have you seen how people treat each other when they get behind the wheel?"

"I guess."

"You guess. Damn right. You're getting cut off all the time by drivers, are you not?"

"Sometimes."

"A lot," Levett said.

William conceded more out of politeness.

They drank to a point made and taken, if not well taken.

"What instead?"

Levett lubricated his speech with a brave slug of lager and set the glass down on a soggy cardboard coaster: "Our transportation technology is so clunky. We move ourselves around in such a primitive way. With fossil fuels, at right angles, on a grid. People will laugh at us in a hundred years. An entire species of buffoons." His tone condescended to the issue. "There's technology, like maglev, energy like solar, and manufacturing capacity, like, umm, a little thing called mass production—all in place and waiting to be implemented, but we can't get off this fucking car idea. Automotive companies and oil companies are running this planet, and running it into the ground."

They drank again to another point made and another round of points taken well, more a pummelling than a conversation.

"So, like them maglev trains they have in China? That float on the track?" William asked.

Levett glared at him.

"I'm just tryin' to get a sense."

"Maglev tubes, modular, so they can be adjusted according to need. Architecture designed and buildings built to accommodate this. They take up a fraction of the space that roads and cars take up and use a fraction of the energy. It's like what Elon Musk wants to do with the Hyperloop, but he's thinking macro, I'm thinking micro. Roads and cars aren't necessarily as problematic outside the city. But in the city they are *the* problem. People can't afford their bills because space is so expensive. Is it necessary, William, for you and the lads to live eleven to a house?"

"We're Irish," William stated. That was not a point to dispute.

"Fair enough. But check it out. Build homes where the roads are, move people around like blood in your body, like the veins in your arm, underground, ground level, in the open sky."

"I see, like them pneumatic tubes, for messages at the turn of the century."

"'Zactly. And of course trams, trains, subways, all that, anything that moves a maximum load of people or goods efficiently through space with a minimum use of space and energy."

"So *that's* your equation. I like it. Kinda science fiction-y."

Kristine had mostly stayed out of it. Every once in a while she checked her phone.

William drank and his drinking activated Levett's thirst and he too drank.

"How do ye s'pose the economy would recover from it, ye know, a complete turn away from the automobile and fossil fuels."

"Reorient industrial capacities."

"How so?"

"Well, you like history, William: What happened during the world wars when entire national industries readjusted toward the war effort? They did it. It took a year or two. And at a loss. But look at the Brits, they were churning out Spitfires in less than two years, had it down to a science, many of the production workers were women, and that plane won the *Luftkrieg*."

"I see."

"Yeah, you see, I know, you're not dumb. Industrial and economic capacities can be oriented any which way. And right now it's war."

"Against who?"

"Against ourselves. Our fetish for fossil fuels and automobiles is turning us into an endangered species, and it's turning our cities into Dickensian nightmares."

"You're on fire tonight," Kristine declared.

"A car on fire," William said. His eyes lit up and twinkled for a second, but no smile. Irish mirth there. All the politics behind it. "But is there anyone at the wheel?" he said.

Levett hardly heard it. He was checking out Kristine, below the horizon, while she blinked at her phone.

William craned his neck to one side. He'd done it before. He might have neck problems, Levett thought. I've never heard him complain about it.

The music stopped. The lights got bright. He didn't remember them announcing last call. They were the only ones left. Stool and chair legs pointed at the ceiling.

The trio of them filed out. William lit a spliff. They walked and smoked. Talked little. William turned east waving goodnight as he jogged toward an SFU-bound 95 B-Line.

They went south along the sloping park and the Great War cenotaph with the down-pointing claymore in relief, ghoulish people loitering all around.

Quiet night. The odd taxi.

"Where are we going?" Kristine said.

"I'm heading home," Levett said.

Hardly a figure. They were quiet for half a block and she spoke. "I'm worried about school."

"What are you worried about?" He felt a yawn swell in his throat and stifled it.

"Just the money stuff, you know—and not succeeding."

"What about student loans?"

"They don't last very long. And you gotta pay 'em back."

"I always got like, almost seven grand." He'd quit reading their warning letters months ago. They called his mother once a week.

"I don't get near that," she said, metallic flats padding the sidewalk. She had a little black leather purse, thin strap diagonal across her chest, tasteful but plain. He looked at her in the street light. Her face was extremely beautiful. Her eyes were small and bright and pretty and they held much. Whether it was what Levett wanted, he couldn't say.

The street lamps laid alternating triangles of light down the avenue, turning it into a zipper, or a mouth full of sharp teeth, something to join together or something to tear apart. They would pass under a lamp and her shoes would flicker reddish pink in the corner of his eye and he would look away.

"I mean, if I don't succeed, I don't know, probably end up on the street."

He chuckled. "You're not going to end up on the street." It sounded avuncular and dismissive.

"I can't go home."

"Why not?"

"My mom is, she's... physically violent toward my dad."

"What?"

"Yeah. They're the same body size. She beats him."

"Why?"

"She claims he doesn't appreciate her. Like, my mother's a writer, actually a really good one. My ex is a writer too."

"Any good?"

"Mediocre. That's why I'm taking my New York trip."

"Because your ex-boyfriend can't write?"

"We were together for six years. Why so long, I don't even know. It became habitual. I need to, like, reset."

"Trips are new beginnings." Now he was sounding like a talk therapist.

They were silent.

"You can be whoever you want," he added.

"My mom, though, she's good. She writes horror. And she screams at my dad: 'You don't have any appreciation for literature!' 'You're an illiterate dumb-ass!' Stuff like that. Then hammers on him."

"Are you in communication with your parents?"

"My father yes, mom no. It's kind of difficult because they still live together."

"How do you talk to him?"

"He calls me when he's on his work breaks. I don't talk to my mother."

"That's harsh."

They walked for a block silently.

"Is it weird, like, that I said that? From what you knew of me, did it seem like I had that type of family?"

"You're a kind person. I figured you had a solid family background. But I don't know, like, if a person's family influences the way they socialize in any predictable way. Like, my brother is pretty quiet, he's partially deaf, but whatever though, he talks to me, he's a chiller, not a big talker. I'm more of a talker, more high-strung. My dad's quiet, but can be a talker, my mom's more of a full-on talker."

"You're quiet sometimes."

"I guess. Sometimes. I mean, sometimes I don't feel like it, like talking. Some days I don't wanna do dishes. I don't wanna be in there."

"I totally respect that."

He knew it now. She was earnest to a fault. She said the most obvious, idiotic things.

"Plus, lately, with this eviction shit, I'm not always in the mood to hobnob with co-workers."

"When I first started working at the Wild Rose, I didn't think you liked me."

"I like you. Yer cool."

"I like you too."

Levett's last university course was astronomy. It was like the cosmos had brought them together in tandem up and around that curving road. Neither had enough escape velocity to go their separate way, and neither could attract the other with their own gravity.

They had gotten as far as a vast boulevard and were looking down Aquarius Mews at False Creek and in the smooth water they saw shyly lit sailboats anchored for the night.

Whatever it was they admitted to clung like a vine.

"I know where we are, this is Robson." Pacific Boulevard was a far cry from Robson.

He wanted to laugh. "Are you going to get a taxi?"

"No."

He could tell she hoped he would walk her back to the West End. Or should he take her back to his powerless unit. They could bang all night and she could tell the whole Wild Rose crew tomorrow. It would be great.

"You should get a cab."

"I'm gonna walk."

"You sure?"

"I'm too cheap."

He remembered her silos of cash.

She took out her phone and asked him for his number. He had to tell her he didn't have one. He didn't get into any of the anarcho-jive some people had recently found themselves on the wrong end of. He kept it quick. She seemed to not believe it.

"So, let's continue the conversation next time..."

A man lurked by a bench in an empty park. He stood in the lamp-light taking drinks of diluted red liquid from a clear two-litre plastic bottle. They paused and watched him.

"Well, take care," he said, and stepped in to hug her. She held her arms up, gave him a stiff squeeze and turned away. He backed off and watched her recede down another darker street he did not know the name of and looked toward the park again. The same figure repeated a groping gesture, goading him, fluting the words in a mocking falsetto: "Take care, take care, baby." Levett looked on at this gyrating man, as if fashioned from plasticine, then back at her. Darkness absorbed the last red flicker of her shoes.

▽ ▽ ▽

It was blistering. Umbrellas raised against a zenith of white heat. People tight to buildings in meagre wedges of shade, fanning themselves with reading material. A bus hissed and beeped as the wheelchair ramp folded back upon itself. Four deafening triplets signalled its locked position.

GG flagged Levett. "Hey man."

"Yo GG."

A queue flowed round them onto the bus.

She wore a butterfly t-shirt. Bedazzle beads marked forking points in the wing venation.

He smells like beer in the afternoon, she thought.

"What are you doing about this stuff?" GG asked.

"What stuff."

"The Vaughn guy."

"Vaughn's a fiend. Don't trust him."

"What am I supposed to say to him?"

"I'm fighting the notice. You can challenge it too."

"I can't handle that. I can't challenge stuff." She clutched her skull. "I can't even remember you telling me that."

"I didn't think I did."

"This is gonna mess up my head for sure. It's already a mess. You should see my place. Can't find anything."

"Talk to the RTB. Get Lane to help. He'll use the same argument he's using for me. You'll have a stronger position than me even. You've got more rights. There's empty suites in the building. They should relocate you if they need access to your suite."

"I've got a learning disability dude. Everything you just said—it goes into my head and poof, gone. Everything's on computers. I can't work computers." She smiled at Levett. A fearful smile.

"You've got all the help you need. There's at least ten people in the building ready and willing to walk you through the process. That includes me."

"I don't know man."

She shook her head, crossed her arms over her chest and held herself. He gave her a quick hug. He clapped her on the shoulder.

"Oww."

"Sorry."

"Careful with me. I'm a dust particle in a … in a … in a raging sea. Melting out there."

"You're not a dust particle." That's all he had.

"Sure feels like it. Feels like a spinny cloud flyin' in one eye out the other."

"That uh, that sounds shitty. But, GG—"

"What already."

"Did you get a notice?"

"Not yet."

"But you think you'll get one."

"That's what the Mac Bundy guy said. Vaughn. How can you trust a guy named after a goalie pad?"

This caught him off guard and he laughed, but she wasn't laughing.

"Is he for real? Is he trying to give me a heart attack?"

"Possibly."

"That's crazy."

"I'm stressed out too, but we're all here for each other. The whole Bellevue crew. Don't say yes to any money."

"There's money?"

"He didn't offer you money?"

"No."

"Really?"

"Nothing."

"Rotter."

Levett imagined cutting Vaughn's brake cables. Vaughn impaled on the steering column of his silver RAV4, eyeball dangling from the rear-view mirror by its optic nerve.

"He talked about compendiums, but I don't know."

"Compendiums?"

"That's what he wants to meet up about next."

Don't correct her. "Compendiums mean money, GG. It's not enough though. You can't take it. There's fuck all for cheap apartments in the city. Where you gonna go? You gotta hold out."

She shook her fists in the air. Then her shoulders dropped and she looked even smaller.

"I gotta get to work man."

It was his understanding that she was not employed, nor had she been for the last six years.

"Reach out."

She shook her head no to it all.

"Talk to John. He's just across the hall from y—"

Before he could complete the sentence she had slipped away into the midday crowd.

An elderly gentleman with hound-like jowls shuffled by holding a cane, paused, turned and doffed his cap. Levett nodded.

"My, she's really cookin', in't she?"

"Is it ever brutal."

"*Savage* weather," the senior replied. He set the cap atop his flaking scalp and went on.

▽ ▽ ▽

He sat in the dark on the toilet. There was a knock at the door.

"Hey Dylan." It was Jim Auerbach.

"What?" Levett snapped.

"I got something for you."

"I'm taking a shit."

An envelope slid through the mail slot and fell to the floor.

"You're welcome, Dylan." Steps receded down the corridor.

▽ ▽ ▽

At Gene Cafe Levett downloaded Lane's file. The tenants union keyfist emblazoned the top left corner of the document.

"I like the letterhead," Levett commented.

Lane didn't react. Levett sipped the coffee Lane had bought him.

Blade Girl was outside speaking to a young woman. She thumbed through the window in Levett's direction. He glanced up at her and thought he could read her lips forming "violator."

"Numbered paragraphs," he said.

Lane stood to the left offering commentary and counsel while Levett scrolled through the document.

"Legal papers are done that way to cite within the text. There's over a hundred footnotes in this thing." His smirk grew into a smile.

Levett glanced down at the footnotes. The notes consisted of tenants' names followed by the date and a page number from the compiled document.

"All the Bellevue tenant statements."

"Yeah, statements and corresponding evidence, also previous cases, some legislation."

Levett bent toward his screen scrolling through the pages fast and bringing it back to the top, the key-fist. Wringing his hands, he began to read what he later described to John as "a textual rotary cannon."

The prose was substantial but glided too.

"You're a good writer dude."

Lane's chest went convex and he smiled. He thanked Levett with the modesty of someone who takes pride in their prose style but would never waste their breath admitting it.

He reached paragraph 9, which stated, *The tenant seeks to be compensated for loss of quiet enjoyment in his rental unit; due to repeated loss of his water service his tenancy has been further devalued; and lastly, the tenant seeks additional damages because of stress caused to him by the landlords' issuance of this notice in bad faith.* "Bad faith"—it was an odd phrase that to Levett just meant devilish.

Lane looked away. He sent a text. Vehicles idled at a red light, choking the coffee house goers with their obnoxious tailpipe fumes.

"Even if we don't get them to pay damages, it's another thing we can use against them."

Blade Girl was trying to draw another attractive woman's attention to Levett.

He read as Lane talked. "My friend Roxanne, who's almost finished articling—pretty soon she'll take the bar—she says a good strategy is to keep harping on all the points we have against them, over and over, or as much as we're allowed to talk. I can do most of the talking if you want. Especially with regard to RTB rules, they're incapable of going outside their own technicalities. She said it's imperative we make it as clear as possible for the arbitrator in their own language."

To confirm his landlords' audacity Levett turned to Lane's text and read in a gentle clear voice paragraph 12, under the heading for section II—*CANCELLATION OF TWO-MONTH NOTICE—Improperly Completed Two-Month Notice to End Tenancy for Landlord Use: "The landlords' agent has not properly completed the Two-Month Notice to End Tenancy for Landlord Use form. The form requires that the 'Landlord Address' field be completed so that the recipient can respond to the notice. The agent has stated the landlord address as the street number of Bellevue Heights, which is not the landlords' service address, and not a deliverable address because the apartment building has multiple units. We request the notice be struck because it provides incorrect and incomplete information.* Drawing on your postal service background I see. Nice argumentation."

Lane nodded while checking his phone.

"Vaughn fucked up the form. What a yob," Levett said.

They laughed together. Lane silently, Levett aloud in the triangular cafe.

"The RTB is receptive to anything represented in a form," Lane explained.

He got to paragraph 18. Here Lane cited *Berry and Kloet v. British Columbia,* case in which the Act's own policy was invoked to make a strong point about vague wording, and here Levett read aloud, "*While the Act is in place to make uniform the rights of landlords and tenants, it favours tenants in situations where ambiguous language is used; in these cases the dispute should be resolved in the tenant's favour*. Excellent, dude. So you found this in a case-law database?"

"It was the example best suited to your situation."

He read on. "They haven't filed with WorkSafeBC. So they're not insured."

Lane shook his head. Levett read the cited regulations. Then Lane brought it back around to the Residential Tenancy Branch in paragraph 27. Levett read aloud, "*Section 59(8) of the Act requires that prior to the issuance of a Two-Month Notice to End Tenancy for Landlord's Use of Property the landlord must be fully permitted and have all the approvals required by law. These requirements have not been met.*"

The argument was sound. By now Levett openly admired Lane's robust intellect and resorted to sycophancy. "I love your prose style."

Lane turned away smiling. His mood oscillated as he rocked to favour the opposite foot. He faced Levett squarely. "Like I said, I don't want to put a number on it, but I'm really confident we can win, like 96 percent sure. Even if we get an incompetent arbitrator, it's not the last step we can take. We can apply for a review of the decision by the Supreme Court."

"I'm thinking it won't get to that. There's more to this thing, right?" Levett scrolled down through the pages of the document. They blurred in the word processor as he flicked the touchpad. "Yeah… there's… like… thirty-some pages," he said, tensing up and leaning into the computer screen, smiling. "Okay, lemme keep reading man. This is good."

"Take your time."

"This is really good man."

"We'll need a quiet place with power to do the conference call."

"Conference call?"

"Yeah, the hearing is done over the phone."

"That doesn't sound too nice."

"I can put it on speaker. My phone though, the battery drains really fast on speaker. I'll need to plug it in."

Levett thought about it for a second. "I'll ask John. It was his idea in the first place."

II

PAUSE

Point seven vacancy rate right now. That ain't a crisis, that's an opportunity. If I could get these assholes out of here it'd be so easy to charge seventeen hundo, eighteen, nineteen hundo. Some could be bought, literally for a song, others are taking it to the RTB. *They won the first time. I didn't have my shit together. Fuck it though, stresses them out, right? When I got the place painted I told the crew not to worry about the windows. "Don't bother taping them off," I said. "They're being replaced." They went ahead and painted right over them. Forest green, almost black. Then I put my phone on silent for a couple months. I stopped paying that sponge caretaker Willy. Never saw a person melt into thin air like that. Nobody had the key to the dumpster. The trash built up. It was like a garbage strike, my garbage strike. Perfectly good windows. That's what I call collateral damage. I finally hired four college students to razor blade the paint off. I said do it fast, don't worry about it too much. I gave them an extra dollar an hour, which to them didn't make sense based on their performance, but they weren't arguing. My biggest mistake was renting out the empty suites again. This hurt me at the second hearing. They got this guy, Roth, Lane Roth. The tenants. Yeah, he's an advocate. Said I was evicting in bad faith, which is true, but fuck it, it's my property. I'm gonna put up cameras next. That always pisses people off. There's also this bum Cam I let into the basement sometimes on cold rainy nights. That's where the laundry room is. He's harmless. Pretty sure. Stinks to high heaven, that I know. They'll say something at the next hearing. Fuck it though. What's the Tenancy Branch gonna do, fine me two Gs? That ain't a slap on the wrist, that's a sexy stroke. That's the cost of doing business. It's a pleasure and an honour to do business. Seriously, once these dough heads are out I'll be clearin' thirty a month on this place, easy. After taxes. The* RTB *labels you a deadbeat landlord after three successful arbitration attempts. Fuck it. What are they gonna do, take my property away?*

WILDFIRES burned in the hundreds that summer. Bolts of lightning forked the midsummer woodland and the parched fir, spruce and pine went up like so much kindling. Authorities declared a province-wide state of emergency. Through rust-coloured air, the vulcanized land evoked a planet in the hot tumult of its own creation.

"Hello officer."

"I'm sorry ma'am, the road is closed."

"I need to get Homer."

"Is Homer your son?"

"Homer is my three-year-old Shih Tzu."

"Ma'am, you can't go in there. Ma'am..."

Thirty homes in Boston Flats burned. A pair of flamingos collapsed into puddles of pink. Charred palings of aspen and birch probed upward from the singed lawns. A gutted Taurus knelt on bald rims, black aureoles of radial cord ply where tires were the day before. Down the lots, twisted chassis enclosed the scorched carapace of here a furnace, there a washing machine, refrigerators, all carbonized. The skeleton of a box spring, another, another, at the back end of each mobile home, in what would have been the master bedroom.

On a dairy south of Cache Creek, a farmer and his lead hand chased eight hundred head through the drive bay of a burning barn, its timber joists sagging, the udders of the farmer's livestock swollen with milk. In the neighbouring corral, a horse on fire, writhing and trying to buck the flames off. Swine stood upon embers in the midst of their own shrieking, cloven hooves melting into size. Twenty thousand worth in bell peppers. Ruminants with nary a grazing field. Tears running down sooty cheeks. Bad smoke inhalation.

The haze drifted southwest. As the rain clouds parted it blanketed the city. North Vancouver and the Coast Mountains were blotted out completely. It occluded Burrard Inlet and it shrouded the port's gantry cranes. They might have been gangly martial vehicles in some harsh future.

A molten disc cut its sky arc daily through the murk.

At night the moon went bloody.

Tempting to read the gloom and word of fire biblically.

Sometimes it felt like a torch in his belly. Sometimes he wanted to douse Vaughn's face in hydrochloric acid, watch the skin melt like a plastic bag in a bonfire.

Fleck of ash on the pant leg. Before work he drank a coffee and smoked a joint out his unit window—a hippie speedball. There was a mural festival on. Funded by real estate–developer dollars, Lane had said, increasing property values by supporting the arts. They were doing one on the Bellevue right now. Whenever the media came by to interview the artists and they took a photo of the building facing his unit, he put up his middle fingers.

Outside he saw the lean figure in pink spandex wheeling by Tim's. Blade Girl wove through a crossing mass of pedestrians, spun round, coasted backwards and scolded the drivers at the red light with one outstretched finger. He took the back way instead.

▽ ▽ ▽

On up the Cambie Bridge's incline and cresting. The smoke-swaddled buildings shone golden yellow in diffuse southwesterly light. A bloated sun redshifted in all that vertical glass.

Down the pigtailing ramp. Ground level. Beneath this canopy of road, blocks of deep shadow. It was no cooler. A small tent attached itself to a thick column like a barnacle. Two calloused feet protruded from the nylon structure, filthy toes wriggling.

There was a large sign on the corner. The sign had a picture of an unbuilt building on it, plugged into a 3-D rendering of the current landscape. Below this, the Concord Pacific logo with a slogan: CANADA'S LARGEST COMMUNITY BUILDER. It read like a kick in the teeth.

Later that night he remembered the slogan and googled the developer. At concordpacific.com this same text is set in stylishly sinister block caps upon an image of downtown, girdled darkly inside a glowing hem of outer towers as seen from a helicopter or drone. On the website these luminescent structures wrap around False Creek's littoral. Where the viaducts now stand, the buildings glow fainter because they are speculative. The viaducts have yet to be razed. Concord Pacific owned part of the land they were on. He looked at the computer-generated illustration and wondered what kind of lethal metastasis this protoplasmic fringe had visited upon the city, got a bit sentimental about it. Where were the foo dogs at Millennium Gate, the floaty nollie heelflips over the hip at Plaza, the improvised shelters and one-man tents in the shade of the east wall outside Dr. Sun Yat-Sen Classical Chinese Garden, when the sun is high in the west? Levett thought. Before he closed the browser tab he looked one last time at the glowing crust of towers, the slogan, and wondered, in the developer's mind, exactly what these hermetic phalli had to do with building community.

On past the signboard and he could see down into the pit. Through a lattice of rebar he watched sparks fan off a grinder. They settled upon the newly poured concrete formwork and expired. The goggled worker stood up like a simian fish, his eyewear two glinting ducats in the jaundiced light.

▽ ▽ ▽

At chin level, the stainless-steel shelf was a mess. A gelato bucket full of gunky steel wool in the wrong place. The Spic and Span and degreaser spray bottles off to the right way out of reach. Bleach bottle in front of his face. He stood in front of the shelf for a while putzing around, organizing it, lining up the cleansers, putting those he used more often closer and those he used less often farther away. He wiped down the surface of the shelf and dried it with paper towel.

"Hi," a voice said behind him.

It was Kristine tying on her apron, lips done, cheekbones blushed. Gorgeous face, he thought.

"How's it going Kristine?" Levett smiled.

"It's goin' pretty good."

"You made it home."

"I did. Funny though. I read in the news today that a fifty-seven-year-old woman was raped and murdered last night, close to where we parted ways."

"Yeah right."

"Google it."

"Okay." He waited for her to crack up and they could have a laugh about it but she did not. "I found a new app that has all the sex crimes in an area mapped." Levett emptied a bus bin. He organized the crockery in separate piles as she spoke.

"I'm totally gonna get that app," she said, ponytail flipping sassily as she spun around and walked down the line.

Levett kept putzing. Cleaned and set things in order leisurely. He sprayed off a few ovals and set them in the far left corner of the rack, sprayed off share plates and set them beside the ovals, switched to round dinner plates, spraying off the canola oil and ketchup pools and cheese. What if she did get raped and worse? he thought, sliding the rack in and closing the Hobart. Like Black Dahlia? he thought grimly. That would be burdensome, knowing you could have walked her home.

The groaning Hobart clouded his thoughts.

There was that weird dude in the park when we said good night.

He put a long chrome plug into the large sink. He set chicken-wing pans in edgewise, flicked on the hot water and sprayed in the orange degreaser. It made him cough. There was d-limonene in it, cyclohexane. He racked another cycle of dishes. When the clean dishes cooled enough, he shelved them. When the dishes were done, he sprayed off the stainless-steel counter and squeegeed all the debris into the small sink. He scooped dross from the catch with three fingers and flung it in the garbage, did it again, waited for the cloudy grey spiral in the water.

▽ ▽ ▽

Instead of emailing, one day he decided to just call Dion. He found his new number in an old email thread and used the restaurant's land line. It rang eight times and he hung up.

Canada celebrated its sesquicentennial. Gastown was closed off to vehicular traffic. Stage components lay half-assembled in the street. Sound technicians rigged up PA monitors on stands and chained them to lampposts. Labourers unloaded black risers from a flatbed Hino around each set of speakers. International tourists wore t-shirts with the official Canada Day emblem, a polygonal maple leaf composed of thirteen diamonds. The symbology was lost on him.

A massive stage stood erect at the intersection beside the Wild Rose. The Rose was already packed.

"That entire table of eight can't fuckin' speak English," Heather growled under her breath. Kristine sat at the bar with an orange spritzer, writing with a felt-tipped pen in her Moleskine. Levett ignored everyone.

In the restroom he took off his nice jeans and clean t-shirt. He rifled around in his backpack for the shorts. There was only an extra shirt. "Fuck." His good clothes would be soiled and soaked by the end of his shift. He looked up at a pair of green cords hanging off the rack that had always just been there. He put them on and cuffed them up. The trousers itched and clung to his legs. They were loose on the waist. He tucked his shirt in. They were still loose.

Rivulets of sweat ran down his torso. In five minutes his body was soaked. He kept having to drag paper towel off the dispenser and mop the sweat from his brow and eyelids and the back of his neck. His glasses were all misted over and splashed.

Dirty mixing bowls, tongs and inserts piled high on two full bus bins. He hadn't even started and he was already slammed.

Heather brought in another heaping bus bin. "Want this underneath?" Heather slid the bin underneath the sink, went to the restroom and locked herself in.

Levett hitched up the cords again. Sweat stung his eyes. He pulled another wad of paper towel off the dispenser and mopped his face and splashed cold water on the back of his neck.

The printer spat out a series of chits. Henry was working. They never worked together.

"Fuck off," Henry told the crowd thickening in the pub. "Fuck off and die you assholes." He walked over to Levett, who stood on the threshold of the dish pit chugging ice water. "Today's gonna be insane," he said, averting his eyes. "Do your best on the prep. If you can't get to it, don't worry."

Levett looked at the whiteboard. *Portion pickles, mayo × 3, garlic butter × 2, margarine × 2, feta × 6. Wings.*

"The easy stuff isn't a problem," Levett said, "but if it stays like this I doubt I'll get to the wings."

"Just do your best. Get outside whenever there's a lull."

Bobby showed up clutching her skateboard by the trucks. Her t-shirt said *Killjoy Feminist.*

"H-he-hey Bobby," Jacob stuttered from behind the freezer door.

"What's up Bobby?" Henry said.

"Livin' the dream."

Henry rang the bell. Kristine poked in and ran the order.

William came. He greeted those on the line and then Levett, who tipped back his one-litre between loads, cold water running down his chin and neck. More chits. William tore them off the printer and stuck them with the rest. Heather brought in another heaping bus bin, slid it under the sink beside the other one. An hour went by. Progress negated by more dishes, burnt pans, inserts and empty sauce bottles.

The cords fell halfway down his ass whenever he stood for any length of time spraying and racking dishes or whenever he scrubbed pans. They stuck to his legs, obstructing his movement whenever he bent down to replace dish racks. His face kept dripping. The sweat lubricated his spectacles. They slid down his nostrils and slid down his nostrils and slid down. He pushed them up and smudged the lenses he just cleaned and they slid down.

The chits kept chittering.

Bobby pulled one off and stuck it up with the others and called out the order with a hard, rattled voice: "Adding on! deep-fried pickles, wings, one hot, one honey garlic, beef burger with cheese, black-bean burger without the bun."

Henry walked over and snapped up the bill, toque pulled down over his eyebrows. He reviled the customers, loathed cooking, numbed it all with drink and NHL hockey. "Burger without the bun. You retarded loser," he said to the chit. "Jacob."

"Yeah Henry," Jacob said while sending burger buns through the toaster. He wore his scarlet bandana for Canada Day. Henry slapped down five plates on the stainless-steel counter, garnished them with lemon wedges and his own resentment. "Put on an RTJ mix," he ordered. "Now."

"R-r-right away." Jacob thumbed the touchscreen on his phone, queued up a playlist on Spotify. El-P and Killer Mike began to absorb the nervous tension mounting in the kitchen.

Levett watched the bun halves slowly level and disappear on a circulating track inside the toaster.

He went out for more water. All the tables were occupied. Standing room only. Kristine stomped by with a tray of martinis. He looked over at Lowell, who shook his head at the cocktail-guzzling revellers on the ottomans by the smoking deck. Heather punched orders into the touchscreen, hammering at the interface, hand like a demented tarantula, new windows popping up rapidly in new configurations and others disappearing, special requests ill-typed or forgotten.

At the broiler Henry pressed beef patties with a metal flipper. White runnels of sweat dripped from the edge of his toque and down a sallow cheek. Levett thought he might punch a hole through the range. The line was all chits.

Bobby's drill-sergeant bark: "Adding on! Hummus, green-onion cakes, fish and chips—two pieces."

"Get fucked," Henry said to the add-on.

William dropped down tenders and yam fries. He pulled a warmed roast-veggie wrap off the flat-top then halved and plated it with a garden salad and dinged the bell, all with a kind of blinky panache that convinced Levett without a doubt that young William was an old pro.

They were two hours in. It felt like forever already. Forever's a long time.

No progress. Three full bus bins beneath the counter, three more full ones on the counter. No room to put anything.

The belly of his t-shirt and his underwear were soaked. It felt like someone had thrown a wet blanket over him.

Six hours to go.

He had drunk four litres of water so far and did not need to urinate.

Lowell brought in another bus bin. "Can we get another bus bin Dylan?" he said, visibly shaken. "These fucking idiots man. A whole crowd comes up to the door, says, 'Table for twelve please.' Like fuck, do you not see what is happening right now?"

Levett lifted a bin off the floor, spilt it gently and set it in the Hobart. "Twenty seconds," he told Lowell, who paced some in the back hallway and pushed through the swing door without knocking. He could have cracked someone right in the face with that door.

Levett was getting hotheaded too.

"Uh, you-you g-got ramekins?" Jake said, peering into the mess.

"Yeah hold on," Levett snapped. He tossed objects around, threw the mass to one side and hoisted up another bin, unloaded its contents. He set all the ramekins in the bottom of the sink and sprayed them out. Lowell brought in another heaping bus bin.

"Uh, where do you want this one?"

"Anywhere. Under the big sink."

Lowell shoved it down under, straightened up and shook his head, paused indignantly, went back out.

"Fucking shit," Levett said, hating it all of a sudden. He threw a cutting board in the big sink. Loud *bong* heard on the line. He sprayed out a strainer, muttering, "Canada Day, what a farce."

Lowell grabbed the steaming bus bin. In five minutes he brought it back full.

"We need cutlery," Heather said.

"Okay," Levett said. The Hobart's water had to be changed. Delay in the workflow. He got some latex gloves to insulate his hands from the hot water and parts. He pulled out the smoking catch, set it upside down on the removable rails above the sink and sprayed out the debris. He brought out the flat guard and the plug, had to put his hand in the dirty scorching water. He looked at the dish shelf on the line and it was near empty. The cooks were resorting to takeout ramekins. He realized he was grinding his teeth, tried to relax his clenched jaw. As the water drained he shelved dishes and containers, rubber spatulas, wooden spoons. He brought out a flat rack and dumped out the jangling cutlery bucket. Smell of chlorine. He sprayed out the bucket and sprinkled in some disinfectant crystals, let hot water drop in full valve. He smoothed out the cutlery, sprayed off the disinfectant, twisted round and flipped the small lever inside the dishwasher and lowered the door to refill it, then twisted back round and arranged the cutlery by utensil in a compartmentalized basket. He tried to do it fast, sighting butter knives, grabbing as many facing the same way as he could and slotting them, forks, steak knives, teaspoons. He set the basket on the flat rack and slid it inside the purified Hobart. He tried to keep the dishwasher going all the time, to always have something in there, but it was difficult to time properly and all the while he felt more oppressed by the rote actions. He would race to fill a rack, fill it, but the dishwasher was not through its cycle, so he would shelve dishes, clearing room for the newly clean to slide out in a hot fog, spectacles opaque in the maddening jungle-like atmosphere. Wait for those ones to cool, doing something else, and so on, unable to coordinate his actions.

He took a break and emailed Dion. He needed to jam, craved the outlet. Dion had not responded to his last five emails.

The arbitration hearing was in two weeks. He wasn't looking forward to it.

Jacob set an empty plastic insert on the mess in front of Levett and Levett flung the insert to the far end of the counter at the wall and it bounced and crashed off the piles of other smattered hardware.

"This job sucks shit," he muttered a bit too loud.

Nearby William set buns in the toaster. He looked up quizzically at Levett, who had taken on a darker cast. The muscle twitched in his clamped jaw. He scowled, plucking up one-litres and stacking them. The strainer and first aid kit tumbled down.

"Fuck me," he said. The cooks noticed, heard his percussion. I'm trying to get fired, he decided. Five months in and he had lost interest in the position, kept trying to convince himself the gig was easy money. It was only as easy as boring drudgery could be. "I'm gonna quit this fucking job," Levett said openly.

Heather set another bus bin on the rails above the sink. He pushed it away.

Rough music emanating from his area. He picked up the bus bin with one hand, straight-armed it and the contents clattered out on the steel counter. A couple of plates broke. It felt good doing it.

"Oh and I *love* my job," Bobby whimpered. "Everybody's getting killed Dylan," she shouted.

"I didn't say you weren't," he snapped.

He was trying to make it through what was there, then another voice called out "Behind!" and another mess appeared. Always voices from behind and arms reaching around and more work in front of him.

It did not end for another five hours. And then it slowed down completely. Only a dozen casual drinkers in the pub. Levett grabbed a one-litre of iced cola and saw workers disassembling the big stage outside, setting pipework on lengths of dunnage parallel to the stone curbs.

All night, an unbroken line of chits staring at the cooks' faces and the cooks jumping around in the grease and trodden vegetables. Levett back and forth between the cooks to shelve the clean dishes and mixing bowls, the knives, having to say "Behind," and "Sharp," with the knives pointing down. He always thought someone might slip and the knife would pierce a throat or a belly, an eye, run across a major vein.

Jacob worked late. He had been there since nine in the morning. In the basement he was taking the first opportunity that day to restock the upstairs freezer. Levett appeared before him.

"That was psycho."

"Uh, y-yeah. I've been here for like two years, and that was, that was, ea-ea-easily the busiest day I've ever worked here."

"My ginch are completely wet."

"Yeah, I-I c-can imagine. You were in the dish pit for an entire eight hours. That's crazy. One t-t-time I was s-stuck in there for three hours and it was hell. So good on ya."

Levett went into the cooler to fetch his beers.

Jacob appeared. "I-I put some smelly steaks and schnitzel in that bucket of yours."

"Thanks, I appreciate that Jacob," he said and turned away, taking the steps in threes and coming out the clamorous steel door.

The streets were hazed over. He went across Water, up Cambie toward Cordova. The westing sun was swollen pink like a chafed nipple.

▽ ▽ ▽

The clouds parted. The tower's shadow knifed across Broadway. The two of them walked into it and out of it. Levett noshed on a croissant, the foil wrapper pressed around his mouth like a feed bag.

Lane looked at his watch: twenty-five after ten. They caught the red. Blade Girl escorted pedestrians across Main Street, admonished drivers.

As Levett let them into the Bellevue, Tom Ford walked by the entrance but did not come in. He was not in his work clothes. Instead of the mesh Canucks cap, his white hair was combed straight downward. He carried what looked to Levett like a deerskin document pouch.

In the elevator Levett pushed 4. The doors slowly closed and the lift slowly rose. Lane shifted his weight from one foot to the other and looked at his watch. He glanced around the confines of the lift, at the fake wood panelling, the placard with a stylized fireball hovering over a zag of staircase. Lane glanced at the four stainless-steel vents, two on each side near the floor. He checked his watch. Half past ten by Levett's estimation. Eight seconds a floor. The hoist laboured and the carriage swayed under the cables. It stopped. A mechanism beneath their feet went *pwong* and the door scraped open. He led Lane to John's unit, 401, knocked firmly on the door.

"Hello?" an agitated voice said.

"It's D."

"I thought I told you quarter to," John snapped from behind the door.

"I told you man, we need time to set up, get ready and shit. We need power."

John didn't say anything for a little while.

"I told you it required an hour set-up time," Levett said.

Shambling noises inside the apartment. "Just a second."

The voice was groggy and frustrated. Levett shook his head and rolled his eyes. Lane looked as though something was in his way.

The door popped open. John's hair was on end, his back turned. He wore sweatpants and a wrinkled undershirt.

The room was stuffy, pregnant with sleep. To the right, at the foot of the bed, a coat rack, and beside it a wicker chest. A set of weights braced the wicker chest. The lupine fleece comforter lay twisted on the mattress—contorted howling wolves. A work table overflowed with papers, periodicals and books. Well beyond its planned obsolescence, the printer sat dormant under a ream of scrap loose-leaf. A pair of his girlfriend's dirty ankle socks lay folded on the table against an empty can of beer. Electric bill. Cable bill. John pulled out a chair and faced it toward the bowed couch and the sticky coffee table. Lane immediately sat down. "Is there an outlet somewhere?"

Levett thumbed at a power bar directly to his right. Lane plugged his phone in and began to riffle through his papers.

"Just lemme have a bath," John said.

I knew this would happen, Levett thought. He looked at the time. It was twenty to.

Lane dialled. Automatic prompts. He stated his name. A recorded voice responded, "You are currently the only participant in this conference."

New country piped thinly from the phone.

John made his way out of the bathroom fully dressed and with his hair hurriedly combed to the left.

"You guys mind if I stick around?" he joshed.

He removed a card from a picture frame and handed it to Levett. "This'll help."

It was an icon of St. Expeditus.

Levett snapped it down on the coffee table's laminate surface. "Thanks for donating your space."

"Good luck," he said, held his keys up and set them on the table. "Lock up when you're done."

Lane flipped through his papers and added marginal notes.

"Announcing participant," said the text-to-speech voice.

Lane was getting squirrelly. He set his papers on the bed, laid his laptop on his lap for a surface, tested his papers. This wouldn't do. He removed the laptop, set it aside on the bed, motioned with his head toward a coffee table book on John's old TV/VCR combo. Levett handed over Ansel Adams's *Landscapes of the American West*. Lane tested it and liked it.

A female voice confirmed the participants. Vaughn MacDunn and Tom Ford were on the line.

"I can't hear you," the arbitrator said over the crackling line. "There's way too much background noise."

Is she referring to the refrigerator or the traffic? Levett thought, as Lane tended to his phone. He disengaged the speaker.

"Hello?! Hello?!" The arbitrator's compressed voice called through the phone speaker.

"We're here," Lane said, hunched over his notes. He shrugged his shoulders at Levett.

"I'm confirming that the landlords are proceeding with the notice and the tenant is pursuing the hearing," said the arbitrator.

"Well, Madame Arbitrator," Vaughn said, "we've not been able to find an engineer to give testimony. We'd like to adjourn the hearing."

"We want to resolve the matter," Lane said.

"You've had plenty of time, though, two months, to find an engineer. I'm denying the adjournment," the arbitrator said.

Vaughn: "But Madame Arbitrator, Mr. Levett initially agreed to a settlement until," he paused and continued vehemently, "until Mr. Roth came into the picture. The landlords have the permit… we've secured permits from the City of Vancouver for this work project, and they include Mr. Levett's unit."

"When did you receive the applicant's request to cancel the notice?" the arbitrator said. Lane held the phone away from his ear cranked to maximum volume so Levett could hear.

"It seems I don't have the exact date handy," Vaughn said.

"I've still not seen the landlords' evidence package, it's nowhere on my file. You had just shy of two months to serve evidence. Is that not correct?"

"I completely understand. We weren't able to schedule an engineer to attend the hearing. We had hoped for an adjournment to the hearing, Madame Arbitrator."

As soon as he finished she countered with, "I've denied your request for adjournment. There would be no guarantee the hearing would happen before the notice takes effect. We are proceeding with the hearing," she snapped.

"I do not have any letters from the engineers," she said. You could hear typing over the phone.

"I did receive Mr. Levett's evidence package," the arbitrator continued. "What is the monthly rental amount?"

"Five hundred dollars per month," Lane said.

"Madame Arbitrator, the suite below Mr. Levett and the suite above have been vacated."

The line was silent.

"Madame Arbitrator, I'd like to draw your attention to the permit again."

"When was the permit issued?" the arbitrator said.

"The middle of February."

Tom Ford was speaking now, tone calm, speech measured.

"The mistake on the permit was a clerical error. Mr. Levett's unit, 310, should have been on the permit. Structural drawings that implicate his unit were included in the permit application."

"It's still difficult to hear you with all the background noise," the arbitrator complained. The noise was obviously, and intentionally, coming from Ford and MacDunn's end. They sat in a loud coffee shop. Crockery rattled in the background, people chatted, it was another one of their strategies to foil the hearing.

"Can you tell me anything about the building's history?" the arbitrator said.

"The building was constructed in 1914," said Ford. "It's under new ownership and has been neglected for years. Really, the issue centres on a rotting beam in the basement of the building directly under Mr. Levett's unit. A hole in the roof that leaked for many years drained directly onto this structural component. The units located above the beam must be vacated, as indicated quite clearly by the building engineers—and shoring is very disruptive."

Like fuck it is, Levett thought. You jack up the surrounding structure and replace the beam.

"What is the timeline for the project? How long is this supposed to take?" the arbitrator asked.

Ford hesitated. "I do not have a pertinent document in front of me."

"The only one holding up the project is Mr. Levett," Vaughn added, sounding like a daft provincial councilman.

"How many unoccupied units exist in the building?" the arbitrator asked.

"Several, Madame Arbitrator, several, all uninhabitable," Vaughn said.

"I want to reiterate," Ford said, "that the original permit does not include the unit, but the permit has since been amended to include the unit. Not much was known about the beam problem until we removed several truckloads of miscellaneous junk from the basement and the extent of the problem was physically revealed and discovered by us."

"By whom? Were you involved in this?" the arbitrator said.

"Yes," Ford confirmed. "I'm the general contractor in charge of renovations of the building."

"Madame Arbitrator," Vaughn added, "it's important to emphasize the permits issued by the City. There has been a second permit issued with Mr. Levett's unit stated in the permit."

"I've got that in front of me," she spat.

"Mr. Ford has been in the business for about thirty years, and he's the main contractor on this building. He knows more about the building than anyone," Vaughn declared.

"Tom Ford?" Lane said.

"Yes."

"Can I ask you a few direct questions?"

"Sure."

"Is it true that you are acting as the building manager of Bellevue Heights?"

"No."

"Are you an engineer?"

"No."

"Have you ever been in Dylan's unit to inspect it?"

"No—I don't believe I have."

More silence on the line.

"Mr. Roth," the arbitrator said, "are you still on the line?"

"Yes," he said, clearing his throat silently and rearranging his papers. "The building has actually had the same corporate owners since 1980. There has been continuous responsibility of maintenance and the landlords have had over thirty years to monitor the structural problem. Mr. Levett takes issue with Mr. MacDunn's conduct toward him. He was never offered an option to relocate. As the landlords' agent, MacDunn made the inflexible offer of a compensation package. It is Mr. Levett's right to oppose the notice and continue his tenancy. Currently the building is being prepared to re-rent to higher-income tenants and this within the context of a concerted effort by the landlords to evict tenants. I find it completely reasonable to forward allegations against the landlords of an extralegal strategy to remove Bellevue tenants. Mr. Levett's ability to respond to the notice was precluded because the address of the building on the notice submission is not a deliverable address. It listed the street address of Bellevue Heights as the landlords' address, when in fact that is not their address. How was Mr. Levett supposed to respond to and contest the notice?

"In addition to the city permit," Lane continued, "we submit that several other permits are lacking, firstly a WorkSafeBC permit. In addition, there is no evidence of a trades permit, either from the landlords or from the City. Moving on to the most substantive matter," Lane swallowed, lightly cleared his throat again, "I cite Berry and Kloet at paragraph 18: *ambiguities in the language of the Act are to be resolved in favour of the tenant*. Firstly, for vacancy to be required, the nature, extent, and duration of work must absolutely necessitate the vacancy of the unit. No pertinent drawings or evidence related to prospective work have been provided. Secondly, and in opposition to Mr. Ford's statement, I want to draw attention to Jim Auerbach's statement from page eight of our submission."

Levett remembered the circumstances in which the letter came to him. Jim's "You're welcome, Dylan" repeating in his head.

Roth read Auerbach's letter in full: "*I have information that Mr. Levett is being evicted from his unit on the third floor of Bellevue Heights because there is a failed beam on the ground floor. This beam has failed due to rot caused by a water leak which continued for nearly four decades and was left unaddressed by the landlords of Bellevue Heights. I've seen the beam first-hand and it needs to be fixed. This can be done without displacing Mr. Levett. As a woodworker and carpenter, I've spent several years repairing buildings just like this one throughout Gastown for Reedijk and Sons contracting, some of the most sought-after and experienced outfits in heritage restoration who have been responsible for 60 percent of all heritage restorations on the 100 block of Hastings between 2011 and 2013, among many, many others. I've seen far worse than what I saw with my own eyes in the basement of Bellevue Heights. The best example would be 261 Powell Street, now home of Cuchillo restaurant. Any diner can look at the roof and note the massive beams and how several of them had entire parts removed, replaced with completely new sections, and reinforced with steel.*

"Without an engineer's testimony," Lane stated, "there can be no decision on the matter, because we have no expert opinion to base it on. I also want to suggest that Mr. Ford is taking on management tasks, thus is not an independent party. This implicates him in the landlords' attempt to evict Bellevue residents. Mr. Ford was quoted saying 'renovations would last about two months.'"

Lane leafed through his papers in search of the citation. "I refer you to Berry and Kloet. Paragraph 22 sets out the second stem of the test for establishing whether the 49(6)(b) vacancy requirement is met: *It must be the case that the only manner in which to achieve the necessary vacancy, or emptiness, is by terminating the tenancy. I say this based upon the purpose of section 49(6). The purpose of section 49(6) is not to give landlords a means for evicting tenants; rather, it is to ensure that landlords are able to carry out renovations. Therefore, where it is possible to carry out renovations without ending the tenancy, there is no need to apply section 49(6). On the other hand, where the only way in which the landlord would be able to obtain an empty unit is through termination of the tenancy, section 49(6) will apply.* In my opinion," Lane continued, "the notice was issued in bad faith. Several suites are vacant in the building. The caretaker's keys have been confiscated. As a result, the sprinkler flood last Christmas rendered four suites uninhabitable. Evidence of protracted repairs on these suites can be found on the USB flash drive included in the submission. On it you'll find video and audio evidence to support claims that several units in the building are vacant."

"But, but, Madame Arbitrator, I didn't receive any flash drive," Vaughn said.

"Flash drive—I don't think I see one here. I don't believe one was ever on file," said the arbitrator.

"Flash drives were included in all three packages I sent by registered mail. Anyway, most of the evidence on USB referred to monetary claims. We can defer those for now."

The arbitrator looked for the flash drive. The line was silent.

"No, it's not here. I have no USB drive in the case dossier," the compressed voice said, louder now. Lane pulled the phone farther away from his ear.

Levett shook his head. He sat back on the bowed couch with folded arms, jaw locked, scowling at the blinking cursor on his laptop screen, dumbly marking off the seconds, tonguing the cracked enamel of a molar.

"We'd be happy to re-submit these claims," Lane said, glancing at Levett. Levett nodded.

Much half-audible deliberation on the line.

"The most urgent thing we are responding to is the cancellation of the notice," Lane said. "I want to highlight the fact that there are vacant units in the building. No evidence suggests the suite needs vacating while the beam is under repair. Also, two months is not long, certainly not long enough to justify Mr. Levett ending his tenancy. This suggests that the notice has been issued in bad faith. I refer to the RTB decision made in September 2012 when similar circumstances allowed the landlord to re-rent the vacated suite at a new, exorbitant price, unattainable for the original tenant. A standard bachelor suite price is double Mr. Levett's rental amount. We also believe repairs in the building have been prolonged artificially or unnecessarily, or both. Please see Osman's conversation with Mr. Ford here. The landlords used the flood damage as a pretext to completely remodel unit 206 for re-rental, going as far as removing walls, while using the lengthy timespan as leverage to convince one of the affected tenants to sign a new rental agreement on his 'temporary' apartment. Hakim, the former occupant of unit 206, was told by Mr. Ford to 'give up' on ever returning to his suite. The tenant of 406, who persisted with reclaiming her unit—in contrast with the others—faced a number of incomplete repairs when she returned to her 'filthy space.'"

The hearing had gone on for two and a half hours when Vaughn requested Levett's participation.

"Mr. Levett," Vaughn said.

"Yes, hi."

"How ya doin' Dylan?"

"Alright."

"I just have one question for you," Vaughn said in his warbling tenor.

"What's that?"

"Did you, during one of our initial meetings, agree to accept compensation from the landlord to end your tenancy?"

Lane held his thumb to the phone mic whispering, "It's your right to negotiate."

"At one point I requested an amount, but the offer was well below what I requested."

"Oh, so you did agree to compensation," Vaughn chuckled.

"It's your legal right to negotiate," Lane whispered.

"I agreed... at one point, but... I'm allowed to... to... it's my right to negotiate."

"Well, thank you for your candid response, Dylan," Vaughn said. "Madame Arbitrator, I would like to emphasize that, prior to Mr.

Roth getting involved, this agreement was finalized. Now, what about *Mr. Levett's* bad faith?"

More distorted phrases from the arbitrator. Something about the estimated time frame for a decision. Official conclusion to the hearing. Termination of the phone call.

They were silent, Levett confused about how the hearing actually went, Lane exhausted. Levett's foot was asleep. Pricks ran up his leg. He gathered John's keys.

In the corridor. Walls skeined with putty. Another half-finished job.

They turned to face each other.

"What do you think?"

Lane looked away.

"Do you think it went okay?"

Lane met Levett's eyes. He looked troubled.

"I don't know."

"You can't tell if it went well or not."

"I really don't know what to expect," Lane said. "She didn't give me any indication of who she'd decide in favour of." He turned away and walked down the corridor.

Levett stood alone by the fire door, John's keys in his hand, overcome by a totally uncertain feeling.

▽ ▽ ▽

He was scrubbing the dish pit wall tiles with the rough side of a sponge when Jacob appeared at the threshold. His large hands dangled, with dimpled knuckles like children have.

"H-hey, dude."

"Yeah."

"H-Henry wants to… w-wants to talk to you in the office."

He stopped scrubbing, looked around. Jacob wore a pink t-shirt and his turquoise bandana. Levett dropped the sponge. It smacked down in a dirty pool of water upon the ridged counter. He slid by edgewise.

Henry sat at the desk in the big brick office. The walls were lined with electronic equipment, amplifiers for the sound system and a receiver for the satellite television. Rows of dimmer dials and light switches. Levett figured he was going to be dismissed for his outburst on Canada Day. He readily accepted it as a favourable and deserved outcome. Lately he'd walked away from shifts feeling short a pre-frontal lobe.

"What's up?"

"Yeah, so..." Henry looked at a point in the corner vaguely right of Levett's hip. "Yeah." He exhaled through his nose, knuckled an irregular pattern on the desk. Levett stood by, as if he was the rebuker. "So, there's been a few comments about you in the kitchen..." He paused again.

"What, like about me freaking out?"

"Yeah," Henry said, with reluctance, and regret—a statement he did not want to have to make.

"Look, it's okay, I understand..." if you want to let me go, he could not finish saying.

"So lately we hired a few more young people, and Rosy will be working Saturdays all summer. She's sixteen. Marie's sister Astrid is coming to work in the kitchen too."

"Perfectly understandable Henry. I can..." find something else, he almost said.

"Like, it's almost a prerequisite that people be kinda crazy, and I'm not sayin' yer crazy, I mean, I went to bat for you all the way with that Vikram stuff, that guy's psycho, but we have to all, me included, try to keep our cool. Like earlier today I flipped out on Tanya because she wasn't knocking out the ramekins before she put them in the bus bin. It's been company policy for like, ever. There was a big thing. We had to work it out."

"Yeah man, I get it. Sorry. I'm feeling the pressure. I still haven't heard back about my place. If I don't win I don't really know—"

"For sure, I feel that. A lot of us in the kitchen are going through shit right now. Well, I don't know about Jacob, his life's pretty nerfy. But otherwise, we get it, we understand, but..." He paused and glanced up from the spot in the corner. For the first time during the remonstrance, Henry met Levett's eyes.

"It's totally fine," Levett said. "I'll..." sign out, thanks for the work.

Henry opened a desk drawer. Levett expected him to draw out a prepared record of employment with *TERMINATION* the reason for leaving. It was a floppy Duo-Tang. He opened the creased blue folio and flipped to a clean page with headings for DATE, TIME, EMPLOYEE NAME, SUPERVISOR and REASON in block caps.

"I gotta write you up, Dylan. I'm sorry. You're a cool guy, you're good here, you're well liked... Bobby loves you, she thinks you're the shit—and I'm not worried about it, it's just parta my job. Protocol. I took this on as the general manager."

Levett stared at him.

"Sign the bottom. I'll write the reason as *losing temper*."

Levett took the pen and initialled the bottom.

"That all?"

"Yeah. Don't worry about it. No biggie. Technically I have to do this sort of thing." He bunny eared technically. "It's routine shit D. No worries."

▽ ▽ ▽

He knew something would happen between Kristine and William when William joined her at the bar one night after his shift.

Levett saw him leave the kitchen at eleven sharp. On the lead-up to it he restlessly paced and wiped surfaces down with a scuzzy rag. At a minute to, he stepped into the bathroom and exited wearing his generic street clothes.

Through the swing door he saw William settle at the bar and saw Kristine twirl her straw in the cocktail glass eyeing up William. As he walked by the swing door Levett admired the contrast of her fresh lipstick and white teeth, her lips closing on the straw, admiring the black low-cut blouse against her pale shoulders. Razor-thin clavicle shadow in the swing-back of the door—her goodly hue there and gone like a spliced frame, like a jump-cut in a film.

She had been talking about wanting to see a movie. He figured it was a hint and she wanted him to ask her, but he was not quite sure.

The dish pit was dead.

If Bobby let me go I could join them, I could out-charm him, I could save it.

"Hey Bobby," Levett said.

She brought a sizzling lasagna out of the oven with a long pair of tongs and plated the boat and hung the tongs back on the oven handle. "What's up man?" she boomed, looking up with her young boyish face.

"Can I get off?"

"Not yet, I wanna keep you 'til at least midnight. I don't wanna get a rush without a dishwasher."

"Sure."

He went and stood by the Hobart and played the part of an indolent dishwasher.

He got bored and cleaned the whole space. Cleaned the tiles behind the organics bin, the tiles along the counter, the counter itself, the sinks, internally and externally, the trolley, the Hobart. If he could only clean up his life the same way.

Then there was no action. Slacking there on the dish pit threshold, he saw William dart into the kitchen and check his schedule.

An hour later Levett looked through the swing door. They were both gone.

▽ ▽ ▽

Next day Kristine made sure to tell Bella in front of Levett that she had "news" and they needed to "talk in the alley." Whether they had fucked or not, Levett assumed they had at least made a date to see a movie the coming week. She's probably gunning for Tuesday cheap night, he thought.

Day after that, a few of the lads came to the Rose for drinks. Henry was their host, half-cut before suppertime. Levett was on until eight. When he punched out and made his way by their table, Henry grabbed his arm. "Dylan," he slurred, "how's it goin'? You wanna sit down fer a drink with the Irish?" Henry gestured toward William and his roommates.

▽ ▽ ▽

It was scalding and hazy out. The sun just a shinier area of sky. People were moving slower. Some wore thin scarves or dust masks. He thought about going into the street. Thought it might be a mistake. He had about five dollars in change on the bookshelf.

I could get a slice of pizza, he thought.

Outside. Looking west, the Federal Store at the end of the block wasn't even visible. Looking east, the unfinished tower rose up like a ruin from battle smoke.

Tom Ford and his crew were gathered round a tall plywood cart along the south side of the building. Ford with his Craigslist crew who seemed to have flipped the work–break ratio on its head. Levett turned and walked over to them. Ford was entertaining his guys with a routine about drinking the tin can of solvent on the cart ledge. They laughed. As Levett approached, the hulking British foreman Reg said, "How's it goin' man?"

"Alright, you?"

"Not bad, man, not bad."

Levett stopped and looked up at him. "Why?"

"What?" The laughing continued.

"Why would you be?"

Reg was perplexed.

Levett came round the crew's pair of rugby youth labourers. To Tom: "Are you Tom Ford?"

Ford squared off to Levett. He looked down at him with very blue irises. Large shrewd eyes. Pale skin. Rugby build.

"Yeah, what can I do for you?" he said, almost shouting it down at him.

"Fuck you is what you can do." Ford leaned back. The laughter died off.

"Excuse me?"

"It's 'bout to fuckin' go down mate," Reg said to the old Welsh painter, Harold.

"Did he just say that?" Harold said.

"Has the guy gone 'n lost it?" Reg said.

Levett stared at Ford, thought he might get hit. "You're a lying bottom-feeder," he said, and crossed the street. "*Not managing the building*. You're a top-tier bullshitter is what."

"He's in 311," Alex the Maori rugby player said in his low drawl, wrongly identifying Levett with Osman's suite.

Nathan, the English rugby player built like a brick shitter, said, "Bollocks," as if that said it all.

"Have a nice day!" Ford called across the street.

"Go fuck yourself!" Levett barked over his shoulder.

▽ ▽ ▽

GG had some leftover Pepsi in the fridge. It was flat, but the chemical sweetness was still there. She thought about tidying. She looked around at the piles. Every time she tried to clean up it got messier. She sat down on a stepping stool and drained the Pepsi. There was a wire grid embedded in the window glass. For the better part of an hour she watched its shadow drift over the floorboards from left to right, the sun going east to south, small hexagonal shadows widening and narrowing again as she bounced the empty plastic bottle on her knee, keeping her own elastic time. A minute could feel like a week, or a day like ten minutes.

Vaughn liked to arrive somewhat early or the slightest bit late, armed with a traffic excuse: it was smooth sailing coming in from the suburbs this morning; it was ass to nose on the Lions Gate—some pileup at the entrance to Stanley Park—even if he wasn't in North Vancouver that day. Really it could be anything.

He nursed a cream-and-sugared Dunkin's, none of that Timmy's swill, and never not a cruller. He would cut it in quadrants to pick at at red lights. Brekky on the go.

Vaughn thought about that Dylan Levett character. What a dishonourable sneak. But he had it coming to him.

Twenty to. GG said ten even. He'd make it three to.

This was what he loved: to sit and think and plot in his vehicle. It all went so smoothly in his mind and at least he had that.

Out of the smoky heat, sweat broke. First on his throat, then the armpits and back, the jock, the inside of each calf despite having switched to cotton. They itched fiercely. He refrained—if he started rubbing then he'd start raking them with his fingernails until they bled.

He turned the ignition and rolled up the window. Starter's sounding funny lately, he thought. The air-con was already cranked.

He hadn't seen any do-good tree-huggers around. The Bellevue was full of social-justice warriors. With Roth at the helm, too, what an upstart hotshot. Pro bono gets old real fast. I wouldn't be surprised if a placarded faction surrounded my idling vehicle right now and launched into a martial chant about climate change, he thought. You know what I'd say? I'd say, Oh yeah, I was changing my climate.

A few weeks ago he admitted to his wife and grown daughters during a ritual Sunday night barbecue that he continued to see the world through a cop's eyes, even though he'd been out of the force going on a decade. They all, including his one son-in-law, gave him frowny poor-you faces. The last thing he had expected was pity, and fake pity at that. What was wrong with a quasi-philosophical conversation, nothing too deep, a measured dialogue, objective yet compassionate, what about that was so hard?

Vaughn looked up out the passenger-side window through the federal building's windows. Part of an X-shaped steel bracing system was visible behind the brickwork facade. Just like his former cop self, he looked up through the building windows and saw the ceiling panels dotted with blackened hemispheres. You couldn't see the little cameras in them but you knew they were there. Vaughn looked ahead at the next vehicle and involuntarily memorized the licence-plate number.

It was five to.

He went into his bag to make sure the pertinent documents and cheque were there. Yes. Then he got out, nearly dooring a cyclist.

There was a jaunty rapping on GG's door.

"Come in. Let's get this over with."

"Oh, hi GG. May I..." He stood in the corridor.

"I said come in."

"Did you?" he said.

She stood there.

"Of course," he said. Vaughn stepped inside her unit. If anything, the place looked worse.

"Spending much time at home GG?"

"I'm a total shut-in lately. Can't seem to tie this place together."

"It's difficult with such limited square footage."

"Tea?" GG offered.

Vaughn stepped up to the kitchen. She was using it for extra magazine storage. The only food in sight was a mouldy bag of panini buns. The sink was framed by a chrome shirt rack on casters.

"No thanks GG, got my Dunkin's."

"I don't think I actually even have any."

"So the landlords have made you an offer."

"Like a money offering?"

"It's quite good. I mean, technically they don't have to offer you anything. We're talking two thousand dollars, GG, plus your last month's rent free. They've written me a cheque—"

"I'll take it."

"—for a thousand dollars. What I have here is a document, see, it says, *I, Greta Guzman*—lovely name by the way—*I, Greta Guzman, agree to end my tenancy in unit 410 at Bellevue Heights. From the first day of September 2017, my residence at the current address will be cancelled.*"

"Read it again. I never catch anything first try."

"Not a problem," Vaughn said, and read the three-line document through again.

"So, you give me the money, I move. Finished?"

"That's right."

"Can't wait."

"Okay, good. We've got a deal."

"It's a deal."

He enclosed her small hand in his.

"I just can't deal with all this right now."

"Yes, and really GG, why should you? This is an opportunity to move forward."

"I don't have a pen."

"One sec." He withdrew a Mac Bundy pen sealed in a transparent baggie. He fussed with opening it, furled the plastic down the pen and held it out. She carefully wrote her signature in a loopy cursive. He signed as a witness.

"Can I have my money?"

Vaughn withheld the limp cheque so she had to reach out for it and tug it from his hand.

He took a long languid look around, exhaled. "You know Ms. Guzman, you're gonna have to get rid of all this stuff."

"All this was already here when I moved in."

▽ ▽ ▽

Levett walked into shade, into patches of sun, along a sordid bas-relief of addicts and dealers. Semicircled in the raking sunlight, users blocked the sidewalks. They fussed over paraphernalia and bartered supplies and searched for veins below waistband tourniquets. Street people getting cut off by Audis and Land Rovers turning right on reds, sealed and drifting away from the cursed pantomimes and toothless affronts.

He walked by a man laying on the sidewalk. Filthy. Back arched. A frothy pus leaking out the corner of his sore-covered rictus. Quaking, contorted, coiling back, turning, turning, beyond his own personal event horizon. Something hairy going down up ahead.

Outside the women's shelter a police cruiser sat wedged into the curb blocking oncoming traffic. The officer had a man pinned and cuffed on the sidewalk. The captive's t-shirt rode his nipples and his gelatinous gut was pressed against the cement. Levett caught sight of the bifurcated forehead and the flash of pink spandex off to the side. Blade Girl was filming the arrest on a tablet. Blade Girl backed away from the arrest, deeply preoccupied with her frame. She did not notice Levett. The police cruiser caused minor motorist confusion and delays.

He had his earbuds in and wondered what the cuffed man's crime was. Blade Girl crouched and sidestepped bow-legged like a latter-day Gorgon. He still regretted pinning her in the door. Levett would come down the street by the pool hall, the bookstore, the diner, and see her sitting there, waiting for him.

Yesterday Blade Girl had walked by Levett. Skates slung over the shoulder. A man in his thirties accompanied her, possibly her mental-health chaperone. "This is my manager," she said to Levett. "You're lucky I'm gonna be a star, or I'd bash your head in."

Levett drank his coffee. He was with a couple of friends he frequently met and chatted with at the coffee shop. Leaving would have made him look guilty.

"Don't worry about Blade Whore," Adam said. "She's off her rocker."

"Just expunge that from your mind," Ryan told Levett.

In a minute she came back alone. "I'm runnin' fer mayor. Gonna get you locked up. *Woman beater.*" A few women walked out of the diner. "Watch out for the guy with glasses sitting over there," Blade Girl said to them. "He's a predator!"

Whenever Levett spotted her brightly coloured clothing, her mannish muscular form on the squared logs outside Gene, he froze, did an about-face, and walked around the block to the other side. Gene had two entrances. It was located in the corner of a building facing one street cloven in two. Main Street and Kingsway. She never caught on to his presence on the opposite side of Gene, though she waited there in order to publicly shame him. She never clued in to the fact that her high-vis clothing was noticeable not only to motorists but to any semi-lucid pedestrian as well, that her adversary could see her a mile away.

He turned west on Cordova along the Army & Navy's expansive show windows. Blouses and neon workwear stiff on the mannequins. Dull neoclassical facade. The plaster columns and Ionic capitals bore no load but their accreted layers of paint. He focused on the complacent drivers turning left on a green. He sauntered across a side street and stranded a queue of luxury automobiles in the middle of the intersection.

A maintenance worker power-washed the opposite sidewalk. Levett found himself in stride with an old fellow. He wore a green cap. Its flat brim ran flush with a grey unibrow. His lower jaw protruded indignantly. "I guess the sidewalk needed a cool-down."

"I guess."

"You heard Nestlé's got a water-bottling plant up in Hope?"

"I heard."

"Do you know its source?"

"Not sure."

"The Kawkawa Lake aquifer." He didn't allow Levett to respond.

"Canada. Pathetic. We can't even bottle our own water."

Levett stepped in the wake of the old-timer's scorn as if scorn itself were a kind of tradition with footsteps you followed in.

At work but with no shift to work, he did some drinking. He went into the customer bathroom and took a leak. In front of the urinal was a poster that said THE GOOD SAMARITAN ACT MEANS YOU ARE LIABLE IF YOU DON'T ASSIST.

▽ ▽ ▽

The kitchen gate clanged shut behind as a fat rat popped out from a shrub. It waddled across the alley, skirted the wall, scaled the dumpster's vertical side like an insect, paused at the lip and disappeared inside. Judging by its circumference, the rodent did this with calibrated regularity.

In the alley a suspicious pair muttered about a stolen phone. They chicken-necked around, observed their perimeter, eyed Levett walking by, reciting a convoluted plan in the shadows of the marshalling yard barbed wire. The guy told the girl he would meet her in fifteen. She told him they weren't splitting up. "I gotta use buddy's phone. Then I'm comin'."

A thin hooker rifled through a plastic purse.

"Got a light?" she asked Levett.

"I don't," he said, patting the pockets of his swim trunks.

"Wanna date?"

"No thanks. Just on my work break."

"Sure," she said, in the incredulous tone of her vocation, shifted her bony knees, clasped a lighter in her bag.

"Ha! Found the fucker." She scoffed affably, the cigarette clamped in her lips.

"Have a good night," he said.

She nodded yes and shook her head in a big wide no, cupping her cigarette to the flame. The flame lit up the hollows of her cheeks. "I'll try," she said, sucking at the cigarette. "Be better once I make some *cash*." She croaked the word and began to hack violently. She turned and spat out a massive clot of yellow sputum as Levett went on. He saw the projectile leave her face then turned, heard it smack the asphalt.

Exiting the liquor store, a cajoling voice said to the passing crowd, "Come on over, talk to me, we'll talk about *Jesus*." He stood on the curb in a faded black overcoat, more an outgrowth of the man than a garment worn. Levett walked over under the pretext of dropping a few dimes in the empty Tim's cup.

Thin wisps of greasy white hair wetted back over the skull. Glassy fathomless eyes perched above the Dracula nose. A constellation of wens on the foremost point of the chin. In one hand a pew bible with dully shining gold letters, in the other the empty cup held out. As Levett reached to drop the coins in, he noticed the hand was badly psoriatic, and was careful not to graze it with his own.

The coins made tiny thudding sounds hitting the bottom of the cup and this interrupted the man in his phrase, "I got Jesus on the brain so come—" He paused and appraised the sum of his alms with a squint. He shrugged and looked up from the floor of the takeout cup and regarded Levett.

"Take care man," Levett said.

The man looked at the passing crowd and at Levett with his head cocked upward as if the gesture itself was insult enough. His cold detachment was like ice to the base of the skull. "Man, I don't take care. Guy, I'm from Ontario, *Ontario*. There ain't nothin' in me that takes care," and he motioned down along his form, open palms toward the frayed overcoat lapels.

What kinda yegg lingo… he thought, and without thinking looked back down at the infected hand. "Take care."

"I *said* man, *I told ya,* I don't take care, does it look like a take care?" shaking his head, still smiling.

Time span of a ciliary twitch. The shallow warmth in his eyes turned reptile. He eyed Levett with a stillness now, a stillness and a silence, with the quiet of a tomb, as Levett walked away considering the abyss packed into that seamy overcoat.

He threaded through the slow walkers. A dense wall of Japanese tourists encircled the steam clock. An older gentleman held up his phone clipped to a retractable selfie stick. Levett would have knocked the rig out of his hand but the man intuitively leaned back and brought the selfie stick out of the way then straightened and pointed it up at the clock again all in one cyclical motion.

He returned through the pub's front entrance passing the bored doorman. In the basement he scooped ice into the bag of beer and stashed it in the cooler. Upstairs on the line Bobby griped to Kristine about her absentee boyfriend. Her voice boomed. Levett heard it caroming down the basement stairwell.

"I have to deal with this fucking flood on my own. He's not even worried about it. He thinks it's no big deal. He doesn't even want to FaceTime me, he texts me like once every three days. I was like, 'Sorry bud, not good enough.' Meanwhile, after my shifts I have to go back to a soggy shithole, sorting through all the damaged stuff and throwing out all this paper—bills and journals and shit, half of it I can't even read. And the sprinklers loosened all the dirt on the walls. Now they look like someone rubbed mud all over them. And he doesn't even give a shit."

"Wanna share a smoke?" Kristine said.

"Fuck yeah man," Bobby said. "I'm out of smokes. Astrid?"

Astrid looked up from the onions she was peeling.

"Wanna come for a smoke?"

Astrid nodded and set down her knife.

Levett was racking a bin of dinner plates when Jacob walked over and stood at the threshold of the dish pit.

"H-How's things goin'?" he said.

"Alright I guess."

"Any news about y-your place?"

Levett looked up from his work. "I haven't heard."

Jacob shook his head, wincing. "Sorry to hear that." The consolatory words had the opposite effect. Levett turned around and slammed the Hobart. It made a terrific racket. His stomach was a pit of pain.

Astrid finished prepping the onions. Bobby got out the twelve-gallon pot to caramelize them. Once they were simmering, she herded Astrid out for another cigarette. On their way out Levett approached Bobby. "Hey Bobby."

"Yeah?" she said, half-smoked butt sticking out of her pierced lips.

"When you caramelize the onions can you not burn the bottom of the pot? I'm tired of scraping it."

"Do you wanna do it?" Bobby snapped. "Wanna switch spots? You cook, I'll do dishes."

"Not really, but I can fuck off and you can do both if you want."

"I'm not in the mood for this bullshit," she barked. "I got enough going on, I ain't takin that." She returned from the bathroom with her leather jacket on over her chef jacket. "Did you punch out when you went to get beer Dylan?" Bobby said.

"Why would I have to punch out? I was gone for a ten-minute break."

"Henry told me to tell you to punch out if you run to the store."

He must have been wearing the sour mask of a face.

"Let's not have a repeat of Canada Day man."

"Fuck you," he said, could tell it hurt. "Sorry."

"Why can't Henry tell me?" he said. He untied his apron and spiked it into the dirty-linen bucket. In the bathroom he changed into his jeans and t-shirt and wetted down his frizzy mullet. There was nobody on the line when he stepped out front to clock out.

"You're off?" Kristine said.

"Yep," he said, halfway back through the swing door. In the basement he gathered his beer and, thinking it was time to get square, collected his meat from the freezer. He went to the icemaker, popped off the lid of the bucket and scooped cubes in up to the brim. The gate clashed behind him. A car shot by as he stepped into the alley and just missed him.

His place was dark and hot and musty. The weighted window slid open easily and a cool gust of fresh air came in. A bus puffed and beeped at the transit stop.

He removed the racks from the empty refrigerator, leaned them vertically inside. He realized the fridge interior was covered with black mould. He set the racks back in the refrigerator and closed the door trying not to inhale.

He loaded the air pistol and put it aside on a stack of books rising from the sofa. He got out his rolling surface from the cupboard and chopped up a pungent bud with a small pair of scissors he sometimes trimmed his nose hairs with. He cracked a beer and lit the cone-shaped joint.

The weed and the iced beer tasted good.

The breeze was silk. The city lights twinkled. The mountains were a slightly darker shade of blue than the sky. You could see the Grouse Mountain slopes constellated up and out there, stealing back a bit of the darkness. There were no stars. There was only smoke you couldn't see.

He was pretty sure he wouldn't go back to the Wild Rose.

A mouse sniffed gingerly around the corner by the fridge. Levett reached slowly for the gun, turned on the sight, sighted ahead at the threshold of his closet. As it came to meet this point it lifted up as if on a small jet of air and lay still and dead on the hardwood. He scooped it up with the dustpan and flung it out the window onto the neighbouring roof for the gulls. He cocked and loaded the pistol again and set it on a closer stack of books.

A tall silhouette darkened the crack under Levett's door.

"Hello?"

That sombre adenoidal voice bending down at the end of each phrase: "Hi Dy*lan*, it's Vir*gil*." His travel mug brimmed with vodka soda. A lime wedge and some ice cubes bobbed on the surface.

"Hi Verge."

"Would you like to come down for a drink?" he said, taking drunken care with his syllables, enunciating each term singly, carefully.

"I'll come by."

"Okay," Virgil hesitated, stepped away, turned, turned back, paused. "Now?" he asked.

"Yeah Verge, gimme five minutes."

"Okay," he said and bowed his head. "Right on. I feel like I haven't seen you in forever."

Levett thought about the eighty bucks he still owed him.

Virgil walked away, ice cubes tinkling in his cup.

Levett sat there for five minutes and went down, bag of ice and beer in hand.

"Thanks for coming by." Virgil hugged him.

"Pleasure."

Virgil let go and made like a carny with his sweeping arm gesturing inside. "Do you have any, uh… weed?"

"I brought my satchel."

"Thank god. I need to smoke a joint. So. Fucking. Bad."

"Where's your snips?"

"I wanna smoke a joint so fucking bad Dylan, my job is driving me—crazy." He stomped his heel on the word "crazy." Then his face relaxed.

Calmly, Virgil asked, "Can I offer you a drink?"

"Hell yeah."

"Would you like vodka or beer?"

"Beer."

Virgil was listening to *The Signal.*

Vase of fresh lilies.

Virgil set down a Corona and some scissors and sat opposite. He crossed his long legs and lit a cigarette and blew a sizeable cloud into the yellowy haze. "It's nice to see you Dylan. Did you get your power back on?"

He cut up the buds, shook his head.

"How the fuck are you surviving without power?"

"I'm charging my devices at the cafe or the Rose. Well, I was."

"Did you hear back about your place?"

"I'm still waiting."

"I can't *fucking STAND* my job." Virgil's acerbic tone cut through the radio banter.

"Pissing you off lately?" Levett said as he held the rolling paper beneath the lip of the table, dragged the weed into it, tamped it down with the side of his finger, licked the glue side and taped it down. "Light?"

Virgil handed him a Bic. "My co-workers are such pieces of shit."

"What do they do?"

"Fuck all," Virgil growled and sucked on his cigarette.

Levett laughed.

"They can't get off their goddamn phones. They refuse to speak English in the staff room, even though it's *policy*." Virgil was practically screaming. He stamped his boot down twice on the word "policy." Levett passed the joint. "Oh my god. Thank you so much."

"So your workplace has an English-only policy?"

"It says so on the goddamn staff room wall," Virgil hollered, thumbing over his shoulder.

"Do they leave all the anal stims to you too?"

Virgil laughed. "I wanna quit so, fucking, *bad*."

The joint had gone out.

"Pass that," Levett said.

"Oh, sorry." Virgil held it out.

Levett took it back and hauled on it.

"How have you been Dylan?"

"Alright I guess." Levett smoked.

"How's the Wild Rose?"

"Sucks shit."

"Really?" Virgil's tone was flat, nasal, incredulous.

"It's a dish-pit gig. What do you expect me to say?" He was going to mention the row with Bobby but didn't feel like revisiting it.

"You're totally right," Virgil said. He held his open palm toward an old cabinet with a stereo amplifier, orange tubes glowing through the dials. "Actually, Dylan, we've got to keep it down, cuz we might disturb Little Miss Princess." Virgil thrust his chin at the shared wall.

"Absolutely, no problem. I'll come on over and keep my lips sealed."

Virgil guffawed. He set his glass down and gave the finger to the shared wall. "I am so upset she did that to me, Dylan."

"I know dude. It's harsh as hell."

"And to think what she said about me, like I'm prowling outside her window like a jaguar ready to pounce. Gimme a break."

"I know dude, it's wack. She shouldn'ta done that."

"Like, I don't need this shit Dylan. My mother just passed away. My garden is gone. They gave me three days to remove a garden I've kept for twelve years. Those asshole Lam twins, they are such pieces of shit, and they replace my garden with a noisy *tarp*. Can you believe it?" He was almost screeching now.

"The drawing didn't help?"

"For a minute."

"After they neglected that beam for thirty years."

"Fucking morons."

"Can I see the drawing?"

"Sure, I guess, but it's not that good."

Virgil slid it from a recess in the closet. He had coloured it with pencil crayon. The plots were laid out from a vantage point corresponding to Levett's window, like Virgil's dream. All the line work was surely done. Each plant had been labelled, some with the common name, others according to the Linnaean system. The flora had parallel forms in Levett's imagination: oriental poppies were orange ovals; pampas grass like quills stuck in the earth; the Japanese blood grass, red spikes; the dahlias, orange stars; the irises, scarlet leaves like a pile of vaginas; the *Cedrus* was a bushy green scribble; the *Vaccinium parvifolium*, an ice-blue fractal; hovering red dots for nasturtium; radiating green tongues for *Ligularia*; the *Delphinium* was a quick explorer's map, blue lines that might have been hearsay tributaries on a fragment of vellum.

Below the ashtray it said *lung cancer*. The chair by the table was a hybrid seat-person, floating over the backrest: its face with two eyes and a downturned mouth—one solitary pen stroke saying despair. An empty pot had *future plant* written beside it. In one of the windows there stood a faintly pencilled figure, arms outstretched with the dour phrase *hopeless dreams*.

Levett thought it was a very fine picture. All of it dense together in the middle of the page, a band of blank white paper on the top and bottom and along one side, as if the garden emerged from negative space, like a person from the fog. "What were you thinking when you were drawing it?"

"It reminded me how upset I was taking it down."

"Like reliving it?"

"I had to give away my garden of twelve years. It's spread out all over the suburbs. The English guy, the worker, knocked on my door, told me it had to go, told me I had two days to take it apart. That's what I did. I hauled it away in pieces. You watched me do it."

Levett remembered, regretted not offering to help.

Virgil swerved heavy-footed into the kitchen. He was deep in the cups. Racket ensued in the kitchen, accompanied by muttering. He came back with a fresh drink.

"You draw well, Verge."

"Really?"

"You should make more pictures."

Virgil pressed a thumbnail into his bottom lip. He took a drag off his smoke. He took the drawing away and slid it into the recess in the closet where it had formerly been. He shouted at the wall, "I don't need this bitch telling me to be quiet on the weekend in my home. *My* home. I've been here twenty years."

"Is she here?"

"I heard her leave," Virgil whispered, holding an outstretched finger over his lips, leering at the wall.

"She shouldn't have written that slanderous public email, and she shouldn't've called the cops on you either. I have to say though..." Levett paused. "At times you're an animal. Man, I used to get so pissed off at you and Shane carrying on all night."

Virgil laughed. "Oh yeah..." Then he paused. Access-memory look. Eyeballs casting off backwards into the past. "Yes, Shane got hysterical a few times, near the end."

"I know. I bloody well heard it. He'd go off."

"That reminds me."

"Sorry, I shouldn't bring up Shane."

"No, I totally don't care. It's fine." Virgil waved it off with his smoking hand. It was no infraction to bring up his dead friend. "Just reminds me. A few nights ago Magnus and I were watching a movie. I got bored, or I just got sick of it and shut it off. Well, Magnus lost it. He was saying 'Why do you have to cut something off like that, cut it short?' And then he was like, 'Cut things short, Virgil, that's you, cutting everything short,' and then he slapped me in the face, said, 'You know, Virgil, *I blame you for Shane's death*.'"

It surprised Levett. Virgil and Magnus were such close friends.

"He said this to me."

"He slapped you?"

"Yes."

"Then you did what?"

"I very calmly asked him to leave my apartment."

"Seriously?"

"Yes, I said, 'Please leave my apartment, Magnus.'"

"And he peaced?"

"He left."

"Why is he blaming you for Shane's death?"

"Because he's being a fucking idiot," Virgil snapped. "If it's anybody's fault, it's Tara and Adrienne's fault."

"How did he justify accusing you? Why are you accusing Tara and Adrienne?" Levett heard himself sounding like a gossip columnist. He liked gossip, the saltier the better.

"He thinks that when Tara and Adrienne called me at work and were like, 'Shane's threatening to kill himself,' and I was like, 'Call 911,' and they didn't, they waited like an hour to call 911, and because they waited, Shane died. That was Magnus's point, that *I* should've called 911. That if I had called then we could've saved him. We could've interrupted him. I was like, 'Magnus, you're a fucking moron if that's what you think.' That's when he slapped me.

"Then I said, 'Shane took five Xanax, twelve Dexedrine, three Adderall and some other shit that was laying around, and drank a bottle of Hennessy while gassing himself to death, and threatening to blow the building sky high if anyone tried to stop him. Okay Magnus, dummy, I mean, I love ya man, but you're so fucking *wrong*,' and then I told him he needed to leave."

Levett remembered the day well and remembered Shane well. Shane always lifted his head and said hello when they met in the corridor. He would smile brokenly. Eyes loving and sad. The day Shane committed suicide, Levett remembered seeing him in the liquor store. He was chatting with someone at the cash register with a forty-pounder of Hennessy on the counter. Levett had noted on his way by that Shane looked especially glad. Really warm. But there was despair too. Now that he thought about it, that's what it was, it was dread and despair and relief that it would be over finally.

Returning home from a second run to the liquor store that day, Levett had encountered a fire engine and an ambulance with its lights on in front of the building. The entrance was taped off in yellow. John was out there with a couple other residents, very downcast, and told Levett Shane had killed himself. Levett stood there with John describing the paramedics wheeling out the body bag on a gurney, John saying, "It's crazy, I just said hi to him in the foyer." And all this followed by other restrained half sentences and long pauses, trite in the face of death.

"Shane was in a bad way," Virgil stated.

"I got that off him."

"Would you like another drink?"

"I would."

Virgil came back with an IPA. It was bitter and cold.

"Unlike Magnus, I know why Shane killed himself," Virgil said.

"You know?"

"I know. I know what was going on between him and Tara, and Adrienne's just a poisonous extension of Tara, so there ya go. They blackmailed Shane."

"Tara. That's the disabled girl he was always—"

"He was in love with."

"I always used to see him helping her up the stairs to the building because there's no wheelchair access."

"Yeah, that's Tara. Bitch. They blackmailed him. I'm certain if Shane hadn't done what he did, and Tara didn't deal with it the way she did, Shane would still be alive." He walked back to the kitchen.

Virgil popped out ice cubes and poured vodka on them. Levett heard the cubes stress and pop in a silent second of the broadcast. When Virgil set the cup down Levett heard the soda sizzle. Then a free jazz tune came on that Levett dug. A velvety female voice said it was "The Pharaoh."

"The week before Shane offed himself I took him to my parents'. The mission was: we'd get away for the weekend to Nelson, paint my parents' kitchen and relax, have some drinks, chill out on the deck."

"Was he weirded out at your folks' place?"

"Not really, a bit squirrelly, not bad, pretty normal for Shane. We painted the kitchen, did a great job, parents were happy, I mean, they couldn't do it. It was great, it was excellent. Had a great time. It was only on the way back that I noticed a change."

"On the bus?"

"On the plane."

"What'd he say?"

"He wasn't saying anything. That was the problem. He was just kind of gloomy, he avoided eye contact, he was very troubled. It was obvious. I was like, 'Shane, what is wrong with you?' And then he told me.

"He confided in me. He told me that one night he had taken advantage of Tara. They had been drinking and doing whatever else, pills and shit, and she passed out. On the plane he said, 'I kinda took her clothes off and positioned her certain ways and took pictures of her. Then another time I was the one passed out, and her and Adrienne found the photos on my computer. They're trying to blackmail me now, for money, or they're going to the police. I'm fucked Virgil, I'm so fucked, I can't pay. I'll go to jail,' he says to me, on the goddamn airplane."

"How much did they want?"

"Like ten thousand dollars or some shit. Money Shane didn't have. He owed me so much money. I didn't care if I ever got it back, knew I wasn't getting it back. 'I'm fucked,' he whimpered to me on the plane, whispering, you know, whispering and whimpering. He was very messed up. Very, very stressed out. Having a nervous breakdown, Dylan."

"He was really tripping eh?"

"Big time."

"I don't blame him—for tripping."

"It wasn't a matter of life or death."

"What did you tell him?"

"I said they weren't going to do that. They weren't going to rat him out. 'I fucking deserve it,' he said to me. 'I can't believe I did that,' he said, on the bloody airplane." Virgil replayed the conversation behind his eyes.

"I don't know what to say Virgil."

"You don't have to say anything. He was such a sweet man. He wasn't thinking straight that night. It was a mistake." Virgil exhaled another plume of smoke. The candles flickered. Soft light wavered over the large Persian rug.

"You guys were close."

"I miss him, Dylan."

"Yeah."

"He was my best friend."

A puddle had expanded around the bag of melting ice.

Levett stumbled down the back stairwell of the Bellevue, knocking into the walls, a cold can in his hand left over from the bag. He was drunk and uninhibited. At the bottom of the stairs he pulled down his shorts and flashed the video camera. Then he stumbled outside.

▽ ▽ ▽

Caden and Terry Lam sat in front of their desktop computers blasting hell out of their respective avatars. It was dark in the office. Each brother hunched forward in their own corona. The relaxation fountain glowed pink and blue. The wall held a lit shelving unit filled with complete sets of M.U.S.C.L.E. Kinkeshi, Monster in My Pocket, Gorelords, BigManToys, Akira Gashapon and various other Keshi.

It had started to rain and from the Lams' panoramic viewpoint the city lights trembled ever so slightly.

"This is going to hurt," Terry said and Caden's man was knocked senseless, his assets dislodged from the figure as a scattering of icons representing strength, money, tools, devices, weaponry, health, food, armour.

The game had a dystopian *Spy vs. Spy* concept. It was called *WIRETAP*. You walked around getting informational tips from people, acquiring tools designed for sabotage. You went shopping, collected outfits in order to disguise yourself so you could infiltrate your opponent's friend groups, associated businesses, hangouts and the like. You could have open altercations with your opponent that amounted to great discharges of human malice and technological power: micron-thin whips, air displacers, different kinds of sprays (nausea inducers, cough inducers, anaesthetics which numb the face and limbs), super-gauntlets that require the player to have expensive surgery so the annihilating gloves will interface with the avatar's nervous system. You can choose one side or another: the side of DEK, standing for Direct Electronic Knowledge, a bodyware company so ubiquitous it controls the entire global population's access to information, and over its thirty years has rendered state power a mere formality; or the side of a small cohort of military generals and intelligence officers plotting to dismantle and destroy DEK, whom they term "Slave Master." The clandestine cell, known as the Sad Horse, is constantly dispatching operators into the field to do missions as delicate as they are elaborate. You had to create false relationships with people, brawl, go to cyber cafes and check deep-web image boards, follow enigmatic clues through a virtual, fully realized city called Rasa.

Caden played for DEK as a hacker double agent with a hopeless crush on an enemy agent; Terry for the Sad Horse as a fearless mercenary with PTSD.

"You made me lose my trench coat, cowboy boots and most of my pairs of sunglasses, plus I had five sandwiches on me and you snagged those."

"I'll make you lose a lot more than that." Terry's avatar tossed a bottle of hydrochloric acid that chewed off part of Caden's avatar's face. The meat and circuitry showed. Almost every character in the game was part machine.

Suddenly their screens automatically flipped to the Bellevue feed.

"I thought I disabled the motion sensors before we started playing," said Caden.

"That sounds like an excuse for why you're losing."

"Check out the back staircase," said Caden.

Terry selected it. A drunk man descended the staircase. They recognized the tenant when he looked up at the camera. Terry struck the hot key to record. The red circle began to pulse in the corner screen as Levett pulled down his shorts and flashed the camera, clumsily put his goods back in his shorts and stumbled out of the frame. Caden rewound the footage, played to the point where Levett is looking up and his pants are down, paused, took a screenshot and emailed it to Vaughn.

▽ ▽ ▽

As the sun met its purple mountain edge Levett rose. The smoke had cleared some. He had an apocalyptic hangover and only a few scattered memories of the previous night. It was a little after six in the morning. He cleared the counter then spread newsprint over it in layers. He uncapped the bucket and a rich vapour of putrefaction wafted up out of it. Made him flinch. In a pair of underwear torn at the elastic he began to slice the beefsteak, schnitzel, chicken breast and albacore into strips on a small plastic cutting board which had stood clean in the drying rack and was now lathered in gore. After he had a fair pile, he bunched it up in a sheet of newsprint and laid it on the dirty dishes piled in the sink. He sliced patiently, nervously, and soon there were five sizeable packets of raw meat.

Once he had to puke. The vomit was surprisingly red.

The white counter tiles were marbled pink. Bloody water had collected in the bottom of the bucket. He dumped it in the toilet and flushed it down, had another puke, put his mouth under the tap and rinsed his mouth out, went back to the kitchen and set the packets of minced meat in the bucket.

He lay in the tub in semi-darkness and watched the apartment gradually lighten from coral pink to white gold, heard moulting seagulls in their rooftop nest, heard roofers on the building, one calling out orders to another in Mandarin, and knew it was time.

The bag of birdseed was in the cupboard. He put that in the bucket, then put the lid back on.

A rented dumpster stood in the alley next to the back exit. The cold green form startled him. He set the bucket next to it, peeked up and down Tenth. Tom Ford's crew stood by the entrance to the basement.

No sign of Ford. Levett leaned against the retaining wall across from the church out of the southeast camera's field of vision. There was a camera on the southwest corner but it was pointing at the dumpster skid. He monitored the groggy workers with cigarettes sticking out of their faces until they extinguished them on the pavement underneath their steel toecaps and went back inside the building.

He stashed the bucket behind one of the hydrangeas and went around the block west, north, east, south to the empty store in the bottom corner of the Bellevue. He was out of breath. He reached up to the low mounted camera facing west and pulled it back on its adjustable base so it faced south. It made a sharp ratcheting sound like something forced the wrong way. He jogged around the block again.

Levett scanned the vehicles parked on either side of Tenth Avenue on his way to the Federal Store and none of them was the one. Lauren served him, his favourite. She looked fresh and well rested and nodded coming over from the machine.

"An Americano please, to go."

"Twelve seventy-five," she said.

He laughed. Her eyes were light brown with dark-red flecks.

"I gotta owe you, like, nine, Lauren," he said, placing the stack of coins in her palm.

"That's okay, I got you."

If you only knew what I was up to right now, he thought, checking her tightly curving back.

He went and stood outside to keep an eye on the corner. She brought it outside to him. He went back in and put cream in it and brought it back out to a table. Some daffodils in a pot hanging from the eaves by three strands of wire. They were growing lemongrass in driftwood planters along the east side of the cafe. There were other herbs too: mint, dill and parsley. He thought he recognized fennel.

The Americano was rich and full-bodied. He tried not to drink it too quickly. He noted each vehicle turning. It didn't take long: there was the black Dakota coasting through the stop sign going left. Ford did a three-point turn and parallel parked on the north side of Tenth. Levett finished his coffee, watching the building manager go toward the apartment. He followed along at a distance, watched him enter the building at the side, into the basement.

Levett hopped up and sat on the retaining wall and reached for the bucket. He undid the top fold of a packet, held the packet in the palm of his hand and smacked it on the hood, quickly scattered the meat, looked at the side entrance. No sign of Ford or his crew. He undid another bundle, smacked it on the hood, scattered it quickly, smeared schnitzel on the windshield. The truck's tailgate was open and there was lumber sticking out. He spread the last of the meat there, avoiding a pedestrian as she came by on the passenger side. He glanced at the side entrance. Nobody. He tore the bag of birdseed and scattered it liberally over the canopy and cargo rack, inside the box and all over the hood. Then he stashed the bucket back in the hydrangeas. If anyone was looking, Levett didn't see it.

"Back for more?" Lauren said. He imagined the two of them together on a clean white duvet, the morning light shining in.

He squirted soap on his hands and passed them under hot water looking in the restroom mirror and knowing some people would consider him not quite right in the head.

He considered getting Lauren's contact information. But it would be a red flag for her if he insisted on email addresses instead of phone numbers. He paid, put cream in the coffee and went back outside.

Ford's Dakota looked like it had been assailed by some new type of leech. Five seagulls alighted. Some crows circled before claiming an area on the hood by the windshield, an area soon joined by two more raucous crows. Some pigeons pecked at tuna near the antenna. The birds began to defecate. Some stayed and some collected food and flew off to their nests. A round of robins fed on the seed and two flew off together with a morsel of chicken. Each bird repeatedly shat on the Dakota. One of the seagulls got too close to a crow. They engaged in an irate contest of flapping wing and snapping beak, shitting all the while.

Now Tom Ford approached. He was tending to his phone and did not see it at first. Not until he was right there. When he looked up and saw the pickup his head bounced back as if on a taut spring. He tried to swipe at a gull. The bird pinwheeled and divebombed Ford, knocking off his Canucks cap. He tried shouting at them. Nothing was going to interrupt this bonanza. He swiped at a crow. The bird hopped two steps over with indifference, cawed, two more alighted. All three flew away with the schnitzel. Ford paced in disbelief next to his spackled vehicle, picked up his hat, balled it up in his fist.

▽ ▽ ▽

He felt a slight pressure on the bench beside him. There was Dion smiling. He wore bug-eye women's shades, *Jaws*-print board shorts and a light-blue t-shirt with a fish skeleton graphic. His skin was baked and the long bleached mullet grown out even longer.

Levett reluctantly marked his page. "Thought you'd show yourself?"

"Just in time it looks like."

"Every time I settle down to read, you're right around the corner."

"Ready to strike."

"How ya doin' man?"

"Pfew, slept like twenty-eight hours."

"That's a long doze."

"Got off work, was super tired, didn't get a good sleep the day before, didn't wanna go to sleep, chowed, got a few tallboys, went to the shop, just smoked, got a bit tipsy, went home, crashed, woke up, thought it was dusk, like, yeah, but it was dusk the next day."

"That was yesterday?"

"Schedule chews up my time having to catch up on sleep."

"You got some days off?"

"I might work Sunday. You?"

"I don't think I'm goin' back to the Rose man."

"'Nuff 'a that."

"You know me."

"Par for the course."

"I'm just gonna chill a second and find somethin' else."

"Can't imagine it's that good."

"I have to apply for graduation. Then maybe I could do better."

"You have to apply?"

"Yeah, you finish your coursework and then apply for graduation, and a committee decides."

"Hmph, they're really bleedin' ya dry up there mate."

"It's a racket."

"But you got the degree."

"True."

"Took you long enough."

"Way too long. Man, I didn't give a fuck. There were some moments, but overall it was annoying."

"Oh, *I know*."

"You of all people. Sorry about all the pissin' 'n moanin'."

"Better be."

"You took on a lot."

"Yer tellin' *me*."

They laughed.

They sipped their coffees. A refrigerated delivery van pulled up. The driver left it running as he dollied in four crates of milk. It moaned and sputtered and shrouded them in diesel fumes.

"So," Dion said, raising his voice, sipping on his cup, "I'm gettin' back into graffiti, as I might've mentioned, can't exactly remember, can't fuckin' remember everything."

"I remember."

Dion pulled out his cracked phone and said, "My new piece."

"That's outta hand dawg."

The burner went across the wall of a rooftop shack. Dion did it in brown, mint green and pink, with touches of Dijon yellow.

"It was hard man, the caps kept clogging up on me, didn't have any spares. Hard on the fingers and hands."

Dylan held the cracked phone and studied the piece.

"Thing was, it was on my shift that I did it."

"What?"

"Yeah dawg. No way was anyone coming out there, way out in the burbs, out passed 'em even."

"That's ballsy man." Levett handed back the phone, thinking it was pretty crazy that he painted it while on guard duty.

"Thing was, when I was throwin' up the outline, gettin' into the background fill, I thought I just had to do it naked."

"Yeah right."

"Yep, it was, uh, pretty fucked, like," Dion scrolled to some selfies of him naked with an aerosol can, crouched down to get a low spot, dick hidden behind his left thigh, "like, I knew, I was like, 'kay man, if they come and catch you doin' this, it's gonna be super fucked."

"Dude."

Dion looked at Levett through his bug-eye shades like some anthropoid moth.

"Your brother got you that job. He's one of the captains."

"I know man, and it's not like we're on good terms. I've been late a lot. A couple captains won't work with me anymore."

"Almost looks like self-sabotage."

"I knew no one was comin'."

"It's probably the baddest thing I've ever seen any of my friends do. I couldn't even imagine doing that, let alone the execution."

Dion laughed. "That's what it's all about mate."

"What's that?"

"Execution."

"So that's what you've been up to."

"Yup. Busy gettin' up."

"You wanna hit the shop tonight? Make a song, get faded?"

"Yeah man, I'm down. Anytime after, like, four, four thirty."

"Right on."

He was going to mention the birds but decided to keep it for himself.

▽ ▽ ▽

A third camera he had not noticed was mounted high on the south wall aimed down the street at the Federal Store. He saw it when he saw the Two Small Men with Big Hearts moving van parked along the south wall. It was three beanpole Pakistani guys. They moved with a spare fluidity. They made chains at the mouth of the van. Each brought an item, then set up in sequence: one on the ground, one up on the back bumper, one at the back of the van who organized the cargo.

On his way to the laundromat to unload a dryer Levett noticed Hakim's hands-off supervision of the movers. There with his hired hands instead of being the hired hand.

"Dylan, Dylan, how are you?" Hakim lightly clasped his hand and drew it away.

"Not worth a shit."

Hakim recoiled, wincing vicariously.

"Yer movin'?"

"Yes."

"Where to?"

"A place on the south side."

"You like it?"

"It's good. It's a fine place."

Levett had heard it was a damp basement suite that cost eight fifty a month.

"All the best Hakim." He started to walk away.

"Dylan."

He faced him again. "Yeah?"

"I have to tell you."

"What's up?"

"You were the most conscientious neighbour. Thank you for being so respectful. You've been so quiet."

That'd be on account of the power, he thought. He would have been blasting drone metal otherwise.

"Thanks for saying that."

"Be well Dylan."

Levett went back to the laundromat. Hakim moseyed over to the cube van, braced the small of his back and watched the movers with his stuff.

I

EXIT

Over a hundred days of elevator failure. I've had to sleep in the lobby multiple times, harassed by drunks coming in and out of Legendary's—you've got whores and pimps, dealers, cracked-out thugs. For weeks on end not a single security guard at the desk. Saturday morning, out of eggs. It's a beautiful day out there. Birds are chirping, people are laughing, nothing's wrong—elevator's out of service. Until my auxiliary gets here I'm stuck. And I'm not her only client. I was there until five p.m. that day. I have to make sure I go out with people, friends or my auxiliary so I know I have help when I get back. What's it to them, the landlords. They live in the suburbs. Why would they care. When did they ever have to stay here. See that one. Rat the size of your cat. They've come up onto my bed. I've felt their tails slither on my neck. They've sniffed in my ear. Their mincing rodent language. I've thought about rolling my chair down the stairs. I figured it would just hurt me, not kill me. The best option is a B-Line at full speed trying to beat a yellow light. Or a SkyTrain at the last second. You might think it's harsh, but living this way is demeaning. You can get your eggs Saturday. I'll be here waiting on the stairhead.

LEVETT stomped down the hill with his laptop bag and a bag of beer. He saw her across the street. Neon pink flashing through the gaps in traffic. Blade Girl slowly ascending the grade in her skates, chopping at the cement, damp hair popping up off her neck with each stride, arms swaying, face mean and calm, slowly ascending the grade, *chop, chop, chop, chop.*

Dirty dusk. Tall cloud piled up in the western sky. It looked like a smeared carnation.

He waited for left-turning traffic and crossed. Passed the body shops and import auto mechanics and the quick lubes all gathered together in one zone. He let himself in with a key. Deep Blue. An art studio and event space named after a chess-playing supercomputer.

Voices. Music.

An event was scheduled that weekend. Upstairs people were decorating the central area. Potted ferns made peninsulas on the old timber floorboards, hung above from the ceiling laths, flanked the turntables. A soundman adjusted the faders on a large mixing board off to one side. Volunteer grips hung black velour curtains over the raw panels of drywall.

Levett slipped into the space. Dion had not arrived. The air conditioner laboured beneath the small window. It pushed coolish air weakly through the oblong space. An exhaust hose curved from the machine to a square of plywood with a circle bored out of it to accept the hose end, the plywood piece clamped in place by the sliding window. Rooftop pigeons cooed on the other side of the window.

He set his keys and change on the corner of his work table. A red strip of LEDs spanned the bottom of a long shelf. It gave the room a darkroom glow. He set the beer on a small brown sectional and poked around for the remote, found it on a two-by-four protruding from Dion's work table and changed the colour to pale amber. Four large screens on articulating arms tilted over Dion's table, a crooked black chart against the white wall. On one small table a Gordian knot of cables. Levett puzzled over how it could ever have gotten that way. What nimble-fingered negligent mind?

Tunes, he thought. Tunes first. He opened his laptop and plugged in the power supply and let the computer's dead battery charge briefly so it would turn on. He flicked the monitor switches. He plugged in his interface. His computer recognized the hardware. The interface made a hollow metallic click. He typed in *YouTube* on the browser. A vocal house track played in the main area. He buried it with D.A.F.'s *Verschwende deine Jugend.*

The tallcan Buds and Sapporos were still cold. He had a pre-rolled joint in the front pocket of his laptop bag. He lit the joint, inhaled deeply, exhaled a large cloud of dopesmoke toward the wall.

From his angle the rhombus of sky in the window was a citrusy rose. He appreciated the colour, drank deeply from the tallboy, pouring it down his neck in three cold gulps leaving only a quarter of it left, frowned when he looked down at three remaining, knew three more was not enough.

He opened another tab and emailed Dion—*Hey dawg, if you haven't gone to the vendors yet could you pick me up two or three more beer? I have cash*—clicked *send,* looked left. The AKAI MPC 1000 sat dormant off to one side. He reached behind along the stubby tube-like jacks and found the small spring-loaded button. The square display screen lit up yellow with black lettering. He sat down again. He leaned back into one slice of the brown sectional and smoked, looking at the opposite wall. He finished his beer. They cranked the bass outside. Levett turned the volume knob on his interface to match it, felt in his fingertips the fine notching of the dial inside the knob, each a tiny little trigger saying more amplitude.

And so it was. Levett sometimes heard ringing in his ears.

He leaned back in the sectional.

The sky through the window was a dusty bluish grey now.

He was kind of antsy.

He checked his email. Dion had replied: *No sweat amigo.*

"Fuck yes," he said to himself, then thought, Wonder if he's got any tabs left?

"Acid would be good," he thought out loud, mute beneath the warring stereos.

He cracked another beer, sat back looking at the opposite wall. Most of Dion's handmade stickers were gone now. Originally they featured the titles of songs and were stuck in one of three bays: A, B or C, in alphabetical order to indicate each song's quality. Mountainous sunny nirvana drawn over A, bridge crossing a rough river over B, chains, lava and a skull over C. They used the chart to organize which songs took priority when, the year before, they mixed their first album with Levett's friend Tyler at his studio Lakeside Sound in Edmonton. Levett still owed Tyler six hundred dollars for the sessions. Tyler invoiced Levett, but the sound engineer said it was "No panic" and Levett mellowed out about it, for a year and a half, spent his extra money on weed and beer. He used to like fashion, hardly bought clothes anymore.

He looked around the room cynically, knew it would probably amount to nothing.

He looked at the naive paintings Scotch-taped to the wall, made by children in the seventies. Dion had found and rescued folders of children's artwork when way back in the day he worked his recycling truck job. The kids had made two-tone optical patterns, a distorted map of Captain Cook's first voyage, and a *Mise en abyme* of a painter in a room painting himself painting in the room, very crude. Behind him was a large Thanksgiving tableau with the Pilgrims and Indigenous peoples feasting together at long trestle tables, a large apple tree in the foreground with an Afro of orange autumnal foliage and square red apples. Near the ceiling, a yellow fish-like shape in profile with a smile and a propeller on its head, also very crude but with limitless energy, ready to fly off the wall and out the window.

Steps approached the door and keys rattled in the doorknob.

Enter Dion. Music swelled from the main area.

Teamster hat. Hair wet from the shower. He looked at Levett and slid by to his work table. He sat down and nodded, smiled, teeth really white in their tanned face.

"Gotchoo a few Saps."

"Thanks bud," Levett handed him a ten.

"That's cool, I got no weed, so."

Levett retracted the ten.

Dion reached around the two PC towers on his table and powered them up. The back-end guts and cooling fans faced outward. A few lines of green code writ fast across the two screens. The red Hackintosh logo appeared on each. Dion popped open a large bottle of IPA. He looked thin, almost wizened.

"How you dawg?" Levett said.

"Pretty tired, slept so long, just made me feel more tired."

"Shoulda grabbed a coffee."

"I know, woulda pepped me right up."

"Smoke one."

"Yeah."

Levett lit a pre-rolled joint, took a hit and passed it over. "Whataya feel like listenin' to?"

"Nothin' too noisy."

"I been diggin' Tricky. Y'ever get inta Tricky?"

"I like him," Dion nodded languidly, hoisted his bottle and took a draught of the bitter microbrew.

Levett typed *Tricky* into the search bar. "Hell Is Round the Corner" came up first and he selected the video. "I wanna do a trip hop tune."

"Definitely, it suits us." Dion held out the half joint.

"We'd sound good in a trip hop vein."

Dion scrolled down his Facebook page. He shifted to a different screen. "Check this out," he said and gestured at a montage of a mountainous landscape Photoshopped across the broad side of a garage. "My friends Christie and Steve have this new Zen garden and they want a mural."

Levett wasn't sure Zen gardens called for murals. He didn't say anything.

Mezzanine was on deck but the video would not roll over. They tested the subs in the main area, buried everything in blocks of bass, in a pounding assault. "When do you start on that?"

"Soon as I get some time and they get back from Hawaii. They're buying the paint."

"Bristle brush or aerosol?"

"Both." Dion smiled.

Levett bumped knuckles with him, saw the paint on his hand from the nude on-duty burner. "I'm happy you're painting again man."

"I'm workin' on a few new masks too."

Levett adored his masks. They were assembled from a diversity of material: glazed clay to electronic detritus to modified visors, old Bluetooths, off-brand shades—myriad castaway junk. "Bring 'em down here when they're ready, I wanna see."

Dion polished off his first bottle. "Fuck man."

"What's up?"

"Something fucked up happened the other day." Dion's fingers extended stiffly like fins. "I hit someone."

Levett took the can back from his mouth. "Like, punched some dude in the head?"

"With my car."

"Oh no."

"Yeah."

"Badly?" Levett asked.

"The guy was okay. It was pissing, low viz fer sure, and I was, like, you know, in a rush, just being a fucking wanker on the road, didn't see this guy walk out, went to turn and smoked 'm. Knocked 'm down."

"Holy Christ."

"Yeah, so I put it in park and got right out and the guy was already up."

"Was he choked?"

"Not really, more just rattled. I mean, I was out there, like thinking I might be taking dude to ER, you know." Dion shook his head in disbelief at his own error. His eyes had gotten serious telling it.

Levett tried to figure out the right thing to say. "It's your chance to learn, just not the hard way. At least the dude was alright."

"I know," Dion whispered in complete agreement.

"Like what if he was seriously injured or killed. Having that on your conscience... Who needs that? Life is hard enough without something like that."

"'Zactly, coulda been a nightmare fer all parties."

"Did you offer him any dough?"

"I was broke."

"The pissing rain makes it hard to see when yer inside a vehicle. Especially at night, all the glare off the road and the wet windows, headlights and shit, everything's all warped as hell."

"*Sacré bleu.*"

"*Porco Dio.*"

"Plus my premiums, like, you kill a guy, insurance is goin' sky high," Dion joked in a bad Bronx accent.

They laughed.

"You got your troubles, I got mine," Levett said.

"What's that?"

"I might be out on my ass. Besides that, Blade Girl won't quit hassling me. She's relentless."

"Cuzza that coffee shop snafu?"

"Yeah man. She keeps rollin' by trying to publicly shame me."

"What's she sayin'?"

"She calls me out. She tells everyone around, especially women, that I'm a predator, and a woman beater, and shit like that. Everyone thinks she's crazy. It's still embarrassing."

"You *did* do that, though, so there's gonna be consequences."

"She can fuck off. Everyone's just gotta take her shit. Fuck that. I watched her pick on those baristas for a month. All the same fucking regulars in there too—no one said a goddamn thing. As if it was cool for her to go on berating them indefinitely. Like, oh, she's bat-shit crazy, let her do whatever she fuckin' wants as long as she wants. Fuck that."

"I know, I know," Dion said gently, "but if you did do that, and Blade Girl's out for blood, she ain't lettin' that go."

"I know man. You're right. But she was lookin' for it. She manipulated that situation."

"But you pinched her in the door."

"She cut me off as I was walking through the door."

Dion laughed. "Just sayin' man."

It bothered him that Dion didn't take his side. "You got any tabs left?"

"I might have one, I recall having one double somewhere."

"Would you do it?"

Dion opened one of the drawers in his steel work table and gently rooted around in there.

"Do you work tomorrow?"

"I haven't heard from dispatch yet. I'm not working in the morning, that's for sure. Might take an afternoon shift."

"So no go on the LSD?"

"I'm not sayin' that," Dion said, rummaging through the second drawer.

"If you feel like it, I'm down. I say we go for it, I mean, we got the supplies," Levett pointed to the beer and weed. "Why not make a night of it?"

"*Night to Remember*," Dion cited. He was referring to one of their guerilla video projects, made drunk, high and on the fly.

"Bloody right mate."

"I'll keep lookin'."

"You wanna hear anything?"

"I'm easy does it, Rico."

Levett typed *Hardrive* into the search bar and selected "Deep Inside." Dion uncapped another IPA, took a long swig of it and began to leaf through some papers and publications on his work table, going through each lyric sheet and doodle, flipping each page, sorting through the old publications. Levett searched up Mr. Flagio and clicked on "Take a Chance." After that he thought of Cybotron, played "Alleys of Your Mind." He did not know much about techno and italo but he knew the songs he liked and that Dion would like. He would have selected Death Grips but Dion did not regularly fuck with Death Grips.

"Here she is." Dion held up a stamp-sized baggie with the small elongated piece of paper inside. It was there between two issues of *Canadian Art*. Dion laid the tabs of acid on the table in plain sight with a kind of delicate veneration, like jewellers do their expensive pieces. It was the way he handled all contraband. Both acid squares had little Bart Simpson heads printed on them.

The two had met under black-market circumstances. Before the dispensaries put solo dealers out of business, Dion sold Levett bud, and over the course of ten years their relationship blossomed, going beyond but not excluding this commercial arrangement. The two of them became artistic collaborators, first through Dion's video projects and later as musical partners. All that seemed to have cooled off now. Sometimes Levett wondered if it might be the twilight of their friendship.

Dion's phone rang. "Hello… sure… ah… pretty good… just chillin'… okay… I'll be there."

"Dispatch."

"Yeah, I took an emergency cover shift tonight."

Levett wondered if he was visibly upset.

"Sorry dawg. I'm a shit bag. It's like five bills and a half. I need the dough."

Levett drank. "Hey man," he said.

"What's up?"

"I hope you weren't mad at me recently, like, I hope I didn't piss you off, like, whining about some bullshit or something, you know, complaining."

"Nah, not at all man."

"I was wondering why you didn't get back to me."

"Aah, sorry, most of the time I've been out on locations with no WiFi. I get home, eat, crash."

"I get it. Sorry dawg, for like, putting you on the stand. Plus, it's me without a phone."

"It's all good." Dion changed the subject. "We could still drop 'em."

"You sure?"

"Yeah, like, I can stay up all night at the location. No one's gonna be there."

"Can I come with?"

"I can't have guests. You gotta be licensed and a Teamster to be on that location."

"I get it. Insurance and whatnot."

Levett eyed the LSD on the table. "Is it the stuff Anne Marie sold us?"

"Yeah, remember, she sold us four, gave us another two, didn't wanna touch them to split up the hits. They were in baggies of three."

"Yeah I remember that. She came by, looked hot as fuck, makin' deals."

Dion nodded in agreement. He put his towers to sleep and gathered up his things. Slid his booze in his packsack and held out the bag with all Levett's beer. Levett pinched him a bud. "You'll need that."

"That's wicked man, thanks."

"We gotta do another song with Anne Marie."

"Definitely." Dion squinted. "Like, I never heard string layers like that, not with a juicy beat, choice bass line, weird rapper, smooth singer."

"Yeah," Levett agreed, "it's sorta like a chamber ensemble on a disco pop song, but like, you know, more ghetto."

"'Zactly." Dion squinted and nodded. He tipped the double out on the table. Levett handed him the scissors and Dion halved it and held them out to Levett. "Take yer pick."

Levett plucked the right one off Dion's long wizard finger and set it on his tongue. He tasted the blot. It tasted like any other chemical. Dion dropped his.

"Yer gonna work on that?"

"Yeah, it's way back in the sticks. Nobody's comin' out there."

"Just you and the gear."

"Yep." He shouldered his backpack, saluted, said, "Take it easy man," and gently closed the door.

Now what the fuck am I gonna do? he thought. Fuckin' flake Dion.

He cracked a beer and rolled one and smoked one to the dome and dumped half a tallcan down his neck. He powered down the machines and gathered up his beer and weed, with the foresight, the restraint, to leave himself two tins and some chronic for the comedown.

The night air was damp. Asphalt exuded the day's heat.

Behind a body shop the husk of a Beamer lay out on blocks beside a loading dock, no windows, no upholstery, no dash. People were using it as a trash can. He went on down the tagged alley: *G4N Crew, Upsy, blite, TETRIX, Lak, ibEX*. Levett thought *TETRIX* and *ibEX* could be the same writer judging by the capital *E* and *X*. At the end of it was his personal favourite, *Treky*, with a flying saucer sigil above the *e* and the *k*.

There was a party somewhere around. Its faint kick and snare rode the dark, nauseous synth bass line knitting the two together. Swish of traffic. Acid coming on strong. Everything started humming with a different vibration and you felt stoned on the greenest crack. He opened a beer and veered off down a back street he could never remember the name of behind some garages and the Fiat dealer and the storage spaces and metal shops and recently installed low-income modular housing on Terminal. Terminal: to terminate, the end. Classical Latin *terminālis*, marking a boundary, marking a conclusion, final. Death and doorways, he thought, noticing the layer of reality the acid put on, it was really something extra. He jaywalked to the other side.

A crust punk paced the meridian with a Gatorade bottle filled with tap water and a squeegee—it was just a cross with the top broken off. Beer-flat placard on gleaned string slung around his neck. It said *LUV 2 GET DRUNK + CHOW BIG MACS*. Vertically up one side he had written *please donate* in a practised calligraphic hand with a chisel-tipped marker. He wore combat boots and rancid cargos, a vest that was all patch or modification: spiked shoulder pads and cuffs, anarcho-truisms, hard-core bands with fan bases in the single digits. Levett met his eyes and it was clear that any caution or fear had long burned out of them and what remained was constant movement, ritual self-abuse and the attendant pain—total freedom at the negligible expense of his donors.

The acid was coming on fast. He marvelled at his chaotic dome. The sutures of his skull tingled. There were so many thoughts all at once and in such quick succession, whole matrices, whole architectures, rushing. They seemed one frozen blur until he could relax, regroup and take stock of his surroundings across the street, the train powering up and accelerating above his head, the dank grounds of the park wafting in his nostrils, and everything was something else: the large orange letters lit up along the north and south wings of the train station, glowing hot like stove elements, its entrance pointing west like a promise, the pediment like an arrow dreaming.

Traversing the park he walked into a dew-soaked spiderweb, structure flashing in a fugitive light beam just as he stepped into it. A radial field of shining white beads. Small lines of cool touched his arms and face. He fogged up his spectacles and wiped them off with his t-shirt and replaced them, looked about. Nylon pupae scattered beneath the trees writhing. Someone from somewhere he could not see asked him if he wanted any down. Levett's head jerked around this way and that way but he could not locate the source of the offer.

The power of a drug-charged world. Levett was overwhelmed. He wanted to talk to everyone, he wanted to say everything. All his words were duds, though, ephemera buffeting the mind. He drank up his beer and tossed the empty aside, cracked another, drank again and looked back where he had tossed the can. It was gone. A silhouette lurched away toward a hedge where a crude duffle had been set out and arranged and was being tallied by the owner.

The Ivanhoe disgorged a group of Indigenous kids in Abercrombie and American Eagle who couldn't have been of age. They all lit up smokes and smoked them as if their lives depended on it. The women eyed Levett. The men turned to him squarely in if-you-dare poses and Levett looked at them out the corner of his eye just where the frame of his spectacles crossed and it looked to the group like the elastic figure was passing indifferently. Levett regarded them: their youth, arrogance and provincial style. He didn't care if they were Indigenous: you were stylish or you weren't. A doorman propped the door open with a stone then went back inside. Levett heard the bar band butchering CCR—reverse the season, "Have You Ever Seen the Rain?" would've been a gross affront.

"I wish that white boy woulda stepped," he heard one of them say as he continued down the side street. Upon the viaduct embankment among the trees there were tents and camps set up. He turned left along the viaduct approach and crossed Main.

A photoshoot was in effect at the skate park.

Pearly bounce flags on C-stands were set up around the picture space.

Someone in Sailor Moon cosplay.

Foot lights around her striking poses on top of the bank in front of the transverse column.

Out of nowhere a female skateboarder bathed in camera flash backside mute alley-ooped the hip.

Trick like a hermetic poem. Monad of perfect clarity and simplicity right down to the decisive snap of the board's tail and the glide of the wheels as she rode away nonchalantly. Nothing could be added to it and nothing taken away. The skate park erupted in unanimous applause. Levett wondered if he was hallucinating, then began to holler and clap himself.

He stayed on the north side of the train along Andy Livingstone Park. A couple shared a crack pipe on the embankment. The woman jiggled the Bic flame under the charred cylinder end.

She inhaled and passed it, said, "It's a matter of human respect man. She takes her dude in, he's stayin' with her and meanwhile she's bringin' in dates and workin' in front of 'im."

"He should kick her out," the man said, holding a dead lighter and an empty pipe in his bony hands.

"It's her place man. She lives in the East End Hotel, right up the street, that SRO above Legendary's. But, you know what I mean, bangin' whoever in front of her boyfriend…" He could hear that her sinuses were fried and there were few teeth left in her mouth. Her cheeks were sunken. Her hair was very thin on top. You could see her scalp.

Levett turned right on Carrall. He cracked the last beer. He kept six for police cruisers. Drank liberally. An occulted fire shone out from the overpass deck. Muffled monologue and shadow play upon the embankment shrubbery as Levett walked along. He thought about words he liked: "surfeit," "renal," "odalisque," "strident," "diapason," "crenel."

Crossing the street, he looked down at a manhole cover with the letters COV.

It had been mellow but once he crossed Pender everything changed. People had been doing drugs here for over a century. The block roiled with addicts. There were ebbers and flailers, dealers galore. An Asian dude bumped electro. He was slanging with a Dre Beats speaker attached to his belt loop with a carabiner.

"Want some speed?" a guy in a pleather coat said. He was tall, with a pitted nose and a faint cleft lip.

"I ain't into that," Levett said.

"You wanna fuckin' merit badge?"

Somebody tried to pedal by on a girl's bike with flat tires.

"You want some speed bud, looks like you could use some."

"Can I borrow your phone?"

"Like fuck," the speed dealer said. "Do I look like a phone booth?" He clearly had a mental rolodex of quips, comebacks and trifling clichés that would never run out as long as he was working a trap.

"Five minutes."

"You can't afford five minutes of my time. Not on my data plan."

"I'll give you this bike."

"I don't want that fuckin' banana-seat piece of shit. I gotta Porsche sittin' right around the corner. You can't see it. Soon as I'm through here I'm gonna walk over, get in and drive away. Now fuck off." He said "porch" instead of "Porsche." Two club girls walked by. "Speed. C'mon ladies, yer gonna dance all night."

Levett went on. To his right an orange neon light said Legendary's. He'd never been.

It was nothing much. A dark amorphous zone with beer-company glow signs hung askew on the walls. Shaped out vaguely by a strip of LEDs framing a few bottles of spirits on the high plank shelf: Red Tassel, Lamb's, Alberta Premium, Gilbey's, Sauza. Empty sun-faded cans of Canadian, Lucky Lager and Bud Light stood beside the hard liquor. The counter was linoleum, corners clad with stair edging. Its construction seemed to anticipate heavy foot traffic. Even the cash register looked like it had been kicked around.

"Wait a sec," a joyless voice said. He came out from a backroom and closed the door behind him, wiggling the knob to ensure it was locked.

The bartender made his way over slow and leaned into the counter wearily. He was tall and corpulent and he regarded Levett with an air of implicit disdain one can never quite put into words. A whiskered dewlap connected his chin to his throat. It inflated and contracted with the erratic tempo of his breathing. He braced himself against the counter. Blue dromedary tattoo on the left forearm.

"Hey man, how's it going?"

"If it was any better I'd be twins." His eyes were a belligerent green colour. They reminded Levett of expired bologna. Everything some other thing. Judging by the sound of his voice, a tracheotomy waited in the tubes of his future.

Levett knew when to drop the small chat. "I'll get a Canadian."

"It's two for five."

He set a five on the lino. "Can I drink one then come back up and get the other?"

"No, you gotta take 'em both at once and let one get warm." He levered both tabs up with a bottle opener and shoved them ahead.

Levett slammed one and set the hollow can down. He collected his full beer and sat down at a semicircular booth against the back wall, could feel the two-by-four framework of the banquette through the seat foam and hard vinyl covering. Half the black laminate on the tabletop was ripped off. Spirals of old glue on the surface. There was a skinny passage lighted with an EXIT sign. The bartender came over. In all seriousness he lifted the sweating can up and set it back down on a wilted cardboard coaster, turned, stared with arms akimbo at the lumpen form slouched below a tinted window in the wall.

"Come on Wendy, get a move on." The senior citizen sat dozing on her walker.

"I gotta a friend comin' and pickin' me up."

"You've been here five hours. Ain't anybody comin.'"

Wendy hung her head, then spoke clearly and automatically: "Well call me a cab."

The tinted window above her was a one-way mirror. People in the SRO corridor checked themselves out in it. All manner of human wreckage. A trans hooker redrew eyebrows in thin arcs on her forehead and touched up her mascara, cussed out somebody's reflection passing behind and studied her face again, practising faces: demure, equable, detached, each one a new parody of seduction.

Levett realized two things at once: that he was extremely stoned now, and that there was no music playing in the bar. He had thought he was stoned before but now it had really come on. Nothing could get him down.

"You got any tunes?" Levett called. Calling out tunes. It seemed like one ear and a nostril generated his voice. And why was he calling out tunes in a strange dive bar on the main floor of a Downtown Eastside SRO?

"If you insist," the barman sneered, plugged his phone into a small jack. He turned the generic blues rock way up so the high frequencies irked.

A guy came in. The barman greeted the customer with his mouldy stare.

"Gimme a double of that rye on the rocks."

"On the rocks," the barman scoffed. He unthreaded the cap on the forty of Alberta Premium and poured a disposable cup half full, bent over an orange camping cooler and with his bare hands plunked a few cubes of bag ice in the cup and set it on the lino. His customer was thinking something but he wasn't saying it, took a crinkled five from his joggers and dropped it on the counter.

"It's six for a double." He turned the information into an injunction.

The guy let a toonie roll on the counter and the barman swatted it down.

He sat at the table beside Wendy, whose head continued to sag. Every so often she would pucker up her face and shake her head remembering a psychic injury that had one time beset her.

The bartender yanked the plug out of his phone and answered it.

"Yeah," he asked. "You need NoteTotes like fuck... No... I'm yer dad I can fuckin' swear when I'm mad... You'll get foolscap like the rest of your classmates and some HB pencils and any extras you can pay for yourself... However you get money... How you get it I shudder to think... No... Not likely... Put your mother on... I took this job to supplement the family income... If I was home, you'd be hiding in your room... I call bullshit spending quality time with your pops, like hell, don't feed me that... Put your mother on Jemma... Unlikely that you'll be taken to the mall school shopping seeing as how it's summer school and it's a punishment... Yeah... Yeah... Well I'm not your mother... You did dick last semester and the semester before that and now you wanna be rewarded for it, not how it works honey, sorry... Jemma... Jemma..." He held the phone out from his face. "Fucking little cuss," he said, with regret, for her or the phrase it was not clear, and then he pocketed the phone and the bar was quiet again save for the melee outside.

A bullet-headed man with a hack crewcut stood facing a cop car, swaying drunkenly. The officer got out and walked up to the man. When he stepped away the drunk was manacled. Levett admired the move, it was kind of like legerdemain. The cop opened the back door allowing for the man to enter the cruiser voluntarily and the bullet-headed man obliged.

Levett studied the shine of neon on the windowpane, the succulent colour, pinkish-orange letters written backwards. That was enough. What else did you need? Just colour and nothing else. He wasn't thinking anymore. It was a real voice.

Without mentally articulating in language, he thought that the cold can on his hand seemed miraculous; it was marvellous he was gripping the can, wondrous he owned a hand.

The guy with the double rye made contemptuous body gestures at the bartender behind his back. Then he picked out the ice and dashed it on the painted concrete floor, put the brittle plastic cup to his creased lips.

Two females walked in. One chunky and the other slim. The bartender served them tequila shots and beers. They both wore skinny jeans with manufactured holes and distress. Jordans that looked fresh in the meagre light. The chunky one had on a tight acid-washed jean jacket, the slim one a Reaper hoodie. They made a point of Levett noticing they were checking him out, the slim one going so far as to lock eyes and cock her head up at him in a thuggish nod and turn back to her girlfriend. He nodded downward once in return.

He saw the dim wash of light from the one-way mirror slip off Wendy's head. A clot of black hoodies and the flat brims of New Era caps filled the window: face tats, neck tats, Teutonic script spelling Indigenous surnames never meant to be spelled with Roman letters. All of them went as one toward the SRO entrance and hairpinned into Legendary's. All four sussing Levett as they approached the counter. They spoke at the two women but got snubbed. The temperature rose suddenly in the bar.

"Can we sit here?" the ladies said to the indignant man.

"I ain't even here." He rose with his arms held palms outward and he went out the door.

"What's your name?" the slim woman said. She was leaning over toward him.

"Dylan."

"Justine," she said and locked hands with him in a solid biker shake as a sour smell flushed their space and they looked up. One of the young men stood in front of their locked hands. They let go of each other and let him pass. He sat down opposite Levett.

"Let me in," a scraped voice said, looming over Levett.

He was going to tell him to scooch in beside his friend but he was huge. Instead Levett got up and let the man in.

"Sit down," another said.

"After you," said Levett.

"Sit down."

"Go head."

"I will. It's our fuckin' booth." It was a spiteful tone. He said "our" like "are."

Levett looked down at the old swirls of glue on the tabletop. "I didn't see your name on it," he said with airs of holding court, but he wasn't the king. Then he sat back down where he was. "Dylan," he said. The bossy one looked at his outstretched hand dismissively.

The third guy was part black. His eyes were large and sad and mean. It looked like he just got up from a bad nap. Like he'd rather punch you in the face than look at you.

Another guy came up, a big unit, larger in scale than the rest but of the same mould, with four Luckys tucked under one arm and two clawed in that hand, four vodka shots on a small circular tray that he set down with the opposite hand. The boys reached out and each claimed one and knocked it back and claimed a beer. The one buying coveted three. He set them in a trine on the empty tray in front of him.

Levett stood up, made way for him to sit down.

"Sit down," he ordered. His hair was long. He had an undercut. There was some obscured design tattooed on the side of his head. When he flicked his hair and brushed it back with his fingers, Levett could make out the skulls and rib cages, some charnel house scene.

"Go 'head."

"You wanna dance bro?"

"Not really."

"Then why're you standin' next to me like you wanna dance." Levett knew dancing was not dancing. The group foreman walked around Justine's table glaring at Levett then peered down at the two women and told them, "I'm takin' this chair." He said it nice. Then he hoisted the chair over their table like a pretend chair and set it at the booth, sat down on it. The frontal pose of ancient statuary. Obviously he was their leader. They all regarded him with a certain deference. He crushed one beer, then sipped delicately at a second.

Not much room in the banquette. He felt the sharp edges of the bench framework. The one next to him sat with his elbows jacked up on the backrest so his forearm rested level with Levett's jaw. The arm had shaky form-line ink all up it past the elbow. Blurred glyphs that said something once across his scabbed swollen knuckles.

The half-black one stared, spinning an Olfa box cutter on the table. It was painted the colour of skin. He felt a cool drag on his cheek and recoiled. They laughed. "It's a key chain," the one at the head of the table said. They laughed again. It sounded cavernous.

He went along with it. He cupped his lukewarm beer, debated getting another two. He needed to piss.

All of them except the big guy wore fitted ballcaps with laser-straight brims and the hologram stickers left on.

"Why ain't this guy callin'?" the first one said. He sank back pocketing the phone in his hoodie, touchscreen glowing through the fabric. He flashed a rotten smile for Levett, steady swivelling eyeballs.

"Ho-lay, Harlan," the one with his forearm in Levett's face said. "You'll be a dead ghost still fiendin'."

"We texted 'im forty-five minutes ago," Harlan said. "I wanna sniff some coke."

"Ten minutes ago chug," the big one said. His diction was slow and sober. What jocular atmosphere there was at the table drifted away.

Harlan fondled the phone in his hoodie pocket. Said gravely, "Quit callin' me chug, Derrick."

"Or what?"

"I'll use what I got left of this bear spray on you."

Derrick leaned across the table toward Harlan without taking his ass off the seat. "Do it—reach for it even. See what goes down bitch. I'll powder your skull. I don't need eyes."

"He's the pussy ass bitch," Harlan said, nodding toward Levett, trying to deflect the power display toward an outsider of no consequence.

The one he'd overheard them call Gibby seemed to harbour a deep-seated enmity for Levett, briefly glancing at his accomplices and returning to meet his eyes in quiet appraisal, likely the satirical narrative of a well-born white boy's upbringing followed by his jacking and proper beatdown.

"Gibby's got it out for you," the one beside Levett said. His breath smelled like butane.

Gibby had the Olfa out again. Extended, retracted the painted blade.

"He wants to filet you." He pronounced the "t."

Derrick continued to goad Harlan with spray-can pantomimes.

"Sheldon," Derrick said.

He looked up from Levett to Derrick, who tucked his hair behind each ear, eyebrows latticed with scars. There was an open viciousness there. The pupil and iris bled together black. Levett saw himself reflected in them; they were looking at Sheldon, Levett two diminutive selves swept away by the hooding of Derrick's eyes looking down to the drinks before him, two crushed tins and one nearing the same fate.

Derrick looked up at Sheldon. "Buy us a round."

Sheldon started pushing Levett off the seat. He stood up and let him out and sat back down, swallowed the final warm mouthful of his drink. He had to piss.

"So what are you doing here?" Derrick accused.

"Chilling, having a beer."

"On whose say-so?"

"Barman doesn't seem to mind."

They looked over at the bartender serving Sheldon. He plucked out the jack from his cellphone. A digital squelch muted the room while he replaced his earbuds saying, "If I get home and there's any trace of that little fucker I'm going to geld him... What... *Geld*... Go to summer school, maybe you'll learn a new word... Yeah... Bullshit... You've been twice in thirty days, liar... Jemma... Fuckin' be quiet... Shut up... Shut up... Shut up Jemma, I'm serious. If I come home and he's there I'm gonna cut his nut sack off with a rusty tuna can..."

"That," Derrick said it in the bartender's direction. "Try me. And these Indians. Fuckin' rez thugs, Little Prince." He hooked his chin in a gesture round the banquette. "Want some down at least? Soften the blows."

"Never got in the habit."

"No time like the present," Harlan chirped, flashing his decayed smile.

"Shut up chug." Derrick didn't take his eyes off Levett. "Why are you here white man? Thieving entitled white man."

"Just grabbin' a drink."

"Move over Jew," Sheldon said with an armful of sweating cans.

Levett rose, stood aside. He did not correct him about "Jew," even if Levett did look Jewish.

Down the narrow hall a door ajar. The red room had a toilet in one corner and a janitor sink in the other. No mirror. He pissed long. Flushed. The toilet sang in his head. About eight different sounds in the one sound. Hot face, he thought. Hot face, felt his face. It was cool, clammy. When he rinsed his hands he saw a disused door next to the big plastic janitor sink.

He headed straight for the front exit. Wendy was being escorted out by an infirm octogenarian using a four-point aluminum cane. The two stood on the threshold waiting for a skirmish to subside outdoors.

Two more, he thought. Justine eyed him up.

"How's it goin'?" Levett asked the bartender.

The bartender plugged his phone back in and set it carefully on the counter.

"Up and down like a whore's panties on payday."

Levett guffawed. The bartender fake-smiled.

"Drink special still on?"

"Last time I checked."

"Hit me."

"You wouldn't want that." The bartender said with a straight face. Not a trace of mirth.

Levett dug out the change in his pocket and placed a poker stack of coins on the counter. The bartender dragged it off the edge in his palm and pocketed the difference. The cans perspired. With the yellow fingernail of each middle finger he snapped them open in unison. They foamed rabidly. Levett slurped them off. He turned back to the banquette, saw Justine. She smiled at him.

To the banquette. They were surprised to see him back.

"You don't belong here," Derrick told.

"I can move to another table."

"This land."

"Call it a twist of destiny."

"Of fate."

"I'm high."

"Where the fuck do you even come from Dilton?" Harlan said.

"Dylan."

"Whatever, geek."

"Alberta originally. But then again, my name goes back a thousand years. My last name is in the Domesday Book."

"Doomsday for you if you don't fuck off now," Derrick said. Gibby kneaded the knuckles of one hand in the opposite palm. The knuckles went *pop pop pop*.

Levett regarded the table's occupants. Were the hemispheres of their brows bulging? Were their eyes serpent eyes? "Normandy before the conquest of my boy William the Conqueror, then we relocated across the English Channel, you know, I see England I see France."

They weren't laughing.

"Lords with demesnes in the Midlands. They had tenants. Clerics too—parish priests, friars, managers and operators of monastic granges, peasants too, rustic folk, one of a dozen souls in a vill, or on the other hand, holding court, mediating disputes like 'My neighbour bit my pig's tail off with his dog,' or 'You, John de Fitzpatrick, were supposed to support our overlord's campaign in Wales this year, but since you were a no-show, pay six ducats three shillings fine.'"

Harlan laughed. Derrick's head rotated to face him. Harlan closed his lips over the stump row—his belly pumped and he vomited and swallowed the vomit.

"Had an uncle Daniel Levett. Held the manor of Middle Haywood along Cannock Forest, Staffordshire. Granted licences to peasants to agist their livestock, permission for fowling and the gleaning of fuelwood and to pannage their swine in the woodland because pigs adore acorns with all their cloven love, all kinds of permission was necessary, anything to do with the forest or the arable land. An eyre retained by my uncle's court, a certain Cooper, travelled from vill to vill and through Cannock itself, issuing amercements. Like, say, if someone had assarted forest land for cultivation and my uncle's eyre Cooper found out, he levied a tax based on the size of the assart. Uncle Daniel maintained a large forge and several smaller ones in and around Cannock, the forest being rich in ore and, of course, fuelwood—"

"Talk English," Derrick said.

They laughed, including Levett.

"I am."

"That ain't English," Gibby said.

"What is it?"

"That some fagotty book talk," Gibby pronounced.

"It's my family."

"I got a dead brother and a crackhead mom in a low-income housing unit back in T.O. for a family and that's as far back as I go." He said it all in one breath with his teeth clenched.

"That's not the half of it," Levett said, about himself.

"When I was five I had to cook my own Kraft Dinner cuz my parents were too hammered to make me dinner, or they were still out getting hammered," Sheldon said.

Harlan's trap ring tone cut through the conversation. He kicked a leg over the seatback and out the booth.

"Yaaay-oh, yaaaay ohhh," Sheldon chanted.

Harlan was back almost immediately. He forced Gibby over and sat down. He slobbered on his fingertip and dipped it in the gram baggie and sucked off the white. They all drew in together with room keys stabbing from their clenched fingers, shovelling them in, pinching one nostril, and sniffing the bumps of debased cocaine. The barman glanced over and looked away out the narrow window.

The pavement quivered in the streetlights. Heavy rain battered the pavement. Like the sound of television static through a low-pass filter. Air fuggy now.

"The heir to Middle Haywood was his only son of four children, John, now Lord John Levett, who received Middle Haywood by impartible inheritance and ran it in exactly the way his father had. Not a lot changed. John had nine children by his three subsequent wives: Mary, Janice, Jacqueline; of the children, five of which survived, four of them were chaps. At the age of forty-two John was kicked in the head by the mule he was kneeling behind, tending to a sore on its inner thigh..."

It was at this point Levett became cognizant of a triangulated pattern of hand ciphers making its way about the table.

"As per the testator's wishes, the nearest heir Greg inherited the estate partible with the lion's share. His younger brothers, Edward Levett, Frank Levett, and my namesake, Dylan Levett, were left consolatory purses, as it were, and all struck out in the world, and to them the world was England, all in their own distinct directions: Edward inherited cash and married the builder Alan Connery's daughter, Kara Connery, of a vill in the neighbouring manor. With her came a dowry consisting of Alan's cornfield and apiary, along with a dilapidated farmhouse and its sparse configuration of outbuildings. From there on Edward was a new rustic and embarked on a life that was simple but totally full up with everything (rather than observing his father overseeing work, he did the work); Frank Levett set up as a cobbler in the city of Ely, it being situated advantageously on the Ouse, having picked up his trade casually from the manor's cobbler Flynn, Flynn being a lilting singer; Dylan, admiring the perpetual motion and contingency of road life, the vicissitudes, spurned the sedentary life, the static life, and sold his portion of the manor forest to his brother Lord Greg Levett of Middle Haywood, and with the profits purchased twenty-four bay horses, three carts with iron-shod wheels, six pack horses, ten oxen, hired five drivers, retained a barge, and started doing business in transport: wax, tallow, canvas, lead and wheat, lumber, wool by the sarplar at four shillings a league, prisoners, high personages, carts full of gold escorted by archers and men-at-arms."

Derrick rubbed his gums with drug residue. He threw a couple quarters on the table in front of Levett, who looked up at him querulously. "Call someone who cares."

Mocking laughter panned around the table, panned back the opposite way. This tripped him out.

"You're a motormouth, White Bread," Sheldon said. He rested his elbow on Dylan's shoulder. Put some weight to it. His armpit smelled like green onion.

"You asked me why I'm here—I'm tellin' ya."

"Yer tellin' me," Derrick said, over a bump of white poised under his wide flared nose. A suture scar protruded from the bridge bone. His head could fit two of Levett's heads. It looked stone. Dual eyeholes of molten slag peering out at a contemptible world. He'd never been asked his consent, would never have given it, had never asked another one for it.

Levett glanced over at Justine standing at the bar waiting for service. The bartender ignored her, on his cellphone. Her friend looked at Levett, concerned.

Harlan had the empty baggie inside out trying to get at the dust in the corner creases. He rubbed his filthy gums with it. "We need another flap," he said.

"On you," Derrick laid a heavy hand on Levett's other shoulder.

"Unhand me."

Derrick's face was now very close. "You will buy it."

"With what?"

"With your bankroll."

"I think you've confused me with someone else. I'm a dishwasher that just quit his dishwashing job. I ain't bankrollin' shit."

"You can buy it."

"With what?"

"If you not buyin' us more coke, we takin' your cash, then we gonna take you down that alley and put the boots to you," Gibby said.

"Like fuck you will. I got five bucks cash on me and my debit card's at home."

"Justine's bought a round on the house," the bartender hollered. Vodka shots lined the counter.

"We'll continue," Derrick said. He squeezed Levett's cheeks and pushed his face away as Sheldon shouldered him off the seat.

He wondered, in all seriousness, if Derrick's head was impervious to a barstool.

Gibby shadowed him. Behind his right ear: "You gettin' robbed, pussy."

They all shot the vodka. Harlan brought Derrick's to him.

Derrick stood in front of the doorway blotting out the threshold. Levett looked at the bartender paying mind to the outsized figure in the doorway.

He reminds me of that bouncer, Jumbo, from all the raves, except he's a total fucker, he thought. He glanced at Justine watching him openly with the same concern as her friend, but with very friendly undertones, looked back at Derrick standing in front of the doorway with his arms crossed and his chin up. It was a contradistinctive pose, evoking bullish thuggery and haughty disdain.

The thought did not cross his mind to hole up in the restroom, he just retreated there. Some far-flung primitive instinct. He thought it was locked at first, wrist-snapped the knob. It was just sticky.

He slid in and locked the door. The knob lock was vertical in the locked position, more a signal of occupancy than a deterrent of entry. The miniature deadbolt at eye level mocked the physical security system idea, fastened to the drywall as it was with four stripped Phillips screws and a layer of flaking paint. Drawing up to the toilet he pulled out his dick and stood there listening to the muffled chatter through the door. But he did not need to pee, and put back his dick.

"Just not here," the bartender said, and then he chuckled.

Levett considered the glass liquor bottles. If I could get to those it would be bedlam. The sharp-edged glow signs are an option providing they come off the wall. They might be held fast by a cord, but how tight was the wiring?

He started rehearsing it.

Walk out, throat punch the first one that gets in your face, grab a bottle and bottle the next guy, throw a stool through the window as signal to the outside world, bottle the next— A pattering knock sounded on the door. He looked up at the ceiling panels, over at the closet door.

"Who is it?"

"Kathy."

He opened the door a hair, squinting out at Justine's stockier friend.

"Wait here for Justine," she said, turned away and receded toward the doorway around Derrick. He locked himself in again.

Muffled deliberation out there.

"Wait 'til he comes out then," the bartender said. "Don't storm the door. You break the door, I call the cops."

He scanned the john for anything he could weaponize. Someone rapped on the door.

"Who is it?"

"Me, Justine."

He let her in, saw Gibby stalk the area next the booth. Derrick stood sentinel. He stared at the restroom door. Levett locked the door.

"Hey," she said. Her voice was deep and gruff but she was small, she was a hard-faced kind of pretty. She squeezed his hand once and went to the disused door and rapped on it. "Rob. Open up. Harlan and them are trying to jack this dude, help him out."

A heavy even pounding on the restroom door.

Levett lifted the ceramic tank lid off the toilet. If the door flew open someone would get it in the mouth.

Justine pounded on the closet door again. "Rob," she called. A resigned protest seeped through from the other side and the door opened onto a brightly lit SRO foyer behind the reception desk. A rockabilly guy with a major sleep deficit waved them in. Another hard pounding on the restroom door. He put the lid in the sink. The restroom door exploded. Rob closed the SRO door and barred it with a length of square steel tubing, already had 911 on the line, fists hammering on the SRO door.

"No, this is good Justine. Motherfuckers fucked around all night. They wanted to get arrested and go to jail," Rob said as Justine led Levett up the rubber-treaded staircase.

The building smelled like dirty diapers.

"We got three big native dudes, you know, all in ballcaps, you know that typical wannabe gangster kit. Fourth guy is black, yeah, black guy, not dark black, light black," Rob's voice fading as they reached the second landing. The way she attacked the stairs made him think she'd been chased before.

He stood by a scoured sink in a room hazed over with dopesmoke. Scattered candles lit the undulant cloud from multiple points like stars forming. She walked out of the bathroom. With the caesarean scar and navel and the small dark-nippled breasts, her torso was a smirking face.

D'Angelo played on her phone. She didn't have any speakers right now.

Not much in the room but clothing strewn around an open suitcase. The bed was a box spring covered with a sweat-stained futon and there were no sheets. She was just staying here for a couple days. Her smile had lipstick on. A bit of colour on the cheekbones. The patterned hum of an electric sign outside the window touched the candle flames and they tilted along with the flawed circuitry. Rippling light played on her skin. He was still stoned but now he was disengaged.

She handed over the warm beer they shared. He drank and handed it back and she shook it off. Setting it in the sink stirred a cockroach from the drain. It scuttled over a moonlit douchebag laying on the soap dish.

He removed his glasses.

She put her tongue in his mouth. Her tongue was thin and tensile. Her small hands searched underneath his shirt up his belly and chest and along the collarbone, strumming his ribcage, fingers keying the vertebrae of his spine and coming back around to unbutton his pants. He placed his glasses on the sink edge and took off his shirt. She pulled his pants down and fellated him. She looked perfect from above, and gloss of sweat on her prim upper lip, pouty lower dragging along the shaft. Levett closed his eyes, raised his head and opened them. Walls scabbed with mould. The back of her throat clicked when she swallowed. That sweet unnameable feeling ran through him, settled in the brain pan, her leaning back smiling and he could see the scar again.

He rather would have fucked standing up. She dragged him by the hand to the bed.

"Don't go down on me." He dragged his mouth across one nipple, the other, bit one tenderly. The suture bumps were tough, from a different body it seemed. "Don't."

The futon was rank. It made his shins and knees itch. As the candles leaned off a gust of wind, he saw the rings of stain, a stratigraphic print of night sweats. His chin rested in her muff. He tried to breath out his mouth.

She slipped away into the bathroom and came back with a strip of them and tore one off.

He heard a high tone somewhere, a humming, or whining.

When he put it in, it clenched. She made the good sad pain face then the canal relaxed and they got a good fuck going.

There were voices outside fading in then trailing off again: "I gotta go show... Grayson... Wait... C'mere... I got cheese for sale... Orange cheddar... That Boston dude... Whatever, he calls himself Boston... I am going to get that goof tortured... I'll find him... He ain't back east, he ain't in T.O.... Don't care... I'll put a private investigator on him man, I'll wait and get him back, like the fuckin' Klingon proverb... I saw this pigeon guy caught, taped its wings with parcel tape threw it into traffic, it popped... That's what I'll do, do 'm like a pigeon."

He had her from behind. He looked at his cock going in and out, at her puckered anus, at the arc of her back.

She kept all her sounds in, except to gasp for air.

On her phone D'Angelo sounded like Jiminy Cricket.

They lay there fully clothed on the floor. He went and took a leak. Her bathroom smelled lemony but it looked dirty. Strands of hair lined the sink. The shower had no curtain.

The whining became a mewling and that became a hoarse cry and the cry died.

She said he could play some songs on her phone. He typed *Satie* into the YouTube search bar and selected *Gymnopédies No. 3: Lent et grave*—that haunted hologram. The narcotic cadence, he thought, the ache of it.

"This is nice," she said.

From where they were a crack of light below the door. Footfall shadows. They lay there pressing the finger pads of his left hand and her right hand together. She had lively eyes but she didn't say much.

"You have a kid?" he said.

"I had a kid. I don't have her anymore. She got adopted. I was only fourteen."

"Where is she?"

"Somewhere in the States. California is where she went, but who knows where she is now. The parents were in their thirties, couldn't have kids. They were well off, she got a break by going with them."

"You seem okay with it.

"It's okay. It's better. For her. I get sad about it too. She's a little munchkin now, four, must be so cute."

He wondered about a downscaled version of her and kissed her forehead, her small aquiline nose, their fingers meshed now.

"I loved how you were fucking with those dudes, that was so funny."

"I didn't think I was."

"Right, they wanted to hurt you. Man, couldn't you tell?"

"I was being straight. I only got a little nervous at the end. Just because if it came down to it, they would've got hurt too. And if they ganged up on me and tooled me I'd come back after I healed and I'd be doing the tooling."

"I don't believe it."

"It doesn't matter what you believe."

"They're really bad people."

"If you corner me I'm the worst person you're ever gonna meet. You better cap me."

"You probably shouldn't have gone in there."

"I thought it was a proper pyramid scheme lounge. I was right too."

She laughed at him and kissed him. Told him she liked his haircut.

They'd been like that for some time holding hands different ways, making different formations. He held his left palm up vertically and she drummed her fingers on it, stopped and ran her thumb across two callouses, where the fingernails of his ring and pinky kneaded and dug.

"How do you get these there?"

"I think I do it when I'm uneasy. But I've caught myself doing it and didn't think I felt uneasy."

"You stressed out right now?"

"Not this instant."

Again that high-pitched sound, that mewling.

A door shot open somewhere along the corridor, bare feet padding. "Oh god," a lady moaned. "He's not fucking breathing, he won't get up. Someone help me," she said cynically, as if no one ever would.

Another door opened and a voice said, "Call a fuckin' ambeelince then you fuckin' hoor."

"Shut up. Fuckin' piece of sh—" She lost her voice.

They heard her mute sobbing, the smack of her bare feet up and down the corridor.

Justine went out in her socks. Levett put his shoes on and followed.

The lady stood two doors away in a children's Pokémon dress. She couldn't have been more than forty but looked undead. Her legs were wrist sized. Her cheeks sank in on toothless gums. Skin a wet putty texture the colour of cigarette ash. Sometimes Levett would sharpen a pencil with a flip knife he had and he would get to where he was just filing away at the graphite so it was a fine pinnacle, so sharp yet ready to break. He felt like that honed bit of graphite now approaching and stopping at the doorway. There was a naked man on the floor sitting up against a trashed couch. To Levett he looked passed out. He had a juvenile sketch of an eagle tattooed on his chest. His penis was uncircumcised.

"What happened?"

"He took a big one, massive," she whined at Justine. "Big big hit."

"Call the paramedics," Justine said.

"I don't want 'em comin' here. I got tonnes a drugs in here. I'm holdin' for a friend. I gotta date comin' over."

Justine went out.

He looked at the guy. "Did you check his pulse?" It sounded like such a stupid question.

"His heart ain't beatin'." She sat back on the floor. Up the t-shirt you could see her curdled thighs and battered cunt.

Justine was back kneeling in front of the guy with a shot of naloxone. She aimed it, back, forth, and jabbed it in his arm.

"Is there supposed to be an immediate result?"

"We gotta call 911," Justine told the hooker.

She went over to him, patted his face, in a sketchy lullaby, "C'man Jay wakey up Jay."

"Hi, there's a man not breathing." Justine gave them the address which got the hooker pacing. Justine checked the door number. "Unit fifty-eight—fifth floor."

"Help me get 'im in the tub," the lady said to Levett and ducked under his armpit.

"I ain't touching him." To Justine: "I think I'm gonna peace."

"So things get heavy and you bail."

"Typical guy," the hooker wheezed.

The man whose heart was not beating had the look people do when aping the mentally ill.

"I just want a bit of time to myself Justine. We can exchange contact info."

"What's your number?"

"I don't have a phone."

"You can just leave."

"I'm serious."

"I'll find you on Facebook."

"I'm not on Facebook."

"Just go."

"Get outta here faggot," the hooker said.

"I'm telling you. I only use email. I gave up my phone."

Both women looked at him, doubting his reality.

"Bye," he said and touched her arm. "Thanks."

"For what?"

"The escape route."

He walked away, down the corridor, down the stairwell, down the inverted cone of his life.

He tossed in his own stale bedding. The drug had worn off but he felt what was left over, the dirtiness of it, and it was impossible to sleep. His head ached. There was some Motrin in the kitchen. He took two with some water and lay down again but his eyes would not close.

The hot water splashed in the scum-lined tub.

He lay back and rewound the night.

Each mental image circling back to the knurled cicatrice smiling across her abdomen. Like railroads on a map, stylized suture marks—tracks stitching a disparate continent together, closer to itself.

He still had the trippy thoughts.

The hot water felt good.

He was back in that stalled train outside Dresden on Christmas Eve 2015, on his way from Berlin to Prague. The train left on schedule from Hauptbahnhof, sliding out from the belly of the station, city lights breaking up, scattering. Soon no view but the blue-and-orange plush interior of the carriage reflected in the windows; the young Taiwanese men across the aisle tucking into an incongruous repast of lager and chocolate cakes. One after the other, small provincial stations expanded, contracted, the blank platforms visible for a breath or two.

In Dresden the pneumatic carriage door hissed open. A couple towed wheeled luggage and small children behind them. The man was tall. He looked down at Levett. He remembered it being ambiguous. It could have been judgmental, but when the man returned to retrieve the rest of their things and met Levett's eyes again, it was clearly holiday stress and fatigue brought on by the perpetual accountability of family life. Perhaps he envied the sight of a bachelor with a reclining, carefree attitude. The young men across the aisle had divided into pairs, one pair asleep and the other pair studying textbooks, diagrams of molecular compounds on the pages.

The pneumatic doors spread again. A ticket inspector informed the riders there would be an unscheduled thirty-minute delay. The seconds rolled by in the cavernous steel interior of the train station, the arcing girders and slanted trestles of its structure appeared mighty and indifferent. Ten minutes went by, then twenty, thirty, forty. It was nine thirty. What would be open in Prague on Christmas Eve at eleven o'clock? In the warm tub coming down he remembered fretting about where he would find food at that hour on that day. Forty-five minutes. Still no movement beyond Dresden. He soaked in the dark remembering the troubled feeling, his empty growling stomach, the Taiwanese dudes and all their cakes, remembered imagining the baroque city all shuttered and desolate on Christmas Eve with nothing to comfort a weary traveller.

As the mental cursing began, he recalled, as the entitled, irrational, unsympathetic cursing thoughts began to circle and collide in his head, the train began to move out of the station, slowly. And slowly it went into the unlit fields. One of the young students said something quietly to another and there was a quieter reply, the train never picking up speed, crawling, as if the conductor was looking for something he mislaid by the tracks. A can of lager snapped open. The train stopped again. Then it crept ahead. A hushed atmosphere took over the carriage as the train entered a milky aureole, the opposing track lit by floodlights on tripods. The train inched along.

A form lay on the gravel bedding. That human form belly down, legs curled back, wet red circles above where the knees ought to be, jacket half up the torso, exposing the pale skin. The green jacket looked like it was pulled over the head, but there was no head. A group of Deutsche Bahn workers in neon coveralls with reflective stripes stood off in a group, about five metres away, talking and looking at the corpse, one leaning on an ice pick.

He pulled the plug. The water made a throaty sound as it drained. He stood ankle deep in the water cowled in his only bath towel. When he brushed his teeth and spat out the froth it was marbled pinkish orange. He ran his tongue along the bottom row of teeth and a trace of scarlet reappeared along the gumline. He rinsed with cold water. The top left molar smarted.

It felt good to put on clean clothes. Everything stiff and fresh smelling. The 501s were crisp and tight on the waist. The new stretchy

Calvin Klein t-shirt felt snug under the old faded black t-shirt, new fabric contrasting with the old. The sport socks were tight and stayed put around the calves. The Adidas looked good with the slight taper of the 501s.

He had started reading *Going After Cacciato* and slid it in the back pocket of his laptop bag. He especially liked Tim O'Brien's rendering of the Vietnamese landscape. It reminded him of how Hemingway depicted the Basque country.

On his way to the coffee shop he saw Blade Girl at a flashing green while motorists turned left. The arrow blinked yellow and she took strides into the crosswalk with an extended finger of admonishment directed at the stranded driver. A chorus of horns flared up behind as Blade Girl drifted by, switching from her index finger to her pinky and then swiping it forward like some androgyne duke, as if the driver and his car stood for the gross indecency of all the people who have taken to the road ever. I'm in total sympathy with her mission, he thought, but why does she have to be such a dick?

People sat on the timber benches around the triangular cafe waiting for the 8 or the 19 or just loitering.

"Hi Juki."

"Hi Dylan," she said, smiling effusively.

"Slow day?"

"Yes, kind of slow."

"Everyone's at the beach."

She agreed with a high hum Levett loved. "I wish I was there," she said. She wore a yukata over her t-shirt that bellied in the breezes coming through the open doors and windows.

"I'll get a medium Americano to go please."

She nodded, plucked a cup from the stack next to the cash register and tapped the item into a touchscreen. "Three twenty-five."

He handed her a five, tipped two quarters and went to an empty table on the shady east side, not the sunny west side, placed his book on it to save the spot.

Before he cracked his book Levett checked his email. There was a new message from Henry: *Hey Dylan, since you never showed up at all this weekend and since I never heard anything from you, I gotta let you go, which sucks because I really liked having you around, you were a big help for us in the kitchen. I left your* ROE *in the office. It'll be there with your tips whenever you come in.*

They were playing some mellow acoustic folk pop in the cafe. Levett plugged in his earbuds and looked for something blackened to listen to on YouTube, something vicious. Lord Mantis, he thought, selected *Pervertor,* turned it up to blot out the weak bubbly tune, opened his book, leaned back, felt free, free and clean. Felt lucky he got away from those assholes at Legendary's. It could've gone the other way.

At the liquor store he walked straight back to the coolers. He picked out a cold Heineken and a cold Budweiser and walked to the registers, watched the security guard daydreaming, dropped the Heineken in his tote. At till two he paid for the Bud and walked out of the liquor store into the lambent afternoon sunshine, crossed Broadway flash flooded with gold from the west. Into the shade of the building along Prince Edward.

He walked across the blighted grass of Dude Chilling Park. A few people were setting up a badminton net. They had a large cooler and a propane barbecue. All the shaded benches were taken. He occupied a bench on Brunswick Street. The bench faced the park but it was in the sun.

He sat here, opened a beer and lit a joint and relaxed in the heat.

A woman wearing ovoid sunglasses and an olive cap stepped here and there around the bench on the opposite side of the path. Plastic bags with recyclables lay off to the side.

"How do you sit in that sun?" she said.

"It's a little hot, but I think it'll go down behind that condo soon."

"I couldn't sit in it. My makeup would melt right off my face."

He laughed. She let out a chortle of her own, pacing around the bench, then over to the waste receptacle where she peeked inside. A dark-plumed seagull ambled up to her in the shade of the tree overarching her bench. It was a chick. She rooted through one of her bags, found some potato chips, scattered a few for the bird, who pecked at the crumbs.

"That bird don't fly."

"Really?" she said, not believing it.

"Watch," he said, as it waddled away into the sun and yellowed grass across the park, toward a group seated around the picnic table under the massive cedar of Lebanon. "It steps around begging. Watch it. He won't ever take wing. I don't think it's fully grown."

"Okay, okay, I'll watch," she tittered.

Properly stoned, he flicked his roach into the dead grass.

"So you think the sun'll go down 'fore long eh?"

Levett looked over his shoulder. "Less than half an hour, probably."

She stopped pacing and regarded the sun dangling over the sharp parapet of the minimalist condo. "We should bet," she said.

"I haven't got any bettin' money."

"No, farmer's bet, just—"

"Like a contest."

"Yeah," she said, "just a competition, you know, to see who guesses right."

Levett took out his iPod, which showed the time. "It's five twenty-one on the dot, and your perspective is different than mine, the sun will go behind the building slightly later for you than it will for me."

"That's cool, that's cool. So, what's your guess?"

He looked back at where it hung. "I'm thinkin'—ten to six, you?"

She stood staring at the sun through her large shades. "Um, uh, four minutes after six."

"Sounds good."

"'Kay, sweet."

She sat down for a moment then stood, turned. "Where is it now?"

Levett looked over toward the desultory badminton players, saw the flightless bird and pointed in that direction. "Over on the far side there."

"Where?"

She looked around, shading her face with an open hand. "I see it, yeah, there it is. Did it fly yet?"

"I don't think it can."

"That's funny. Ha, brown seagull, can't fly. Ha," she guffawed.

He laughed. "What are you up to today?"

"I was just takin' these cans down. Well, I was gonna. Supposed to meet my boyfriend here. But he ain't ready. We're on different schedules."

"Are you taking them down to the depot?"

"Yeah, if it's still open."

"You might not make it. I think it closes at six."

"That's okay, I don't really care. Whatever. Do it tomorrow."

She continued to pace in the shaded territory beneath the tree. She cupped a hand over the visor of her cap to scan the park for the bird. "There it is now." She pointed over to another set of benches, its occupants soused in the late-afternoon heat. At their feet the bird foraged in a pool of vomit.

She fidgeted with an LED flashlight key chain, dropped it, picked it up again and dropped it again. She looked up at the sun.

"What time is it?"

She sat down on her bench.

"It's twenty to six."

He looked over his shoulder. The sun was halfway below the building edge. "Almost gone," he said.

"I can still see it from here."

"I don't think either of us'll be right."

"We'll see."

"What's your name?"

"Alison. You?"

"Dylan."

"Dylan, Dylan. Nice to meet you."

"Nice to meet you too."

She fumbled with a match to light a rolled butt. Her face was sallow and pitted underneath the makeup. "You got a girlfriend?"

"Nah."

"How come? You seem like a pretty laid-back guy."

"I can be, I guess. I don't know. I can hardly take care of myself right now. It'd be hard to sustain a relationship."

"I hear that. Lemme tell ya. You should see me and my boyfriend. Holy fuck man. We can't even leave the house at the same time. You know, different schedules. Takes me forever to get my shit together, then he just wants to sleep. I let him sleep over at my place. Half the time I just leave him there."

She said it all rapidly. He finished the Heineken. Another binner hovered next to the recycling container.

"Get the fuck away from my stash man," Alison barked. The old fellow backed off, hovered momentarily and stared at another group lounging on a blanket near the centre of the park. Levett handed her the can. She dropped it in her empties bag.

She sat down again. "The sun ain't there no more. What time is it?"

"Quarter to six."

"What'd you say again?"

"I said ten to."

"What'd I guess again?"

"You said four after."

"Ah shit. Both of us were wrong."

They laughed.

"I'm startin' to flail now though."

"What's that?"

"You know flail, ebb and flail. Binners, them are junkies that flail. They get enough for a hit and they ebb for a bit. Never lasts. I'm startin' to flail. Not too worried though. Got a stash at home. You don't mind that eh?"

"Not at all. Do whatever the hell you want."

"My boyfriend ain't there anyway. Otherwise it'd be *gone*."

"Yer stash."

"He'd smoke it all in five minutes."

"How's your place? You like it?"

"It's an SRO. Better than the shelter. Fuck, last winter we were in a shelter. Holy shit, in the winter that place turns into a three-ring circus. Fucking crazy."

"It ain't that good."

"Good," she scoffed. "It was a nightmare. How I lived like that, I don't know." Alison's speech got quicker and more agitated. "That was after I lost my son."

"Sorry to hear."

"He's okay. He's seven. The Ministry took him away from us cuz his dad's an idiot."

"How so?"

"Oh he is fucking dumb."

"Like, how?"

"He took my son to the casino at two in the morning. Then he got back in the car and drove away with him, hammered. Casino called the cops. He got arrested, got an impaired and we lost custody of my boy."

"That's horrible."

"I'm tryin' to get my shit together. I don't wanna miss his first day of school. I gave up the file. It's a joint file with his dad. It makes it look like we've broken up in the eyes of the Ministry. It improves my chances of getting my boy back."

"Good luck," he said, drank from the big Bud.

"It'll happen, it'll happen, just gotta get our shit together, you know. This SRO is way better than the shelter, like I'm not complainin' right, but where we live now is still out to lunch. Like, I'm not the cleanliest person. I got a huge mound of clothes in the corner right, most of 'em are clean right, it's no big deal, and I got it how I want. But my boyfriend comes in and complains, and I say fuck man, you got your own room down the hall, and you got it how you like it. And he complains, see, cuz I'm 'messy' he says, and that's why it takes me so long to get ready, 'Can't find nothin',' he says, and I'm like, 'Look guy, whenever I'm ready you're ready for bed.'" Alison dropped her lighter. It was dead. She kept trying to light it. "Hey, where's the nearest store, sells chips and cigarettes and shit?"

He pointed down the block to his right and said, "Kingsgate Mall. There's a shop beside the liquor store."

"Okay, yeah, I know where you mean. I need a lighter."

He held out his. "Thanks, like I need it now, but..." she snapped up a flame for her cigarette, "...but I need to like invest in one you-know-wh'I'm-sayin'?"

Whenever she went on a tangent she stood still again, swaying, crossing and uncrossing her arms. She held the lighter out for him. He pocketed the small yellow Bic.

"Like I don't mind when he comes over to like watch a movie or something or get high or whatever, but don't be criticizin' my room when you got your own and you forgot your key card so you can't get to the other wing. He lives on the left wing. I live on the right wing. There's two big steel doors, fuggin' locked right, in the middle of our floor, between our two rooms. He's on one side and I'm on the other side. So he has to wait until someone comes who lives on the other side, farthest from the stairwell. I'm closest to the stairwell, which means I can't get locked off my floor, but the downside is all kinds of weirdos come in off the street."

"People just come in?"

"All the time man. Whatcher name again?"

"Dylan."

"All the time Dylan. Creeps and shit. Hookers. You name it. And they will walk into your room if it is not closed and locked. If a room is open, you know, for the air circulation or whatever, a person will straight-up walk in uninvited." She paused. "And then you've got Leanne."

"Who's Leanne?"

"She's a dumb-ass fuck is who."

He laughed. Alison dropped the flashlight and stooped to pick it up. One of her ears had long scars radiating out to the edge of the auricle from earrings getting ripped from her head.

"How so?"

"She's got this pit bull, pisses and shits in the hallway. She's a piece of work too, lemme tell you. Out of her mind. She doesn't think she has to clean it up. Leaves her sharps laying around, you know, doesn't put her needles in the rig box. Like, that's a big no-no, right?"

"Does she eventually?"

"No. She waits for someone to do it for her. Maintenance. Or her boyfriend."

"Gal like that's got a partner?"

"Phff, more like a codependent. He's retarded too. They're a match made in heaven. But who am I to talk?"

"Who needs a pit bull pissing and shitting in your apartment building?"

"Errright. That's what I say."

He was near the end of that big beer.

"Hey, I got these canisters," Alison said. "Found 'em. Four of 'em. They're nice. Chinese style. For tea or some shit. Want one?" She pulled them out from her ample baggage and handed him one. It was a square tin with a round lid for Tieguanyin tea. There were little scenes painted on the sides. A father and son fishing beneath a blossoming tree among butterflies, temple in the background, and on the other side a Chinese maiden under the same blossoming tree, mingling with the same butterflies on a promenade by the water, a small junk sailing by a rocky island, distant mountains in the background.

"I can have this?"

"Yeah, I wanna make it a gift."

He studied it, turned it over in his hand.

"It ain't dirty. Might wanna give it a wipe though, I like those Lysol wipes," she said, as he placed it in his tote and stood.

"Thanks."

"I like to give a gift."

"It was nice meeting you Alison. Take care."

"You too man. You're a nice guy."

"Bye."

"Bye."

He smiled at her and waved as he turned away.

Magnus was on the landing cleaning up soiled garments from a torn garbage bag left beside the entrance.

"Hey Magnus."

"Aah, Dylan, hi."

"Someone's Irish luggage?"

"Aah, it's just someone, nowhere to go, nothing doing, no need for this useless clothing," he said, a shit-stained thong dangling from the end of his broom handle.

A rank scent of manure wafted along the south end of the tower site. Watson Street smelled like a barnyard. All day Friday the crane operator hoisted plywood bins loaded with spruce and hemlock up to the rooftop. A landscaping company dumped enriched soil on the sidewalk. Day labourers shovelled it into the emptied plywood bins and these were winched up to bed the conifers.

In the supermarket he went directly to the canned goods aisle with a basket. He grabbed three tins of tomato soup. He really wanted Kraft Dinner and placed two boxes in the basket, went to the dairy section, got the butter for it and half a litre of milk. He chose a loaf of whole wheat bread, some peanut butter and some raspberry jam. In the cookie aisle he noticed a burly man with sharp Indigenous features walking along the deli, looking around and stopping. He drained a bottle of juice, tipping it straight back, almost making a show of it, and placed it in his basket among an implausible combination of items: a box of Kleenex, a tin of sardines, a squeeze bottle of ketchup. He wore plain blue jeans and a green flannel jacket. For a minute Levett pretended to look at some artisanal candied nuts while he watched the man watch someone else.

In cookies and crackers Levett chose a package of lemon creams. As he put them in his basket a female voice on the intercom said, "Code twenty-two. Repeat, code twenty-two."

At the register he watched the items tot up on the screen as the cashier scanned them. It came to just under nineteen dollars.

"Stop!" said a voice as Levett tapped his debit card. The man in the flannel held a tall freckled ginger kid belly-first against the shopping carts, hands held behind his back fussing with a zap strap as he read him his rights. "Don't move around. You're under arrest for theft under ten thousand. Where's your accomplice?" He looked over at the automatic doors. "I see you, I got an ID on you, you better not run."

The shoplifter was stooped straight over the tops of the carts looking out the door, helpless, arms cinched behind his back.

"A cruiser's on the way. Get over here. Get over here now. Join your friend."

And the accomplice did come. The undercover cop seized her too, and led them both through the produce section as if they were on sets of casters. Levett walked out, watched them disappear through a steel swing door into the warehouse.

The flashlight glowed on the white tile counter. A lotus appeared in the dark. He set the pot of water on top. The roundel of blue light throbbed below the aluminum pot.

Slouched on the couch, he still felt funny from the acid.

He snapped open a cold beer and sipped it. He rolled another joint on a book called *Disenchanted Night*. The weed was dryish. He rubbed the buds between his fingers and it crumbled easily. He tore some filter material off the rollie pack, thumbed it into a spiral tip and set it in the rollie's trough, sprinkled in the fluffy indica and pressed the closer edge against the farther, tucked it in, rolled a bat, twisted the end into a fuse.

He heard the water boiling. He went back to the kitchen with the flashlight, fussed with the KD package, pulled out the pouch of powdered mix, dumped the noodles in the pot of boiling water. Fork in his right hand, flashlight in his left, he unstuck the noodles from the bottom of the pot with the fork. Noodles got stuck in the tines.

He took up the lid and pressed it down on the pot. With one hand he turned off the burner and with the other hand, he took up the scorching pot handle with a dishrag, held it over the sink and drained the water. When all the water drained he set the pot back on the burner and tore open the powdered cheese–mix packet and dumped it on the noodles. He pared off a generous pat of butter and dropped that in and dumped milk on that, drank the rest, turned the burner back on and stirred in the dark.

In the chair beside the window he sat and ate the macaroni. It was hot and good and the breeze was warm. He had to remind himself to chew. Tears fell from his eyes down his cheeks into the food. Steam rose up from the KD. He took another forkful and swallowed.

Steady traffic. The 3 passed by, its pantograph sparking and crackling. A tow truck drove past with its snatcher in its vertical position like a rusty crucifix. Ambulance sirens flared up and the maddening sound trailed off. Blade Girl tucked into a speed crouch down the empty sidewalk.

He had only just lit the joint when a mouse crept out of the shadow and he shot it. With the dustpan he launched it out the window onto the neighbouring building.

He relit the joint and drank from his beer.

He thought about the coming eviction date. He had not packed a thing.

Faced with the ordeal, he still could not imagine an alternate living situation.

He finished the joint and flicked it out the window, cherry dot fading to a black speck on the tarpaulin. He listened passively to the street noise.

Someone freaked out on someone.

A skate posse sessioned the waxed curb along the parking lot next to Barney's.

Blade Girl patrolled, thought she was refereeing the situation.

He drained the beer, rinsed out the can and put it with the growing can collection.

The flashlight stood on the ledge above the sink, throwing a ghastly bottom-up light on his face while he brushed his teeth.

The bedding was dank.

He woke in a child-sized bed and turned on a conic light. There were no bedcovers. The bed was a cot. A wall of boxes and packing containers rose up immediately to his left. A roll-up door faced him at the foot of the cot. He pulled himself up in the cot, pulled the clattering apron up and stepped into the corridor. A corridor lined with other slender roll-up doors. Farther on, a man at an easel. On a fold-out stand sat a small radio playing Mahler. Beside this, a thick plate of glass that served as a palette, the man dabbing at a shape of colour on the canvas, then helping himself to a chip from an open bag atop a barstool beside the easel, completely contented.

The corridor went a long way off beyond the painter and he could not make out the end of it. On one side the roll-up doors receded and on the other a corrugated steel wall, caged fluorescent lights above. He locked his door with a padlock and went the other way toward an EXIT light. Outside the city had eaten the landscape. No roads. The odd flying car. He went up a set of stairs, down a narrow pathway, through a green atrium to a small platform. The translucent tube with glossy white ribbing spanned the platform, bolted to the buildings it passed through.

He blinked and the maglev capsule was there on the platform and he boarded and sat down. It shot through the architecture studded with more atria, each a microcosmic woodland. He saw countless other tubes running through the city, merging and branching like the veins in a forearm. Buildings everywhere and he could not distinguish where the earth ended and the buildings began. There was no sky.

He got out. The capsule moaned low and with a short tweet shot off. A short puff of wind at the back of his neck. He entered a monolithic sand-coloured building and went down a space with light panels along the walls, a thought scanner, and he thought of chocolate milk and grilled cheese sandwiches. He could see others forcing happy thoughts too. The corridor split off into pedways. Through squat portholes he could see other pedways leading to an amorphous enclosed area, filtering through a structure of interconnected tiers reaching up through a vast arcade. Paper walls. Catwalks. Beyond the web-like framework of roof glass, more built spaces and green spaces and darting maglevs and still more builtness packed in between.

He went on through the crowded honeycomb of commerce amid stalls the width of a pelvis. In a slender bar he ordered a Sapporo off a ceiling-track robot server, a grey monocular cube with a Victorian accent. "Thirty-seven full and one half units sir," it said. He stacked the tiles on the bar. "I'm sorry, sir, we do not accept physical currency, might I scan your wrist?"

He turned over his wrist. The beam fanned across his arm and drew back inside the top corner of the server. "Transaction cleared. Low unit amount. Work more frequently, replenish units," said the polished voice. With a retractable tri-digited claw, it set the diminutive silver can down. "You may take your cold can of suds sir," it said. "One hundred millilitres of premium lager." The server motored on its track to the far end of the narrow space, turned outward to face the black paper wall.

He heard the floor above him creak and saw above the soles of someone's shoes through the floor's grill and a voice inquiring about a new set of utensils, could hear the sliding doors of a display case. "Hey man, turn on some music," he said to the robot, who swivelled to face him.

"This business does not possess a music licence."

"Fuck that," he said.

"Please avoid vulgar terminology," the irate yet mannerly voice said.

He finished and went out. He went to a stationery dealer through a long series of aisles and bought a notebook, a mechanical pencil and a small vial of graphite from the automated dealer (nothing but a window, a scalloped tray and a holographic touchscreen with an inventory list) and sat down on a ledge, began to write but the thoughts did not show in the words. The characters were unknown to him. He continued to put them down in neat columns on the page anyway and he felt good filling up the page with these ciphers thinking there would be a time when he could read them.

He looked up and saw Magnus standing at a confluence of passageways leading out of the arcade. He followed a set of directions painted with light in the air. Magnus said hello: "Aah, hi, hi Dylan." He stood there in front of the confluence; it was like the threshold of a cubist room, the same point observable from everywhere, everywhere observable from the same point.

"What are you doing Magnus?"

"I'm in the Alpha Zone," he said and turned away muttering and smacking his lips, quietly scatting the remote fragment of a tune, hands tucked in his blazer pockets.

Levett kept walking, through sounds and surfaces grazing his cheek and arms and hands tugging at him through thickets of stalls, one blending into another and up spindly helical staircases gripping the newel and up chain-driven single-body lifts. Dorsal niche at the far wall of the arcade. He wanted to look at his notebook ciphers, now could read them as pictographs resembling gestures, body language, but phonetic, a language against time in time structured by image, he thought, but didn't know. His certainty confused him. Gills of certainty, he thought, didn't know, put away the notebook.

Some droid, like a dustbin with triangular mount tracks, poked at a bedspread tent slanted against vent panels in the wall. Small distensions on the surface of the bedspread. He looked over and the man with the easel painted the rickety superstructure. Beyond him an EXIT light but no visible exit.

Footsteps opened his eyes. He rolled over to face the window. The sky looked like curdled milk. He sighed and let off a gigantic tuba fart.

He bathed. He brushed his teeth. After he dressed he checked his email. There was a message from Lane Roth. He clicked on the message.

We won! it said. *The official decision letter is attached, really happy about this!* Levett didn't bother to read the attachment, shouted "Hell yeah!" in a militant bass. A great sense of relief ran through him as a heavy slam resounded from the suite above, followed by the step of heavy boots with heavy men inside them. Another loud crash from above he could feel in his molars.

He waited there a while sitting on the couch, pleased with himself, that he had gambled. And won. And he had gambled on the most important thing. He was very proud of Lane. Everybody would be so pleased. Every tenant in the Bellevue. What a collective victory, he thought.

A sneaker step neared in the corridor. The mail slot clapped down. A stack of envelopes slid through. He watched the envelopes fall. He looked at them splayed on the floor for a good minute. Creditor, creditor, student loan bill, parcel notification. He could pick up the parcel on his way back from the liquor store.

It was sweltering and overcast. Blade Girl streaked by in full flight. She cut off a car running a stop sign. Its breaks chirped. The passenger's soft serve creamed the dash.

The traffic light blinked red. It was broken.

She circled round as he crossed, joined a group of young women in their corporeal prime, pointed at Levett with a half-cocked Roman salute and said, "He is a violating woman beater!"

"Sidewalk's closed," a snide construction lackey told him, pointing with his outsized cleft chin at the opposite sidewalk. Levett stared at him, thought he'd like to punch that chin, really bear down on it. The ventricles of his heart pulsated.

Crossing the street, a biker blasted by, nearly crushed him. But nothing could get him down today. He figured the parcel would be a care package from his mother.

At the liquor store he went straight to the coolers. I'll start with two tallcans, he thought. The chipper Hispanic clerk was working till. She really caked on the paint. He asked her how it was going.

"Oh you know, not bad, not bad, another day in paradise, can't complain."

"Right on."

He watched her put the beers into a plastic bag. She had fresh shellacked nails. They clicked and tapped on everything she touched and glinted in the heavy lighting. "Oh, sorry, didn't even ask you."

"Bag's good."

"Eight eighty-eight. Whoa. Never saw that price before."

"Debit."

She struck the key command with her mint-green talons.

He tapped. "Have a good one," he said, dragging the beers off the depressed little staging area beside the scanner.

"Will do, will do, I'll try and stay in the shade, melts the paint rat off ma face... How are ya sir?" she transitioned. "Paper or... no bag, all good... Credit—Visa or Mastercard?"

The mall air conditioning was cranked.

Lineup at the post office. He waited there in his glorious mood. Two separate people sat in the chair, stuck their arm in the tube and had their blood pressure checked. Sixteen-packs of toilet paper were on special. Levett noted the pathetic corner aisle of school supplies and stationery, a few Mead spiral notebooks, Bics, pink erasers, neon posterboard.

A pugnacious clerk served him. "This says DD Levett."

"Dylan Delbert Levett."

"DD is not your name?"

"They put it like that to mess with me."

He showed her his expired driver's licence, two student IDs, his SIN card.

She looked over at her colleague, an effeminate man of middle age. He'd issued about seventy money orders to Levett over the years. "That's Dylan," he said to her. She looked him over again.

She reappeared with an envelope. He had to sign on a tablet with a stylus. It always fucked up his signature. He felt like digging it into the pliable tablet screen and snapping it off.

Going out he examined the envelope. That same spidery scrawl. He couldn't not open it. He set his bag of beer beside him on the steel bench in the mall. He slid his middle finger through one end. There was some girth to the document. Several pages.

Following the RTB*'s decision to cancel your landlords' Notice of Eviction, my clients have decided to issue another Notice of Eviction to you, Dylan Levett, effective now. Due to aggressively obscene and bizarrely destructive behaviour in and around Bellevue Heights, the landlords wish to follow through with your removal from the building by the first day of September.* Vaughn MacDunn's name, Vaughn MacDunn's signature.

Levett flipped the page. It was filled with video stills of him toe to toe with Tom Ford outside the building. They were cut and pasted in chronological sequence. Levett flipped to the next page. Several different stills showed him giving the finger to the video cameras, and in the large bottom frame, him flashing his genitals to the camera at the back of the building. His dick was pixelated. He had no memory of this. The face looked wildly drunk. The bottom frame had a band of metadata with it.

Levett flipped the page. The pictures showed him in the distance approaching the curb with a bucket and tossing stuff on the black Dakota. Another chronology. Shots of him passing the entrance in both directions, of the camera he tampered with, penned arrows drawing attention to the highlighted time code captioning each image, which corroborated the evidence.

Levett flipped the page. A full-colour ink-jet form identical to the one he had first received.

The four cold bars of the bench burned his back. A child screamed by the coin-operated amusement ride. Blind man with his seeing eye dog recumbent and panting beside him. Small child in a fury. Levett looked outside at the parking lot. At the empty spaces. At the one car. He sat there for a long time watching people come and go from the drugstore. There was a trash can next to the bench. It took everything he had not to throw the papers away.

The parent relented and planted the child in the ride and fed it with money. It played a three-note song, it moved back and forth with a slight tilt, and that was enough for the child. The blind man took a collapsible cane from his coat pocket and let it fall stiff, was led to the lotto centre. In the big drugstore windows you could see two cashiers. They chatted around a nonplussed shopper waiting between their tills. An elderly woman sat down beside Levett. Her skin was translucent. She was the shape of a question mark. Through the main entrance of the mall he watched light rotating in the parking lot, let it fill up with cars. Windshields flashing in the sun, flashing in his eyes.

He got cold. He went outside into the heat. He went along the mall in a fringe of shadow, passed the loading dock, mounted the steep set of stairs next the dumpsters and tossed the papers in. He continued up the staircase and walked out of the frame.

ACKNOWLEDGEMENTS

Lausanne and Evan Cole, Kyffer Cole and Kaitlin Kirk, Dave and Dianne Ellis, Scott Franchuk and Susan Mikytyshyn, Dave Pullmer, Silas White, Amber McMillan, Emma Skagen, Liam McClure, Richard Mackie, Simon Redekop, Sean MacPherson, Bradley Iles, Matthew Tomkinson, Peter Magnuson, Sam Choo, Adam Dodd, Les Funk, James Steidle, Derya Akay, Braden Jones, Inge Kvemo, Joshua Bartholomew, Daniel Rincon, Mark Hall-Patch, Erin MacSavaney, Ali Ahadi, Ahmad Tabrizi, Glen Alteen, Lawrence Paul Yuxweluptun, Christopher Brayshaw and Steven Tong.

PHOTO CREDIT: SEAN MACPHERSON

ABOUT THE AUTHOR

Dustin Cole was born in Hinton, near Jasper, and raised in the town of High Level, a remote community in northwestern Alberta. He received his B.A. in history from Simon Fraser University and now lives in Vancouver. His collection of oneiric poetry, *Dream Peripheries*, was released through General Delivery in 2015.